Large Print F
Lacy, Al.
The tender flame / DEC 9 9

DWIGHT FOSTER PUBLIC LIBRARY
FORT ATKINSON

W9-BAH-760

WITHDRAWN

The
Tender
Flame

Also by Al & JoAnna Lacy
in Large Print:

Secrets of the Heart (Book One)
A Time to Love (Book Two)

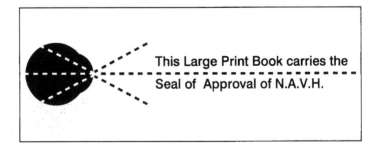

This Large Print Book carries the
Seal of Approval of N.A.V.H.

The Tender Flame

Mail Order Bride Series #3

★ ★ ★

Al & JoAnna Lacy

Dwight Foster Public Library
102 East Milwaukee Ave.
Fort Atkinson, WI 53538

Thorndike Press • Thorndike, Maine

Copyright © 1999 by Lew A. and JoAnna Lacy

All rights reserved.

Published in 1999 by arrangement with Multnomah
Publishers.

This book is a work of fiction. With the exception of
recognized historical figures, the characters in this novel are
fictional. Any resemblance to actual persons, living or dead, is
purely coincidental.

Thorndike Large Print ® Christian Fiction Series.

The tree indicium is a trademark of Thorndike Press.

The text of this Large Print edition is unabridged.
Other aspects of the book may vary from the original edition.

Set in 16 pt. Plantin by Warren S. Doersam.

Printed in the United States on permanent paper.

Library of Congress Cataloging-in-Publication Data

Lacy, Al.
    The tender flame / Al & JoAnna Lacy.
      p. cm. — (Mail order ; 3)
    ISBN 0-7862-2156-9 (lg. print : hc : alk. paper)
    1. Frontier and pioneer life — West (U.S.) Fiction.
2. Mail order brides — West (U.S.) Fiction. 3. Women
pioneers — West (U.S.) Fiction. I. Lacy, JoAnna. II. Title.
III. Series: Lacy, Al. Mail order bride series ; no. 3.
    [PS3562.A256T4 1999]
    813´.54—dc21   99-38786

*With deep affection this book is dedicated to
Deanne Morris,
wife of our beloved editor, Rod Morris.*

*Thank you, Deanne, for your enduring
patience as your husband's attention is drawn
to our manuscripts when deadlines draw near.
Thank you also for being a fan of our books
. . . and a cherished friend.*

*With love and appreciation to you and your
precious family —*

AL AND JOANNA
2 THESSALONIANS 3:16

As for God, his way is perfect.

PSALM 18:30

Prologue

The *Encyclopedia Britannica* reports that the mail order business, also called direct mail marketing, "is a method of merchandising in which the seller's offer is made through mass mailing of a circular or catalog, or advertisement placed in a newspaper or magazine, and in which the buyer places his order by mail."

Britannica goes on to say that "mail order operations have been known in the United States in one form or another since Colonial days, but not until the latter half of the nineteenth century did they assume a significant role in domestic trade."

Thus the mail order market was known when the big gold rush took place in this country in the 1840s and 1850s. At that time prospectors, merchants, and adventurers raced from the East to the newly discovered gold fields in the West. One of the most famous was the California gold rush in 1848–49, when discovery of gold at Sutter's Mill, near Sacramento, brought more than 40,000 men to California.

Though few struck it rich, their presence stimulated economic growth, the lure of which brought even more men to the West.

At this time, the married men who had come sent for their wives and children, desiring to stay and make their home in the West. Most of the gold rush men were single and also desired to stay in the West, but there were about two hundred men for every single woman. Being familiar with the mail order concept, they began advertising in eastern newspapers for women to come west and marry them. Thus was born the "mail order bride."

Women by the hundreds began answering the ads, wanting to be married and to make the move west. Often when men and their prospective brides corresponded, they agreed to send no photographs. They would accept each other by the spirit of the letters rather than on a physical basis. Others, of course, exchanged photographs.

The mail order bride movement accelerated after the Civil War ended in April 1865, when men went west by the thousands to make their fortune on the frontier. Many of the marriages turned out well, while others were disappointing and ended in desertion by one or the other of the mates, or by divorce.

As we embark on this fiction series, we'll tell stories that will grip the heart of the reader, bring some smiles, and maybe wring out some tears. As always, we will weave in the gospel of Jesus Christ and run threads of Bible truth that apply to our lives today.

1

On Monday, January 18, 1841, the brightening sky over Montgomery Village, Maryland, was tinged with the opalescent hues of morning. In moments, the sun peeked over the horizon, sending bony shadows of the naked tree limbs across a layer of snow that had fallen early the night before.

As families throughout the village and the surrounding hills prepared for a new day, thin wisps of smoke floated reluctantly from chimneys, meeting the chill of the air.

Men who worked in Washington, D.C., and other nearby cities left their homes early, riding on horseback or in buggies. By eight-thirty, children were trudging through snow toward the schoolhouse at the south edge of the village.

At the Duane Reynolds home, Beverly Reynolds was making sure her two children — fourteen-year-old Lydia and twelve-year-old Billy — were bundled up.

Beverly tied Billy's scarf about his neck and studied his black eye. "Your father told me that if you have any more trouble with those bullies, he's going to talk to their fathers and see that something is done about it."

On the previous Friday, fifteen-year-old Frederick Kendall and sixteen-year-old Gerald George had decided to walk Lydia home from school, even though she made it clear she didn't want their presence. Billy, as usual, was walking with his sister and told them to leave her alone. An argument ensued, and Gerald punched Billy. The younger boy had fought back, but both of the teenage boys had pounded on him, giving him the black eye.

Lydia pulled a stocking cap over her light brown hair. "Mother, I hope Gerald and Frederick stay away from me; then there won't be any trouble between them and Billy."

"Well, if they do bother you again, just ignore them. I don't want your brother getting in any more fights."

Lydia picked up her schoolbooks. "They're pretty hard to ignore, but we'll try." She placed a hand on her brother's shoulder as he opened the door for her. "I appreciate my little brother protecting me."

Billy, who was almost as tall as Lydia, stood a little straighter and said, "That's

11

what brothers are for, isn't it?"

She gave him a mock scowl. "What about last summer when my brother put a june bug down the back of my dress? Was that protecting me?"

Their breath plumed in the frigid air as they laughed.

"There have to be a few exceptions," Billy said. "Brothers have to have a little fun now and then."

"So do sisters," said Lydia, tucking her books under her left arm. She grabbed a handful of snow off the porch railing and flicked it in his face. "And that was fun!"

Billy had started to retaliate when his gaze fell on his mother, who was shaking her head.

"But Mom!" he protested.

"Son, she's just paying you back."

"That's right!" Lydia said. "And now we're even, William John Reynolds!"

"Ah, but William John Reynolds will have the last word. I don't get even, I get ahead!"

Beverly laughed at her children's sparring and said, "See you two this afternoon."

"Bye, Mother," Lydia said. "I love you."

"I love you too, honey."

"I love you, Mom," Billy said.

"And I love you, son." Beverly rubbed her upper arms against the cold as she watched her children walk as far as the road, then she moved inside and closed the door.

The Reynolds family lived two blocks from the schoolhouse. When Lydia and Billy were almost halfway to school, Lydia saw Frederick Kendall and Gerald George coming from between two houses.

"Uh-oh," she said with a sigh. "Here come Gerald and Frederick. Just ignore them. Pretend they don't exist."

The older boys drew near, their feet crunching the snow. Gerald, who was the bigger of the two, grinned at Lydia and said, "Hello, sweetheart. You know, I think you're absolutely the prettiest girl in all the world. Frederick and I were just arguing about which one of us you'd like to have walkin' beside you to school."

Lydia looked straight ahead, as did Billy.

"Aw, c'mon," Frederick said. "Don't play hard-to-get."

Billy clenched his teeth and tried to ignore them, as his sister was doing. Gerald moved close to Lydia and rubbed his shoulder against hers.

"You two leave my sister alone!" Billy said. "She doesn't want anything to do with either of you, so just go away!"

Frederick looked at Gerald and said, "I guess little brother didn't get enough on Friday. Since he seems to like black eyes so much, I say let's give him another one."

"You two get away from us!" Lydia screamed.

Gerald laughed and put his arm around her, pulling her close. "I can stand it without your ugly little brother, but life without you is getting unbearable. How about a little ol' kiss for Gerry?"

"Let go of me, Gerald!" Lydia tried to twist her shoulder from his grip.

He just laughed and held her more firmly. "Now, you know you like all this attention."

"Move, kid, so I can hug her too," Frederick said. "We want to know which one of us she likes best."

Billy grabbed Gerald's arm and yanked it from Lydia's shoulder. "Take your hands off my sister! Get away from her, you creep!"

Other schoolchildren looked on from a distance, but no one made a move to help.

Gerald stood over Billy, his eyes widening with anger. "If you're man enough to make me get away from her, kid, hop to it!"

Billy glared at him, and Gerald turned back to Lydia and put his arm around her again. Lydia twisted from his grasp, but slipped and fell facedown in the snow. Billy started to help her up, and Frederick shoved the boy's face into a nearby drift.

"Keep his face in the snow for a while," Gerald said, as he took hold of Lydia's arm. "Teach him a lesson."

"Don't you touch me!" Lydia said.

"Aw, c'mon, sweetheart. Let me help you up." He took hold of both her arms.

"I said don't touch me!"

Frederick relaxed his hold on Billy for just a moment, and Billy scrambled to his feet and lunged at Gerald, catching him slightly off balance. Gerald fell heavily in the snow, then jumped up and swore at Billy, threatening to beat him to a pulp.

"You aren't going to beat anybody to a pulp, Gerald!" someone said.

All eyes went to sixteen-year-old Grant Smith, who stood with his feet apart and fists ready for action. While Frederick and Gerald stood motionless, Grant leaned over and helped Lydia to her feet.

"Thank you, Grant," she said.

"Seems I heard Lydia screaming at you two to keep your hands off her," Grant said. "You deaf?"

"We don't have to take this from you, Grant," Gerald said. "If we want to walk Lydia to school, it's none of your business."

"It's my business if Lydia says she doesn't want your company and you try to force yourselves on her."

"Let's teach him a lesson!" said Gerald, making a lunge for Grant.

Grant met Gerald with a fist square on the mouth. In the frosty air it sounded like an ax hitting a tree. Gerald fell sideways, and Frederick stumbled over him but got up fast enough to catch another punch from Grant flat on the nose. He went down hard.

Billy was standing beside Lydia with an arm around her as Gerald got up, swearing at Grant. His lips were split and bleeding, and an upper front tooth was barely clinging to the gum. Gerald held a hand partially over his mouth and said, "Look what you did, Grant! You knocked my tooth loose!"

"You bother Lydia or Billy again," Grant said, "and I'll knock some more loose. You got that?"

Gerald did not reply. His attention went to Frederick, who was just getting up, his nose bleeding profusely.

"Grant," Billy said, "they did this on Friday, and when I tried to fight them off, they gave me this black eye."

Grant nodded. "They better never give you another one." Then he asked Lydia, "You all right?"

"Yes, Grant, I'm fine."

He turned back to the bullies. "I mean what I say: you two stay away from Lydia and don't even think of doing anything else to Billy. If you do, what you just got will seem like nothing compared to what you'll get then."

Gerald ran a hand across his mouth, looked at the blood, and said, "We'll tell Mr. Wilkins what you did."

"Go ahead. I'll tell him what you were doing when I did it too. You boys want him to hear that?"

Without a further word, the two boys turned and walked away.

"Guess we'd better get going," Grant said to Lydia and Billy, "or we'll be late for school."

The three of them made their way as quickly as they could through the slippery snow, and Grant took hold of Lydia's arm to keep her from falling.

That afternoon when school let out at

3:30, Billy was waiting outside Lydia's classroom door when she came out. "Well, big sister," he said, "what did you learn in school today?"

Lydia smiled at him as they headed toward the school's front door behind other students. "I learned that the seventh wonder of the world was not the Pharos lighthouse at Alexandria, Egypt, as some historians have stated, but the gigantic walls of Babylon. I learned that mathematics is not just the science of numbers, but also of space configurations; and I learned how to construct a sentence without ending it in a preposition."

"That's a lot for one day."

Lydia giggled. "I also learned something else. This was before school this morning, though."

"Mm-hmm?"

"I learned that Grant Smith is the most wonderful —"

Lydia's words ended abruptly as she and Billy moved outside and she saw Grant standing there.

"Hello, Lydia, Billy," he said with a smile. "Just thought I'd walk along with you, if it's all right."

"Yes, of course," Lydia said, glancing at Billy's sly grin.

When they reached the street at the edge of the schoolyard, they saw Gerald and Frederick standing beneath a big oak tree, its leafless branches silhouetted against the cold blue sky. There was fear in the two boys' eyes, and they quickly looked away.

"I don't think they'll bother you any-more, Lydia," Grant said.

She looked up at him and smiled. "Thanks to you."

When they reached the end of the first block, Grant slowed his pace and said, "Do you want me to walk you all the way home?"

"That won't be necessary, Grant," Lydia said.

Billy looked over his shoulder. "No sign of you-know-who."

"They know better," Lydia said. "Thank you, Grant. See you in the morning."

Beverly Reynolds greeted her children at the front door as they stomped snow from their shoes on the front porch then stepped inside. "So how was school today?" she asked.

"School as usual," Billy said.

"Yes, but before and after school was anything but usual," Lydia said.

Beverly's eyebrows arched. "You had

trouble with Gerald and Frederick again?"

"Before school, yes. After school, no. And the reason we didn't have trouble after school is what happened before school."

Beverly's gaze ran quickly between her children. "Well, take your wraps off and tell me about it. I don't see any more black-and-blue marks on my boy, so whatever happened on the way to school today must've been better than what happened on the way home from school on Friday."

"A whole lot better," said Lydia, pulling off her stocking cap. "Daddy won't have to talk to Gerald's and Frederick's parents. The problem is solved."

"And who solved it?"

Billy finished hanging up his coat in the nearby closet and turned to take Lydia's.

"Grant took care of it," Lydia said.

"Grant?"

"Yes, ma'am."

"What did he do?"

"Let's sit down and we'll tell you all about it."

The "we" turned out to be mostly Lydia.

Billy got in a few words when Lydia finished telling Beverly about the bloody nose, cut lips, and loose tooth. "Tell you what, Mom," he said, "those two were standing in front of the school when Grant started walking us home, and boy, did they look scared! They won't come near us again."

"Good for Grant," Beverly said. "He sure is a nice boy. Your father and I will let him know how much we appreciate what he did."

When Duane Reynolds came home from work an hour later, he learned about the morning's incident and was glad to hear what Grant Smith had done. He thanked Billy for once again coming to his sister's aid and said he was proud of him for standing up to the two bullies, both older and bigger than he.

When mother and daughter went to the kitchen to start supper, Billy said, "Dad, could we talk for a few minutes?"

"Of course, son. Let's go sit in the parlor."

As soon as they got comfortable, Duane said, "So, what's on your mind?"

"Well, I was just wondering . . . since Grant's a Christian and all, was it right for him to, you know, do what he did today?"

"You mean to use force when he came to your rescue?"

"Yeah, that."

"Just because we're Christians, son,

doesn't mean we have to let people walk all over us."

"But why do people who aren't Christians think we're supposed to let them do anything they want to us, and we're just supposed to take it?"

"Part of it may be that they misunderstand Jesus' words when He said, 'I am meek and lowly in heart.' They think 'meek' means weak. They think 'lowly' means He was to be walked on. Now, it's true that when it came time for Jesus to be crucified, He did not raise a hand to protect Himself. He went as a lamb to the slaughter, Isaiah tells us. He had come to die on the cross for sinners. Therefore, He let them take Him, beat Him, spit on Him, and crucify Him. But when the day comes that sinners who rejected Him must face Him in judgment, He will pour out His wrath on them. He certainly showed that He was no pushover when He went into the temple in Jerusalem and drove out the money changers. What they did was wrong, and He lifted up His hand against them."

Billy nodded. "So what Gerald and Frederick did to Lydia and me was wrong, and Grant was right to lift up his hand against them."

"We're to be meek and lowly like Jesus, and we certainly should never be trouble-makers. But when trouble comes our way, we are not to be cowardly. Jesus was meek in the gentle and patient sense of the word, but He stood up for what was right in the face of all kinds of opposition, and He strongly stood against all that was wrong. His followers should be the same way.

"If Grant had stood by and let those bullies do what they wanted to you and Lydia, Grant would have shown cowardice. Christians are supposed to stand for what is right, and against what is wrong. That's what Grant did."

Billy nodded. "Grant is a good Christian, Dad. I know he witnesses for Jesus at school and has invited kids to church. Some have come and been saved."

"Grant is a fine boy, son, and I think as a family we will go over to the Smith house after supper. I think your mother and I should express our appreciation to Grant in the presence of his parents and sisters."

2

It was a frosty night with a bright winter moon reflecting off the snow, making it easy for the Reynolds family to see as they walked the short distance to the Smith home. The frozen landscape of surrounding hills stretched into the distance like lumps of cold silver dotted with tall trees and bordered in black.

A lone kerosene lantern burned beside the front door, illuminating the snow-laden porch, and the soft glow from the parlor windows offered the Reynoldses a warm welcome. As soon as Duane knocked on the door, the sound of muffled footsteps was heard.

"Well, look who's here!" Scott Smith said upon opening the door. "Come in! Come in!" He hustled the Reynoldses into the warmth of the cozy home and called toward the parlor door, "Marjorie! Kids! We've got company!"

Marjorie Smith's eyes widened with pleasure when she saw who had come visiting, and she embraced Beverly Reynolds as Grant and his sisters came through the parlor door behind her. Thirteen-year-old Sharon and eleven-year-old Theresa moved to Lydia's side, and Grant shook hands with Duane.

Scott reached to take young Billy's coat and eyed the boy's black eye. "Uh-oh! Looks like you and Lydia got into a fight, and she won!"

Billy chuckled. "She's a tough gal, Mr. Smith, that's for sure!"

"Let's go into the parlor, folks," Scott said, ushering them toward the family room.

The Smith home was tastefully furnished, and a feeling of serenity greeted the visitors. A fire crackled in the fireplace.

"Everybody relax, and the girls and I will be back in a few minutes," Marjorie said as soon as her guests were seated comfortably.

"Is there something Lydia and I can do, Marjorie?" Beverly asked.

"Just sit there and soak up some heat from the fire, honey. That's all."

Sharon and Theresa followed their mother to the kitchen, where Marjorie began setting out cups and saucers. "I'll make the coffee, girls. You put those cookies I baked today on a plate."

Sharon took a blue willow china plate from a hutch that stood in one corner of the kitchen, and Theresa opened the large cookie tin. Together, they took out a variety of freshly baked cookies, placing them on the plate in a decorative manner.

When everyone had been served, Scott looked around at his guests and said, "Is this just a social call, or did you folks have another reason for coming by?"

"We always enjoy being with you folks," Duane said, "but we do have a special reason for being here tonight. Beverly and I wish to express our deep appreciation to Grant for what he did this morning."

"What did he do?" Scott asked.

"You don't know?"

"He hasn't said anything . . . Son, what did you do?"

"I . . . ah . . . I just kept a couple of bullies from bothering Lydia and Billy on the way to school."

"He beat 'em up good, that's what he did," Billy said.

"Grant, is Billy talking about Gerald George and Frederick Kendall?" Sharon asked. "Gerald had a swollen lip and a loose tooth when he got to school, and Frederick had a bloody nose. It was them, wasn't it?"

Grant nodded humbly. "Mmm-hmm."

"I thought they had fought each other," Theresa said. "I didn't see any other boys around school who looked like they'd been in a fight."

"Well, I think we need to hear all about it," Marjorie said.

"Can I tell what happened?" Billy asked.

"You were there, son," Duane said. "Tell it."

Billy told the Smiths how he got his black eye, then explained how Gerald and Frederick approached them that morning, wanting to walk Lydia to school. When Billy had finished giving every detail, Duane and Beverly Reynolds expressed their appreciation to Grant for rescuing Lydia and Billy.

"Mr. and Mrs. Reynolds, I only did what any other red-blooded young man would do," Grant said. "Those no-goods were forcing themselves on Lydia, and Billy was doing his best to drive them off."

Beverly looked over at her daughter, whose eyes were fastened on Grant, and smiled to herself.

It was almost ten-thirty that night when Duane Reynolds leaned over and kissed his daughter's cheek as she snuggled beneath the covers. "You sleep tight, honey. I'll see you in the morning. I love you."

"I love you too, Daddy. Good night."

Beverly came in just as Duane reached the door. "Get that boy all tucked in?" he asked.

She nodded. "I think he's asleep already."

"I have a wonderful brother," Lydia said. Grinning, she added, "But don't tell him I said so."

"Oh, we wouldn't think of it," Duane said.

Beverly nodded. "You have to keep that brother-sister war going, don't you?"

"Mm-hmm. What would life in the Reynolds household be like if we didn't pick at each other now and then?"

"Hard to imagine," Duane said. "Good night, sweetheart."

"Good night, Daddy."

Duane moved through the door, and Beverly sat down on the edge of Lydia's bed and blew a stray strand of hair from her own forehead. She wore her hair up-swept, with a bun on top, but the wear and tear of the day had loosened some locks.

"I noticed something tonight that I want to talk to you about," Beverly said.

"Yes, Mother?"

"When . . . well, when Grant was telling us about why he stepped in to help you and Billy, I saw you looking at him. You really like him, don't you?"

Lydia blushed. "Yes, I do."

"You like him more than just as a friend, I mean."

"Yes, Mother. I've had a crush on Grant since I was twelve. I . . . I can't help it. I think he's the most wonderful boy I know. He's so . . . so . . . well, it's hard to find the words."

"When I was thirteen — just a year younger than you — I had a crush on a boy named Marty Foxworth. The problem was, Marty was two years older than I was. I kept hoping that someday he would notice me, but he never did. In his sight, I was just a child. The day he got married, it broke my heart. I pined away for months. I told myself I could never love anyone but Marty, so I would be an old maid all my life."

Lydia smiled faintly. "And you don't want me to have the same kind of broken heart."

"That's right."

"I appreciate your looking out for me, Mother. And I'm sure glad nothing worked out between you and that Marty guy, or I wouldn't have my wonderful daddy."

Beverly smiled. "Me too. Your daddy is the man the Lord had picked out for me all along."

Lydia was quiet for a moment, then said, "I know I'm too young for Grant, Mother. Sixteen-year-old boys look at fourteen-year-old girls almost as being children."

"That's right."

"I've thought a lot about it. By the time Grant and I get old enough to where the two-year age difference wouldn't matter, he'll already have a steady girl, or he might even be married. But . . ."

"But what, honey?"

"I can't help how I feel about him. My crush was big enough before this morning. But after what he did today, it has gotten *really* big."

"I can understand that, Lydia, but I think it would be best if you steered your heart away from Grant."

"How do I do that?"

"Ask the Lord to help you. I just don't want you to suffer the same kind of heartache I did. You see, honey, you belong to Jesus, and He has already picked out your mate for you. Just like He had already picked out your father for me."

Lydia pondered those words for a long

Grant chuckled. "You're right about that."

Sharon looked at Theresa. "See what I mean? He's going to let all that love in Lydia's heart go to waste because he thinks he's a mature man of the world."

"Mm-hmm," Theresa said, nodding sagely.

"Grant," Sharon said, "you'll search a long time to find a girl who walks as close to the Lord as Lydia, and who's as pretty as she is, and who adores you like she does. What's two years? Better make her your girl now, before that love light shines in her eyes for somebody else."

"Well, dear sisters, I appreciate your kind and caring advice. Now it's bedtime. Give me a hug and get yourselves to bed."

When his sisters had gone to their room, Grant picked up his Bible, finished reading the passage he had chosen, and put out the lantern. As he slid between the sheets, he chuckled and said, "So Lydia had love light in her eyes for me, eh?"

He pulled the covers up under his chin and watched the pale moonlight coming through the curtains. *I have noticed her a lot lately*, he thought, *but she's only fourteen. If I courted like her, my friends will accuse me of robbing the cradle.*

moment, then said, "I hadn't thought about it before, but the Lord does plan our lives, doesn't He?"

"He does, and we don't want to get in His way and mess up the plan. Many Christians do that and are sorry for it later, sometimes for the rest of their time on earth."

Lydia smiled slightly. "Well, since the Lord has already picked out the young man I am to marry, I'm sure he'll be a good Christian like Grant, and I hope he'll be as rugged and good-looking too."

Beverly leaned toward Lydia's nightstand and picked up the girl's Bible. Opening it and flipping pages, she said, "I want to read you a verse the Lord has pressed to my heart of late. It will help you as you think about God's will for your life, and His working it out for you as time passes."

Beverly found the page and said, "The entire verse is excellent, but one part of it has really taken hold of my heart. Psalm 18:30 says, 'As for God, his way is perfect: the word of the LORD is tried: he is a buckler to all those that trust in him.' Those first seven words are so powerful: *As for God, his way is perfect.* You need to let Him do His perfect work in your life,

Lydia. Part of that perfection is the man He has chosen to be your mate one day. Do you understand?"

Tears misted the girl's eyes. "Yes, Mother. I'm so glad the Lord cares that much for me."

Beverly swept her daughter's light brown hair aside and kissed her forehead. "In this life, we'll never know just how much He cares for us, sweetheart, but we sure can praise Him for what we *do* know. Good night."

Lydia reached up, pulled her mother's head down, and kissed her cheek. "Good night, Mother. I love you."

"I love you too." Beverly rose from the bed, doused the lantern, then paused at the door. "The Lord will make your life just what He wants it to be, honey. *As for God, his way is perfect.* Don't forget that."

When her mother was gone, Lydia lay in the darkness and said, "Lord, if You make it so Grant loves me like I love him, that really *would* be perfect."

After putting on their robes, Sharon and Theresa Smith chatted with their parents at the door of the front bedroom, then bid them good night and moved down the hall toward their own room. Grant's door was

open, and they paused and looked in. He was sitting on the bed, reading his Bible by the light of a single lantern.

He looked up and smiled. "Good night, girls."

The sisters exchanged a furtive glance and stepped into the room.

"Something I can do for you?"

"No," Sharon said. "We just wanted to tell you what we saw tonight when the Reynolds family was here."

"What you saw?"

"Mm-hmm." Sharon gave her sister a mischievous look. Theresa snorted an covered her mouth.

"All right," Grant said, closing his "What did you see?"

Sharon giggled. "Love light. eyes when she looked at you."

Grant shut his eyes, open and said, "You silly girls, Lydia's eyes was *appreci* ates what I did in pro from those nuisance

"Appreciation ; eyes," Sharon s Lydia's eyes v come of it, 1 older than me, a child."

★ ★ ★

During the next three months, Grant Smith talked often to Lydia Reynolds at church and at school, but he kept a guard on his actions so his kindness and attention toward her would be seen only as friendship.

Lydia tried to keep her heart from reaching out further toward Grant, but she found herself helpless to stop that from happening, whether she was in his presence or simply thinking about him.

Billy kidded his sister about her crush until Beverly sternly told him to stop.

One Sunday night in late April — after Grant had sat beside Lydia in church that day — Beverly sat on the edge of Lydia's bed, as she so often did, and talked to her about it.

Lydia wiped away her tears and said, "Mother, each time Grant speaks to me or goes out of his way to spend time with me, my feelings for him grow stronger. Today when he sat beside me in church, I thought my heart was going to beat itself to death."

Beverly took hold of her daughter's hand. "I know, honey, but you've got to ask the Lord to take those feelings away so you don't get deeply hurt one day when you see Grant fall in love with another girl."

35

Lydia began to sob, and Beverly folded her in her arms.

"Oh, Mother, I want to be that girl. I can't ever love anyone but Grant. If I'm not the one he marries, I'll be unhappy the rest of my life."

"I know it seems that way now, but when that right young man walks into your life, you'll realize that what you felt for Grant really was infatuation, not the marrying kind of love."

The girl wept for several more minutes, then dried her tears. "I love you, Mother. Thank you for spending so much time with me about this."

Beverly kissed Lydia's forehead. "You're my little girl. I care about you with all my heart. I want you to have a wonderful life — the life God has planned for you. Remember, *As for God, his way is perfect.* And that's what I want for you."

Moments later, when she lay alone in her bed, Lydia stared toward the darkness of the ceiling and whispered, "Lord, You know how much I love Grant. I don't think I'd feel this way unless he's the one You've chosen for me. Plenty of girls like him, but he hasn't chosen one to be his girl. Is that because You've marked him as mine, even though he doesn't know it yet? I know he thinks of me as his young friend, but I want to be his girl and someday his wife. Would You please make it so he sees me as more mature than my years?"

The next day as Lydia and Billy walked to school, orioles chirped in the trees, their orange and black feathers glistening in the dappled sunlight. At the first corner, they met up with Angela Dunne and her little brother, Gregory.

"Have you two heard about the new family that moved in on Mulberry Street yesterday?" Angela said. "You know, where Mr. and Mrs. Bangston used to live?"

Lydia shook her head.

"Well, Papa met them yesterday afternoon. Their last name is Lannon, and they're Christians. They told him they'd be coming to our church."

"That's nice," Lydia said. "Do they have any kids?"

"Papa said they have one daughter. She's sixteen."

"Do you know her name?"

"No. I don't think they told Papa what it is. But she'll probably be at school today."

At the Montgomery Village school, grades seven through twelve began each Monday in assembly, where principal

Henry Wilkins talked to the students on different subjects. Sometimes he would bring in a special speaker.

When Lydia and Angela entered the small auditorium, Angela went to sit with the tenth-graders, and Lydia moved to the section reserved for ninth-graders. As she greeted friends, her eyes strayed to the eleventh-grade section. Grant was talking to another boy, but his gaze was on Lydia. He smiled when their eyes met, and Lydia smiled back.

The buzzing of voices faded to silence when Henry Wilkins appeared from a side door and mounted the platform. Wilkins, who was small and thin with a bird-beak nose, smiled as he stepped to the center of the rostrum and said, "Good morning!"

Teachers and students returned the greeting in unison.

"We have a new student in our school," Wilkins said, still smiling. "She's starting today, and I want to introduce her to all of you."

Principal Wilkins gestured toward the eleventh-grade section and said, "Veronica, will you stand, please?"

There was an undercurrent of admiring male voices as the girl stood. Her golden hair was long and shiny and lay in soft swirls on her shoulders.

"Students," the principal said, "this young lady is Veronica Lannon. She and her parents moved here from Baltimore just yesterday. Her father is the new foreman at the lumber mill over by Clarksburg. I want all of you to be sure to introduce yourself to Veronica sometime during the day and make her feel welcome."

Wilkins gave his usual thirty-minute talk, then dismissed the assembly. Since there was a fifteen-minute break before the first class, Lydia got in line to greet the new girl. She found that most of the welcome line ahead of her was made up of boys.

When Lydia finally reached Veronica, she smiled and said, "Hi. My name is Lydia Reynolds. Welcome to our town and our school."

"Thank you, Lydia," Veronica said. "I know I'm going to enjoy it here. Everyone seems so friendly."

"I understand that you and your parents are Christians and will be attending the village church."

"That's right."

"Well, my family and I are Christians, too, and we're members of the church. We'll be very glad to have you. Our pastor's a wonderful man and an excellent preacher. I know you'll like him."

"I'm sure I will."

Lydia glanced behind her and saw that the line had grown longer. "Guess I'd better move on. It was nice to meet you, Veronica."

As Lydia walked away, she saw that Grant was farther back in the line with two of his friends. Moments later she looked on as Grant introduced himself to Veronica. A sharp pain lanced Lydia's heart as she watched the conversation. She was sure Veronica was more friendly toward Grant than she had been with the other boys.

For the next two weeks, Veronica spent most of her free time at school talking to Grant. Lydia's heart felt weighed down. She was sure Grant was falling for the pretty blonde.

On Friday, when school let out, Billy Reynolds found his sister in front of the schoolhouse waiting for him. He noticed her watching Grant and Veronica in conversation near the street.

"Ready to go, sis?"

Lydia pulled her gaze away from the couple and nodded silently. As they walked away, she cast a quick glance over her shoulder, then looked straight ahead.

"Something's bothering you, sis," Billy said. "Want to talk about it?"

"There's nothing bothering me."

"Come on, I know you pretty well. I can tell when you're upset. And I think I know what it is."

"No, you don't."

They walked swiftly and silently for almost a block. Then Billy blurted out, "It's Veronica, isn't it?"

Lydia's lips began to quiver, and she averted her eyes. "Billy, you don't know everything."

"I may not be real smart, but I'm not blind. Ever since Veronica came, Grant's been talking to her a lot. It's eating you up, isn't it?"

They were near the Reynoldses' front yard.

"Okay, Billy, okay, so I'm jealous. Shouldn't I be? Grant is spending a lot of time with that . . . that girl."

"He still talks to you, doesn't he?"

"Well, yes. But not nearly as much as he talks to her."

They were at the front porch.

"Billy . . . don't say anything to Mother and Daddy about this, okay?"

"I won't."

★ ★ ★

Beverly found Lydia preoccupied while they were cooking supper together, but she didn't pry. When the family sat down to eat, Lydia tried to smile and be herself but without much success.

After praying over the food, Duane kept glancing at his daughter. Finally he said, "Lydia, honey, something's bothering you, isn't it?"

"It's nothing important, Daddy."

Duane glanced at Billy, who was busy eating and kept his eyes on his food. "If it's nothing important, why does it show so plainly on your face?"

Sudden tears filmed the girl's eyes, and she laid her fork down. "Daddy, you met the Lannons at church on Sunday."

"Yes . . ."

"You saw how pretty Veronica is."

"Well, I guess you could say she's pretty. Why?"

"Grant seems to think she's pretty. He's spending a lot of time with her."

Duane and Beverly exchanged glances, then Duane said, "Honey, you're too young to set your heart on any young man. You're only fourteen."

"Yes, Daddy."

"You mustn't expect Grant to ignore

girls his age simply because you have a crush on him. Do you understand what I'm saying?"

Lydia sniffed again. "Yes."

"And honey, even when the time comes that you're old enough to set your heart on someone, you must be careful that the young man you choose is not only a Christian, but a dedicated one."

Lydia brushed tears from her cheeks. "You mean I should choose a young man like Grant, don't you, Daddy?"

Duane smiled. "Yes, honey. You should choose a young man like Grant."

That night in her darkened bedroom, Lydia prayed, "Dear Lord, I really need to talk to You. Daddy said that the young man I choose should be like Grant Smith. I have nothing against Veronica, and I don't wish her any heartache, but Lord, I've known Grant a lot longer than she has. There are lots of boys for her to choose from. I'm asking You from the bottom of my heart, please make it so the young man for my life is not like Grant Smith. I want him to *be* Grant Smith!"

3

The school year was over the last week of May, and spring soon turned into summer. Grant Smith had worked the previous summer on a farm near Gaithersburg. The farmer had liked his work so well that he offered him a job again for this summer.

The job kept Grant busy five days a week, and he saw Lydia only on Sundays except for a chance meeting now and then on a Saturday. Yet a Saturday hardly went by without his running into Veronica. He had an idea that she planned those meetings somehow.

On the last Sunday in June, people stood around chatting outside the church building after the morning service. The teenagers were clustered together, laughing and having a good time. Grant was talking to his closest friends, Roy McNay and Orval Proctor, who were telling him they planned to be carpenters once they got out of high school.

Grant nodded. "That's an admirable

plan. We need carpenters, that's for sure."

"So what about you?" Roy asked. "What are your plans for the future?"

"I'm thinking seriously about a military career. I have an uncle who's in the army, and he's talked to me about it. He went to West Point, and now he's a major at a fort in North Carolina. I'm praying about going to West Point myself."

"Well, if you can handle four years of tough academics and hard work, that's the way to go," Orval said. "That way, when you go into the army, you're an officer."

"You'd be commissioned a lieutenant, wouldn't you, Grant?" Roy asked.

Grant noticed Lydia was watching him as she stood with a couple of her friends. He smiled at her and was about to answer Roy's question when he saw Veronica coming his way. But she just scowled at him, stuck her nose in the air, and passed on by.

"Whooey!" Orval said. "What did you do to deserve that, Grant?"

"Must've been pretty bad," Roy said, chuckling. "What *did* you do?"

"Long story. Wouldn't interest you."

"From what I've noticed," Orval said, "Veronica's had a heavy crush on you, ol' pal. Messed it up, eh? Now maybe some of the rest of us will have a chance with her."

"Veronica's a nice girl, but I've got someone else —"

Roy snorted his surprise. "You've *what?* Someone else, you say? And who might that be?"

"Military secret, boys. It's not for public knowledge right now."

Roy and Orval laughed, then began walking away to join their families. Grant turned to leave and saw Lydia standing alone, watching him. He smiled at her and headed her way.

"Hi, Lydia. Some sermon this morning, wasn't it?"

"Yes, very good," she said, giving him her best smile.

"Warm day, isn't it?"

Lydia chuckled. "Didn't look too warm a few minutes ago when Veronica walked past you. Kind of cool, I'd say."

"You noticed, huh?"

"As did several people, I'm sure. Has something . . . has something happened to your friendship with her?"

"I guess you could say that. Veronica's been trying to get something serious started between us, and just yesterday I told her I wasn't interested in her in that way. I just want to be friends."

"Well, Grant, Veronica's a very pretty girl. She won't have any trouble finding plenty of male company. Of course . . . all the girls who are interested in you are pretty."

"I doubt there are all that many girls interested in me. I just know that Veronica's not the type of girl I'm interested in."

Lydia's heart was in her throat as she said, "What type of girl are you interested in, Grant?"

"Oh, well, I suppose I'm interested in . . . in a girl of *your* type, Lydia."

"I take that as a compliment, Grant."

"I meant it that way."

"Lydia!" came a familiar voice from near the parking lot. Billy was standing by the family buggy, and Duane and Beverly were already aboard and ready to leave. "Time to go!" Billy called.

Lydia gave him a tiny wave, then turned to Grant and said, "See you in the service tonight?"

"I'll be there."

Marjorie Smith tapped on Grant's bedroom door one Saturday morning in early August.

"Come in," Grant called. "Oh, hi, Mom.

47

Need me for something?"

"I just need to talk to you for a couple of minutes about your birthday party. You're birthday's only a week away, you know."

"You really don't have to go to all that trouble just for me."

Marjorie put her arms around him. "What do you mean, 'just for me'? You're my only son, aren't you?"

"Well, yes."

"Then let your mother give you a party. What I need to ask you is, do you want Roy and Orval and their parents to come?"

"That would be great."

"We can have one other family. Who would you like to invite?"

"The Reynolds family."

"All right. The McNays, the Proctors, and the Reynoldses it will be."

The guests arrived at six o'clock the day of the party. Though Marjorie had been busy with preparations since sunup, her face was glowing as she greeted everyone then ushered them to the backyard, where a table groaned under all the food Marjorie and the girls had spent the day preparing.

Grant glanced at the place cards on the

table and was pleased that Lydia would be seated directly across from him.

It was a lively group that sat down at the table to enjoy the feast. Roy and Orval were seated on each side of Grant, and though he talked to them throughout the meal, his eyes kept wandering to the girl across from him.

When the meal was over, Scott Smith rose to his feet and said, "All right, folks, it's time for Grant to open all those nice presents you brought. Roy and Orval, would you mind bringing them out here?"

The young men brought the presents to the table, and a place was cleared in front of Grant. When he opened each present, there were oohs! and ahs! and Grant made sure the givers knew he appreciated their kindness and generosity.

Grant opened Lydia's present last, and she watched eagerly as he broke the ribbon and tore the paper loose. It was a Bible with a black leather cover.

"Thank you, Lydia. It's the most beautiful Bible I've ever seen."

"You're very welcome, Grant. There's . . . ah . . . something on the flyleaf."

Grant felt a lump in his throat as he read her beautifully inscribed words:

To Grant, whom I deeply admire.
May this Bible be a lamp unto your feet
and a light unto your path.
Your friend forever,
Lydia

Marjorie suddenly jumped up from the table and beckoned to her daughters, telling the others that she and the girls would return shortly.

Grant leaned across the table. "Lydia, let's take a little walk around the yard."

"All right."

When they were out of earshot from the others, Grant stopped and said, "I don't know how to thank you for that beautiful Bible, Lydia."

"Knowing that you like it is enough thanks for me."

"I'll always treasure it. This is the best birthday I've ever had."

"Seventeen. Do you realize that makes you three years older than me?"

"Not really. It only sounds that way. In fact, it doesn't even seem that we're twenty-five months apart in age, Lydia, because you are so mature."

"Time for birthday cake, everybody!" Marjorie called from the back porch.

She moved down the steps, carrying a

large chocolate cake. It was covered with fluffy white frosting and had seventeen candles burning brightly. Sharon and Theresa followed their mother, carrying pitchers of iced tea and lemonade.

Grant and Lydia joined the others as Marjorie placed the cake on the table, and Scott led the group in singing "Happy Birthday."

When the song ended, Grant leaned over the cake, then glanced at Lydia before he blew out all the candles with one gust of wind.

"What did you wish for, Grant?" Theresa asked as everyone applauded.

"If I tell you it won't come true."

Everyone ate their fill of cake, then the ladies and girls cleared away the dessert dishes and carried them inside the house. In the kitchen, they all offered to help with cleanup, but Marjorie gently shooed them outside into the cool of the evening.

They all continued to visit for a while over iced tea and lemonade; then gradually the guests began to say their good-byes.

Grant quietly thanked Lydia again for his new Bible, and when everyone was gone, he expressed his appreciation to his family for making his birthday such a wonderful day.

★ ★ ★

The following Sunday morning at church, Veronica Lannon sat next to a young man named Luke Denton. Luke was well liked in the community, and Lydia was glad to see them sitting together. Grant talked to Lydia both before and after the service and continued to do so in the weeks that followed. Although Lydia didn't understand why she was getting the added attention, she was glad for it.

School started on Monday, September 6. The following Friday was Lydia's birthday. Beverly had a party planned, which would be preceded by a hearty meal. In accordance with her daughter's wishes, Beverly invited the Smith family along with two families whose teenage daughters were Lydia's closest friends.

Lydia awakened on her fifteenth birthday with an excited flutter in her stomach. "Good morning, Lord. Thank You for fifteen years in this world and for another day to walk with You."

She quickly threw off the covers and began to get ready for school. She must get her morning chores done, even on her birthday!

The day dragged by, but the last bell finally rang. After chatting a few minutes with Grant, Lydia and Billy hurried home to help her mother with preparations for the dinner and the party.

When all was ready, Lydia rushed upstairs to splash cold water on her face and redo her hair, pulling it up on both sides and securing it with a silver barrette. She fluffed her bangs with her fingers. She went to her closet and took out the dark blue dress with the wide white lace collar her mother had made for her in August. It was her very first "grown-up" dress.

She gave herself one last look in the mirror and thought, *Maybe Grant will notice that I really am growing up.* She gave herself an impish grin, then hurried from her room and fairly skipped down the stairs.

In the kitchen, she went to her mother and kissed her on the cheek, thanking her for this most important dinner and party.

Lydia's girlfriends and their families arrived first, and she met them at the door, welcoming them warmly. Moments later there was another knock, and Lydia rushed to greet her guests. In chorus, the Smiths wished her happy birthday. Grant complimented her on the beautiful dress, which brought a thank-you and a wide smile.

After dinner, when Lydia opened

Grant's present, she found a beautiful Bible bound in expensive leather, with a dainty, feminine look to it. A thrill shot through her when she found but three words on the flyleaf: *With love, Grant.* She thanked him and let those three words echo in her mind. Then she scolded herself for actually thinking he meant anything by them.

Later, as the guests were leaving, Lydia thanked them for coming and for their gifts. The last person to leave was Grant.

"Thank you so very much for the Bible, Grant. It's beautiful."

"I'm glad you like it, Lydia. And I meant what I said when I signed it."

"I appreciate that. True friends do have a love for each other, don't they?"

That night, Grant Smith lay awake in the darkness of his bedroom as Lydia's words echoed through his mind: *True friends do have a love for each other.* All the next day he tried to think of some way to stop by the Reynolds house to see her, but he couldn't think of a way to just happen by.

Sunday morning came. Grant was standing in front of the church building talking to some of his friends when he saw the Reynolds buggy pull into the parking lot. Lydia and Billy preceded their parents across the lot, and Grant noticed that Lydia was carrying the Bible he had given her.

During the preaching service, Grant and Lydia sat with their families in their usual pews, directly across the aisle from each other. From time to time Lydia's eyes strayed to Grant, and she found him looking at her. Each time she held his gaze briefly, then looked away.

After church, Lydia stood outside with her parents and Billy as they chatted with people. She saw the Smiths come out the door, and Grant walked toward her, smiling.

"Lydia, could I talk to you for a minute?" Grant said. "In private?"

"Of course."

They walked toward the parking lot, and Grant waited till there was no one else close by before he said, "Lydia, I've been thinking about what you said the other night at the party when I told you I meant what I had signed in your Bible."

"What I said?"

"Yes. Do you remember?"

"You mean about true friends having a love for each other?"

"That's right."

"You've been thinking about that?"

"Yes, and I want you to understand that the love I had in mind when I wrote, 'With love, Grant,' is more than friendship." Grant took a deep breath. "Lydia . . . I've been in love with you for a long time. Do you remember at my birthday party that I looked at you when Theresa asked me what I wished for, and I said if I told her, it wouldn't come true?"

"Yes."

"I didn't really make a wish. I asked the Lord to put a love in your heart for me like I have for you."

Tears misted Lydia's eyes and her pulse raced. "Grant . . . that prayer was answered long ago. I have been in love with you for two years, but I've kept it from you because I was so young. Oh, I've prayed so hard that —"

Lydia's words were cut off by the approach of both their families.

Grant touched her arm and whispered, "It's just too hard to try to talk here at church. I'll see you here this evening, but we'll talk at school tomorrow."

Lydia lay in her bed that night too excited to sleep. "Dear Lord," she whispered, "thank You for what is happening between Grant and me. I just knew You wouldn't let me love him like I do unless he was the one You had chosen for me. Please, oh, please . . . let me one day be his wife."

At the Smith home, sleep was just as elusive for Grant. "Lord," he said, "I don't care if people do tease me about robbing the cradle. I love Lydia, and I'm going to ask her to be my girl. Thank You that You have worked in her heart as well as mine."

4

Lydia Reynolds awakened refreshed the next morning, though she had not fallen asleep until three hours before sunrise. After spending time with her Lord in prayer and praising Him for all His blessings, she left the bed and padded to the dresser, where the mirror showed her a happy face.

"Good morning, Lydia," she said to her reflection. "Know what? The most wonderful young man in all the world loves you! What do you think of that?"

She ran her fingers through her thick hair and let it fall partially over her face. Peeking through the locks, she answered the girl in the mirror, "I think it's marvelous! The Lord is good, isn't He?"

"Yes," said her reflection, "He is so good! He answers prayer. His way is perfect. That's what His Book says, and I believe it!"

She dressed for school and all but floated down the stairs and into the kitchen. "Good morning, sweetest mother in all the world!" she said, kissing Beverly's cheek.

"Well, good morning, Miss Sunshine! My, aren't you chipper today. May I ask why?"

"It's a wonderful day, that's why!"

Duane and Billy were just coming through the kitchen door.

"Of course it's a wonderful day!" said Duane, moving up behind Beverly and putting his arms around her. "I'm married to the most beautiful and wonderful woman in all the world, and God has given me a precious daughter and a precious son." Then to Lydia he said, "And what makes this a wonderful day for you?"

"Why, Daddy, Psalm 118:24 says, 'This is the day that the LORD hath made; we will rejoice and be glad in it.' I'm just being scriptural."

Duane tilted his head and gave her a skeptical look from the tops of his eyes. "Well, then, tell me why you weren't so scriptural yesterday morning, or the day before."

Lydia sighed, looked to her mother, and said, "Can't we females have any little secrets?"

Beverly laughed. "Sure, honey. Keep your little secret. Daddy ought to be glad that his daughter is so happy this morning."

"Oh, I am. She's just got my curiosity up."

"Well, maybe I'll satisfy your curiosity a little later."

"Let's get up to the table," Beverly said. "Breakfast is ready."

As they sat down at their places, Billy eyed his sister suspiciously. "Has it anything to do with Grant, big sister?"

"Billy!" Beverly said. "If your sister wants you to know what she's so happy about, she'll tell you. Don't pry."

"Mom's right, son," Duane said. "Don't pry."

"Girls!" Billy said, rolling his eyes.

All the way to school, Billy wanted to press his sister about her secret, but he refrained.

Lydia's heart warmed when she saw Grant standing outside her classroom, smiling broadly.

"Good morning, Grant," she said.

"Good morning to you. Did you have a good night's rest?"

Lydia sighed. "Do you want the truth?"

"Of course."

"No, I didn't. And do you want to know why?"

"Sure."

"I had a very difficult time getting to sleep because of what you told me yesterday morning."

"You mean — ?"

Lydia smiled. "Yes. You know what I mean."

Leaning close, he said, "I was awake for a long time last night, too. For the same reason."

"I'm glad."

"I've got to get to class, Lydia. How about we meet outside by the children's playground during lunch hour? We'll be where everybody can see us — including the teachers — but we can talk without anyone hearing us. Okay?"

"All right."

Grant turned to head down the hall to the next classroom. He paused and turned back, mouthing silently, *I love you.*

Her lips formed the same words.

Noon came, and at lunch Grant met Lydia at the edge of the playground under a large oak tree amid the laughter of children.

"I've been praising the Lord in a special way ever since yesterday morning, Lydia," Grant said. "I've prayed for so long that the Lord would cause you to love me."

"And I've prayed for so long in the same way about you," she said. "I had a hard time, though. I figured by the time I was old enough that the difference in our ages didn't matter, you would already have a steady girl . . . maybe even be engaged or married."

"Lydia, will you be my steady girl? May I be your beau?"

Tears misted Lydia's eyes. "Oh, Grant, nothing would make me happier. But are you sure? Lots of girls have a crush on you."

Grant shook his head. "I don't know about that, but I'm not interested in lots of girls. There's only one I want, and I'm looking at her." Grant was quiet a moment, then said, "Lydia, I want to do right by your parents in this."

"What do you mean?"

"I think I should talk to your father and ask his permission to be your beau."

Lydia looked at him with admiring eyes. "I think it's wonderful that you would ask my father. Especially because of my age."

"I would do it even if you were my age. I just think it's the proper thing to do."

"Daddy and Mother already think a lot of you, Grant, but this will raise their estimation of you even higher."

"I just want to do what's right."

"That's one of the reasons I love you."

He grinned. "I'm planning on giving you lots of reasons to love me."

"I really don't need any more. I already have plenty."

He shook his head humbly, then said, "Are your parents going to be home tonight?"

"As far as I know."

"Good. I'll be over after supper. Have you said anything to them about our talk yesterday morning?"

"Not yet. I wanted to tell them about us, but at just the right time, and in the right way."

"Is tonight okay for the time? And by my talking to your father, is it the right way?"

"I couldn't think of a better time or way."

"All right. I'll be there tonight."

"I'll be waiting for your knock."

Grant glanced toward the school building. "It's almost time to go back in. Could we just take a moment and thank the Lord for the way He's worked in our lives?"

"Yes, I'd like to do that."

Grant led in prayer as they bowed their heads.

Grant and Lydia were standing in front of the school that afternoon when Billy came out of the building, greeted Grant, and said, "You ready to head for home, sis?"

"Mm-hmm. Let's be going. See you later, Grant."

"Sure will."

"Bye, Grant," said Billy, and walked his sister toward the street.

"Take good care of her, Billy," Grant called.

Billy looked back over his shoulder and smiled. "You can bank on it."

As they walked toward home, Billy said, "Sis, it seems to me that you and Grant have been spending quite a bit of time together lately."

"Oh? What do you mean?"

"Well, I see you together at church a lot and at school too. The past few days, he's been waiting at your classroom door when we get to school. And then, today . . . the two of you spent almost a half hour together on the playground after lunch. Looks suspicious to me."

"Suspicious?"

"Like maybe there's some romance going on."

There was a stretch of silence while Lydia pondered her brother's words. "Little brother," she said finally, "you are a perceptive person."

Billy grinned at her as they crossed the street. "I try to be."

"So you think there's some romance going on, eh?"

"Sure looks like it to me."

"Can you keep a secret?"

Billy leaped in front of her, causing her to stop. There was a sly grin on his face. "There is, isn't there?"

"Yes. Grant has asked me to be his steady girl."

Little brother laughed. "And you turned him down, of course!"

"Oh, sure!"

"Sis, I'm so glad. I know how you feel about him, and I'm glad he feels the same way about you. I really like Grant. In fact, I hope someday he becomes my brother-in-law."

Lydia blushed. "We have to take these things a little at a time, Billy. First there's going steady, then engagement, then marriage. But I don't mind telling you . . . I hope he will become your brother-in-law too."

"So when are you gonna tell Mom and Dad?"

"I'm not going to."

"What?"

"Grant is."

"*Grant* is gonna tell 'em?"

"Mm-hmm."

"When?"

"Tonight. He's coming over after supper. He wants to ask Daddy's permission to be my beau."

"Really? I've never heard of that. I've heard of fathers being asked when it comes to engagements, but not just for going steady."

"You will keep this a secret until Grant talks to Daddy tonight, won't you?"

"Of course."

At supper that evening, Grant told his family that he had asked Lydia to be his steady girl. Scott and Marjorie were pleased. They had seen it coming.

"So what will you do when your friends tease you about robbing the cradle, son?" Scott said.

"I'll tell them that Lydia is more mature for her age then most of them are."

"And you'll be right," Sharon said. "Lydia is very mature for her age, and I really love her. I'm glad you finally took the step and asked her to be your girl."

"Me too," Theresa said. "In fact, I hope you and Lydia get married someday."

"Now, Theresa, let's not rush things," Scott said.

"Lydia and I aren't going to rush into anything," Grant said. "We'll take it one step at a time and let the Lord guide us as time passes."

"That's fine, son," Scott said. "You've always had a level head, and your mother and I appreciate it."

"After supper I'm going over to the Reynoldses' house and ask Mr. Reynolds for permission to be Lydia's beau."

"Son, I'm proud of you for that. I'm sure it will sit well with both Duane and Beverly."

"That it will," Marjorie said. "Grant, please know that if it should turn out that Lydia is the one the Lord has chosen for you to marry, your father and I will be very pleased."

When Grant knocked on the Reynoldses' door, it was Billy who opened it. Billy smiled and said, "Hi, Grant. You all by yourself?"

"Yes. Is your father here?"

"Sure. Come on in."

Billy led Grant into the parlor, where the

family was seated. The young man greeted everyone, then said, "Mr. Reynolds, would you allow me the privilege, sir, of talking to you in private, just for a few minutes?"

"Why, of course, Grant. Let's go into the kitchen."

After Duane and Grant had left the parlor, Beverly looked at her children and noticed a gleam in Lydia's eye. "Lydia, do you know what this is about?"

"I do, Mother. But it would be best that I not say any more until Daddy and Grant come back."

Thirty minutes had passed before Duane and Grant returned to the parlor. Beverly was in her favorite overstuffed chair. Lydia was on the couch, trying to hide her excitement, and Billy was removing himself from his father's chair, which sat close to Beverly's.

Duane gestured toward the couch. "You can sit over there by Lydia, Grant." Duane eased into his chair and said to Beverly, "Grant came here tonight to ask my permission to be our daughter's beau. I gladly gave it."

"Grant, this is highly unusual," Beverly said, "but I want to tell you that I'm very pleased. I appreciate that you've asked

Lydia's father for permission. You are a true Christian gentleman."

"I told him the same thing," Duane said. "Grant and I had a good talk about Christian conduct in dating. I've set down some strict ground rules, for which he thanked me. I'll go over them with Lydia also."

Beverly smiled her approval, then looked at the couple who sat on the couch and said, "So! It's now official! Grant and Lydia are steadies. How about some cool sarsaparilla to celebrate the occasion?"

In the months that followed, Grant and Lydia developed a sweet and pleasant relationship, growing closer together in heart and in the Lord. Both sets of parents were pleased at the way the couple complemented one another, and as each day passed, Grant and Lydia found themselves more and more convinced that the Lord had chosen them for each other. To Grant's surprise, not one of his friends kidded him about robbing the cradle.

In late January 1842, after a church function for the young people, Grant drove Lydia home in the family buggy. One of Duane Reynolds's rules was that the couple was not to be alone except for the few minutes it took them to travel about

Montgomery Village. In the evenings, they were free, however, to sit in the parlor of either home, even after the other family members had retired for the night. In warm weather they could sit on the front porch instead of the parlor.

The Reynoldses were just heading for bed when Grant and Lydia came in from the church activity. They bid the couple good night and left them alone in the parlor, next to the crackling fire.

After some small talk Grant said, "Lydia, I've told you how much I admire my Uncle Rex Swanson, my mother's brother."

"The one who's a major in the army?"

"Right. Well, I know we haven't talked about this much, but I've decided to make a career in the United States Army. I've prayed about it, and my parents feel it's the right thing for me too."

"If you have peace about it, Grant, and your parents believe it's the right thing, then it has to be."

"I'm glad you see it that way. I've looked into going to West Point so I can be an officer when I go into the army. It takes an appointment from a congressman in order to enter the academy, but with the good grades I've received all through school, Uncle Rex says there'll be no problem getting the appointment. It takes four years to graduate."

"Will you be able to come home for the summer?" Lydia asked.

"Partly. There'll be six weeks of practical training in June and half of July, but I'll also be able to come home for two weeks at Christmastime."

Lydia smiled. "Then I will live for the times you can be home during your years at West Point. I'm proud that you want to be a soldier and serve your country."

Grant took her hand, leaned close, and kissed her cheek. "I love you, Lydia."

"And I love you, Grant," she whispered. "With all my heart."

The courtship continued, and as time passed the young couple found their love for each other growing deeper and stronger.

With his father's help, Grant submitted to one of their congressmen his petition to enter West Point in September. A letter came back with forms to fill out. Grant completed the forms and sent them back to the congressman, along with a copy of his grades through the years.

Grant graduated from high school the last week of May and was hired again by the farmer he had worked for the previous summer. Four days after graduating, the notice came that he had been accepted at the U.S. Military Academy in West Point, New York. Marjorie shed some tears as she realized her boy would no longer be living in their home come September.

That evening, Grant and Lydia sat on her front porch, enjoying the moonlight. Crickets were making their night sounds, and the sweet aroma of honeysuckle filled the air. They talked about their day, then Grant said, "Lydia, something came in the mail today." He reached into his shirt pocket as he spoke.

"Oh, I know what it is! You've been accepted at the academy!"

"You guessed it," he said, handing her the folded envelope. She took the paper out, angled it toward the moonlight, and read the acceptance letter. As she placed it back in the envelope, her lower lip quivered. "I'll miss you, Grant, but I'm so proud of you."

Grant embraced her, kissed her cheek, and said, "I'll miss you, too, sweetheart. You *will* wait for me, won't you?"

Lydia drew back, looked up into his eyes, and said, "You *do* know the answer to that question, don't you?"

"Yes, but I just want to hear you say it."

Moonlight reflected in Lydia's emerald eyes. "All right. Mr. Grant Swanson Smith, I, Lydia Jane Reynolds, solemnly promise that I will wait for you during the four years you are getting your military education."

Grant sighed. "Music to my ears. Now, that brings up another subject. Something else I have to ask you."

"All right."

"Since my chosen career is with the United States Army, would you have any problem being an army wife?"

"Grant, if we marry, I'd be happy no matter what because I'd be married to you. Since the army is your chosen profession, then my profession will be as an army officer's wife. I'll back you all the way."

He embraced her again and said, "I know we're too young for a formal engagement, but here and now I am asking you to marry me soon after I graduate from West Point in the spring of 1846."

Lydia pulled back once more to look into his eyes. "The answer is *yes*, my darling Grant," she said through brimming tears. "Eighteen forty-six sounds like a long time from now, but it will be worth the wait. I'm so happy and honored that you want me for your life mate."

On the first Saturday in June, Beverly Reynolds invited the Smiths over for a meal. At the table, in front of the young couple, the parents discussed Grant and Lydia's promise to wait for each other and marry after Grant graduated from West Point. Both sets of parents said they would be very happy if it worked out.

"Grant . . . Lydia," Beverly said, "you are both very young, and things might change between you in the next four years. Your young love is a tender flame. Time will prove if it is the genuine, lasting kind upon which to build a marriage."

"Beverly is right," Marjorie said. "Many things can happen in four years. If the love you have between you is the real thing, it will prove out."

Grant looked around the table at each parent, then settled his gaze on Beverly. "I understand what you've said, Mrs. Reynolds. Lydia and I are very young. But may I say what is on my heart?"

"Of course, dear."

"You've put it in a beautiful way, Mrs. Reynolds . . . our love being a tender flame. In my heart, I know the tender flame between Lydia and me is genuine. It will grow stronger as time passes, even though we'll be apart while I am at West Point."

"I agree with Grant," Lydia said. "Yes, we're young, and life can bring along things we never planned on. But when it comes to my love for Grant, I know it's the genuine thing. I have no doubt at all that the Lord has chosen us for each other, and that He has given us the true, lasting kind of love."

On Monday, September 5, Grant went to Baltimore to board the train for New York. Both fathers had taken off work to be there, though Sharon, Theresa, and Billy had to tell Grant good-bye that morning before leaving for school.

As departure time drew near, Scott and Marjorie hugged their son with tears in their eyes. Grant tried to cheer them by saying he would be home a few days before Christmas. Marjorie kissed his cheek, and they stepped back to allow Duane and Beverly to talk to Grant.

When the Reynoldses were finished, Duane said, "Us old folks will vacate the premises so you young folks can say your good-byes."

Lydia smiled at her father. "Thank you,

Daddy. I'm staying till the train pulls out, if that's all right."

"Sure, honey. We'll meet you out front."

As Duane turned to walk away, Grant said, "Mr. Reynolds . . ."

"Yes, Grant?"

"Sir, begging your understanding, since Lydia and I are promised to each other, and since we'll be apart for nearly four months . . . would it be all right if —"

"Sure, son. It's all right."

"Thank you, sir."

Both sets of parents walked away quickly, not looking back to watch the young couple share a sweet, tender kiss on the lips.

5

On Saturday, August 30, 1845, Duane Reynolds was working in his backyard late in the afternoon when he heard Beverly call from the porch, "Duane, there's somebody here who wants to talk to you!"

"Who is it?"

"Grant. He's in the parlor."

"Just send him out here, will you, honey? I'll talk to him in the yard."

Moments later, the West Point cadet stepped off the porch. "Working hard, sir?"

"Naw. Just making Beverly think I am so she won't come up with some chore I don't like."

"Well, I won't take up a lot of your simulation time, sir."

Duane laughed. "Okay. Let's see, you're heading back to West Point for your senior year on Monday, aren't you?"

"Right, sir. And . . . well, I want to ask you a question."

"Sure. Let's come over here and sit in the shade." They moved to some wooden lawn chairs beneath a pair of elm trees.

"Okay, my boy, what's the question?"

"Mr. Reynolds, you know that I love your daughter and have intentions of marrying her once I'm out of school."

"I'm quite aware of that, yes."

"Well, sir . . . I . . . uh —" He cleared his throat. "I would like your permission to give Lydia an engagement ring."

Duane grinned. "This is no surprise, Grant. And let me say that I am superbly proud and happy that the Lord has given my daughter such a fine Christian young man." He drew a deep breath. "Yes, Grant. You have my permission to become officially engaged to Lydia, and to put a ring on her finger."

"Thank you, sir! I promise I'll be a good husband to her. I will love and cherish her with all my heart. And if God blesses us with children — your grandchildren — I promise you, they'll be raised in the nurture and admonition of the Lord."

"I have no doubt about that, son," said Duane, tears welling up in his eyes. "She's a precious girl, Grant. Always make her happy."

"I'll do my utmost, sir."

"And Grant, thank you for asking me before you made your engagement official."

"I wouldn't do it any other way, sir."

"That's one reason Beverly and I love you so much, son."

"Thank you, sir. Well, I'd better be going. I have a dinner date with Lydia tonight, and I've got several things to do between now and then."

Both men rose from their chairs.

"Grant . . ."

"Yes, sir?"

"What's it look like?"

"Sir?"

"The engagement ring. You've already purchased it, haven't you?"

Grant nodded, a wide grin stretching across his face. "Yes, sir."

"You wouldn't have put that ring on her finger if I had objected, would you?"

"Oh, no, sir."

"Pretty sure of yourself, weren't you?"

"Shouldn't I have been?"

Duane smiled without comment.

"See you later, sir." Grant turned away, then stopped and rubbed his chin. "Ah . . . Mr. Reynolds?"

"Yes?"

"When I put the ring on Lydia's finger, it's going to be a very special moment. Would it be all right if —"

"Of course. An engagement certainly

should be sealed with a kiss."

"Thank you, sir."

That evening Grant took Lydia to nearby Germantown for dinner. When they returned to Montgomery Village, he drove his father's buggy around the town square where kerosene lanterns lit the evening darkness. He noticed an empty bench and said, "Okay if we stop and sit a spell?"

"Of course," Lydia said.

Grant stepped out of the buggy and rubbed the horse's muzzle as he went around to the other side. Extending his hand to Lydia, he said, "May I have the honor of helping you down, miss?"

"It's my pleasure to have such a gallant gentleman help me down."

Grant ushered Lydia to the bench. Seating her first, he then sat down beside her and said, "You look lovely tonight, sweetheart."

"Thank you, but you already told me that three times."

"You'll probably hear it again before you're rid of me tonight." Grant took both of her hands in his. "Lydia, since I first fell in love with you, that love has grown. I love you now more than ever."

"It's been the same for me."

"I'm so thankful for that. Now, I want you to do something for me."

"Of course."

"Close your eyes."

She gave him a quizzical look, then obeyed. When her eyes were closed, Grant let go of her right hand and took the engagement ring from his shirt pocket.

"The next time I do this, it will be when I say, 'With this ring I thee wed.' " As he spoke, he slid the ring onto the third finger of her left hand. "You can open your eyes now."

Lydia's gaze fell on the tiny diamond that glistened in the combination of moonlight and lantern light. She lifted her eyes to look at Grant's face, then raised her hand and kissed the ring. "Darling, I promise I will always love you and be faithful to you."

Grant held her close for a long moment. When they eased apart, she looked at the ring, then threw her arms around his neck and said, "It's so beautiful!"

"I love you so very much."

"And I love you so very much."

"I was at your house today," Grant said. "Your mother told me you were shopping in Gaithersburg with Betty Palmer."

"Yes. Mother said you'd been there to

81

talk to Daddy. Neither one would tell me what it was about."

"Well, now you know. And as you can see, he said I could."

"Daddy loves you, Grant."

"Your father said I could do something else when I gave you the ring."

"And what was that?"

"He said an engagement should be sealed with a kiss."

"Who am I to disagree with Daddy?"

Their lingering kiss was sweet and tender.

As they held each other close, Grant said, "Remember when your mother called the love between us a tender flame?"

"I do."

"She said that time would prove if it was the genuine, lasting kind to build a marriage on. That was three years ago. Three years that we've been apart most of the time. Yet here we are, more in love than ever."

"Yes, more than ever."

Grant kept his arm around Lydia as they sat contentedly without speaking. Then he said, "I wish this moment could last forever, sweetheart, but it's time to take you home."

She looked up at him. "I'll be glad when

taking me home will mean our home."

Ten minutes later, the buggy came to a halt in front of the Reynolds house. Grant helped Lydia out of the buggy and they walked up the porch steps side by side. The lone lantern burned beside the door.

Lydia placed her hand so the flame would find its reflection in the diamond and said, "Oh, Grant, I'm so happy!"

"Before you go in . . ."

"Yes?"

"Your father said that since we are engaged, it would be all right if I kissed you good night. You know, other than on the cheek."

Lydia giggled. "Well, like I said, who am I to disagree with Daddy?"

On Monday morning, the newly engaged couple stood on the platform by the New York-bound train. Scott and Marjorie had already told their son good-bye and were standing some distance away. After a few sweet kisses, Grant boarded the train. Lydia stood on the platform, not moving from the spot until the train had passed from view.

On November 28, the entire student body of cadets at West Point was told to gather in the chapel at ten o'clock that morning for a special assembly. As they gathered, the students speculated what the assembly was about. None of the professors had given out any information when announcing to their classes that the meeting had been called.

Grant Smith was sitting with two of his friends, Keith Killen and Cordell Anderson, when General Forrest Wexford, the academy's president, appeared from a side room and walked across the platform. On his heels was U.S. Army General Zachary Taylor, who was recognized by nearly all of the student body.

Military men, whether students or regular army, had seen Taylor's face in newspapers and old army bulletins. He had joined the army in 1808, and as a major in the 1832 Black Hawk War, had earned the nickname "Old Rough and Ready." The name had become even more popular when, as a colonel, he led campaigns against the Seminole Indians in Florida during the fierce battles of 1835–1842, after which the Seminoles moved to Indian territory east of Texas and became one of the Five Civilized Tribes.

General Wexford called the meeting to order, then said, "Gentlemen, all of you are aware that last March, President Polk announced the intention of the United States to annex the Republic of Texas as our twenty-eighth state. You are also aware that upon that announcement, the government of Mexico denounced our president for such a plan and has severed relations with our country over it.

"Texas won its freedom from Mexico almost ten years ago. Their battle for independence began at the Battle of the Alamo in March 1836 and ended when General Sam Houston defeated the Mexican army at San Jacinto the very next month. I stood before you last March and informed you of the Mexican problem over President Polk's plan to annex Texas. The problem is growing worse, and I think as military men, you need to know what has developed. I learned that my friend, General Zachary Taylor — Old Rough and Ready himself — was nearby, so I collared him and asked him to come and speak to you on the matter."

There was laughter followed by applause.

General Wexford turned to the stately gentleman seated behind him on the platform and called him to the podium as those assembled gave a standing ovation.

The young cadets listened intently as General Taylor told them that just two months before, President Polk had sent American diplomat John Slidell on a secret mission to Mexico to attempt a peaceful settlement of the dispute over the planned annexation of Texas as a U.S. state. The Mexican government had refused to receive him. When Slidell returned to Washington and made his report to President Polk, the president called General Taylor to the White House and told him to make preparations in case of war with Mexico. He feared the Mexican government, still angry over their defeat at San Jacinto, might become an aggressor.

The faculty and students of West Point were stunned to hear such news.

General Taylor advised them to wait for more information from Washington.

On December 13, Lydia was at the Baltimore railroad station, along with both sets of parents, when Grant arrived from New York.

As Duane Reynolds drove the buggy toward Montgomery Village, the conversation soon turned to the Mexican problem. The Smiths and the Reynoldses were interested to learn if Grant had any news, since the newspapers had not mentioned it for a few days.

"We received news just before classes dismissed for the holidays," Grant said. "Things have grown hot between the U.S. and Mexico. The Mexican government declares the Nueces the boundary between Texas and Mexico, which would give them the entire southern tip of the land the Texans claim. President Polk agrees with the Texans that the Rio Grande is the proper boundary."

"Looks like we could have us a war with Mexico," Duane said.

"It's very possible, sir."

Though December was a cold month in Maryland and there was snow on the ground, Grant and Lydia took walks in the evenings to the town square in Montgomery Village and strolled through the adjacent park.

A few days after Grant's return, the Smiths had the Reynolds family to their home for supper. Sixteen-year-old Billy discussed military matters with Grant during the early part of the meal and then asked his opinion of the Mexican crisis, which Billy's history teacher talked about each day.

Grant told him that with the Mexican government so angry at the United States, and now with General Antonio López de Santa Anna once again president of Mexico, he feared there would be war. It was Santa Anna who had led the Mexican army when it attacked the Alamo and when it was defeated at San Jacinto.

"Enough war talk, Billy," Beverly Reynolds said. "I'd like to hear if your sister and her intended have discussed a wedding date."

Grant and Lydia looked at each other and smiled.

"We have, Mrs. Reynolds," Grant said. "We've decided that we'd like to marry on Sunday afternoon, June 7. Since graduation at the academy is May 1, this will give us time to make final preparations for the wedding after graduation."

"Probably the best thing would be to talk to the pastor about it," Scott said. "Make sure the date is all right with him."

Grant smiled. "We already did that, Dad. Just this afternoon. The date is set."

"Well, great!" Scott swung his gaze to Marjorie. "Just think, honey. As of June 7 we'll have us another daughter!"

"Yes!" exclaimed Sharon, who was now a maturing eighteen-year-old. "Theresa and

I have wanted Lydia for our sister for a long time."

"Well, we'll have us another son too," Duane said. "And we're mighty proud of him."

"And I'll finally have a brother!" Billy said. "And Grant is the one I would choose if I had been given a choice."

Grant reached over and mussed Billy's hair. "And I'd choose you too, Billy!"

"So what about your orders upon graduation, Grant?" Duane asked. "Do you have any idea where the army is going to send you?"

"Yes, sir. I received that information just before the semester closed. They gave us opportunity to choose the fort where we would like to be stationed. They don't always meet our requests, but they did mine. I asked to be stationed at Fort McHenry, and they granted it."

"Well, praise the Lord! You and Lydia won't be very far away."

"Lydia and I will be living in the married officers' quarters. General Wexford has seen them and told me they're fairly new and quite comfortable."

Lydia smiled at him. "Even if they weren't comfortable, I'd gladly live there with you."

Scott chuckled. "It's good that you have that attitude, Lydia. Many of the forts around this country aren't so nice."

"No matter, Mr. Smith. As long as I'm with Grant, it'll be a little bit like heaven."

On December 30, the newspapers reported that the strained relations between the United States and Mexico were growing worse. The previous day, the Republic of Texas had become the country's twenty-eighth state. Antonio López de Santa Anna viciously and publicly denounced President James K. Polk and declared the act would forever alienate Mexico from the United States.

When Grant and Lydia got together at the Reynolds' house on New Year's Day, 1846, they couldn't hold in their excitement. They were now in the year that would bring them together as husband and wife.

Grant was scheduled to leave on Monday, January 5. On January 2, the newspapers carried the story that President Polk had dispatched a large number of troops to south Texas, under General Zachary Taylor's command. Taylor would occupy the disputed area between the

Nueces and Rio Grande Rivers. Polk had declared that any move on this territory by Mexican troops would constitute an act of aggression against the United States. Such a move would mean war.

On the same day Grant Smith boarded the train to return to West Point for his final semester, the newspapers reported a message from President Santa Anna. He and his countrymen were demanding that the statehood of Texas be rescinded and that President Polk make a public apology for leading his country to annex Texas.

Two days later the newspapers carried Polk's curt reply, an open letter to Santa Anna:

My dear sir,

Be it understood that Texas will remain the twenty-eighth state of the United States. I emphasize the word "United." The Texas-Mexico border is the Rio Grande, not the Nueces. If Mexican troops cross the Rio Grande, it will be considered a direct act of aggression, and will be met with deadly force and resistance by the UNITED States army.

James K. Polk
President, UNITED States of America

6

The strain between the United States and Mexico continued as the months passed. President Santa Anna continued his verbal attacks from his balcony in Mexico City as great crowds gathered around the presidential palace. His harsh words were reported almost daily in newspapers throughout the United States and kept the American people on edge. There was more and more talk in Washington, and in military installations all over the country, about war.

President Polk delivered a speech in Washington attempting to settle the country's dread of impending war with Mexico. Polk said there was still hope for peace, since it was now mid-April and as yet no Mexican troops had been ordered across the Rio Grande. Polk believed that the Mexican government didn't really want war and that peaceful negotiations could end the hostile feelings. To that end, he was sending John Slidell and a team of negotiators to Mexico to talk to Santa Anna and his military leaders.

The American people were filled with hope by the president's speech, and many were praying for the success of the negotiators.

During these same months, letters flew back and forth between Grant Smith and Lydia Reynolds as they planned their wedding, now only weeks away. They did not mention the Mexican problem in their correspondence. Their letters were filled with love, hope, and the anticipation of becoming husband and wife.

Hopes for a peaceful settlement between the United States and Mexico were shattered when, on April 22, the U.S. negotiators were turned away from the presidential palace in Mexico City. Santa Anna told them that until Texas was removed from statehood, there would be no peace negotiations.

Polk received word of it on April 24, and the next day, General Zachary Taylor and his regiments, occupying Point Isabel on the Rio Grande River, were attacked by Mexican troops who had sneaked across the Rio Grande under cover of darkness. The Mexicans had been driven back across the river, but not before sixteen of Taylor's men were killed and several others wounded.

James Polk learned of the attack four days later. He was furious but kept it from the press. He wanted to meet with Congress before the bad news reached the American people.

Secret emergency joint sessions of Congress were held beginning on Friday, May 1.

On that same day, at the United States Military Academy in West Point, New York, some two thousand people were seated on the wooded academy grounds, attending the open-air graduation ceremonies. In the crowd were Scott and Marjorie Smith, along with their daughters, Sharon and Theresa, and Duane and Beverly Reynolds, Lydia, and Billy.

The academy military band played an exhilarating march while the graduates filed from the main building in perfect step, then onto the platform to join the academy's faculty and administration, along with several army dignitaries. The ceremonies began, and after several brief speeches it was time to call each graduate to the podium to receive his diploma and commission as a lieutenant in the United States Army.

Lydia's golden brown hair glistened in the sun. She had it styled in Grant's favorite way . . . in an upsweep with long, dangling curls on the back and tiny ringlets across her forehead and at her temples. She wore a cool pale yellow dress sprinkled with light green leaves and a pattern of trailing vines. Lydia sat tall and proud, waiting eagerly for Grant's name to be called. Her mind strayed to her wedding, and she pictured herself in the long, flowing white dress, walking down the aisle on the arm of her father, with the pump organ playing. She saw Pastor Britton standing on the platform, wedding manual in hand, looking distinguished in his black suit with his thick head of silver hair.

At the altar, tall and handsome in his officer's uniform, stood Grant, smiling at her.

She pictured Grant and herself rushing up the aisle after taking their vows to enter their new life as Lieutenant and Mrs. Grant Smith. *Mrs. Grant Smith.* She mused over the title for several minutes, feeling the warmth and joy it brought to her heart.

The list of graduates finally reached the Ses, and Lydia's attention came back to the ceremony. Lydia was seated between her parents, and each one took her by the hand as Grant's name was called and the tall, broad-shouldered young man strode across the platform, halted before General Forrest Wexford, and offered a snappy salute.

Tears moistened Lydia's eyes when General Wexford congratulated Grant on being in the top five of his class scholastically and announced that his fellow classmates had voted him the 1846 graduate "most likely to succeed" in his army career.

When Wexford handed Grant his papers and saluted him, Grant proudly returned the salute, pivoted military style, and headed for his seat. He glanced down at Lydia, gave her a wide smile, and winked at her. Lydia gave a tiny wave and smile in return.

In Washington, D.C., the joint sessions of Congress continued into the next week. On May 5, however, President Polk released the story, knowing that he could keep it a secret no longer.

While newspapers across the land reported the Mexican attack on General Taylor and his troops, Congress and the president were carefully deliberating the course of action to take.

The joint sessions were finished on

May 6. Polk took the opinions and suggestions of the congressmen to the Oval Office, and there met with his secretary of war and top military advisers.

Early in May, Lydia Reynolds moved into the house of Captain and Mrs. Nathan Daniels at Fort McHenry. The captain and his wife were friends of Pastor John Britton, who had told them that Lieutenant Grant Smith and his bride-to-be were members of his church, and that Grant would be living in the married officers' quarters with his new bride after they were married on June 7. When Captain Daniels learned that Grant was moving into the apartment upon his arrival from West Point and Lydia wanted to do some fix-up work on it before the wedding, he and his wife gladly offered their spare bedroom to Lydia so she could be at the fort.

The apartment was completely furnished but a bit cramped for space. Lydia decided that a fresh coat of white paint would work wonders at making the place seem larger, and Grant agreed. As they painted, scrubbed, and rearranged furniture, they spun their dreams of a wonderful life together.

Word came to Washington that on the night of May 3, Santa Anna's army had shelled Fort Texas on the Rio Grande from across the river. No one in the fort was killed, but United States property was severely damaged. The U.S. troops fought back, and the Mexicans lost some men as their troops retreated with their cannons.

On May 9, President Polk sat in the Oval Office alone and began to carefully prepare a war message to Congress. The next day, the flag-draped coffins of the American soldiers killed at Point Isabel arrived in Washington, and great crowds of irate citizens gathered to look upon them. The newspapers named the dead men, and the people of the United States felt sure President Polk would ask Congress to back him as he declared war on Mexico.

On Monday morning, May 11, Polk met with Congress and delivered his war message. In the stirring address, Polk stated that Mexico had "boldly and contemptuously invaded United States territory at Port Isabel, and shed American blood on American soil." He further decried the act of aggression at Fort Texas.

Grant and Lydia had just finished polishing the apartment to perfection when there was a tap at the open door. Duane Reynolds was there to pick up his daughter and take her home, where she would remain until after the wedding.

Lydia rushed to the door. "Hello, Daddy! We've got it all done. Come in and take a look."

Duane embraced his daughter, grinned at his future son-in-law, and said, "Looks like this place is just about ready for a happy young couple to occupy."

"Sure is," Grant said. "It's a rather lonely place when I'm here by myself, but that'll change in a little less than a month."

Through the open door, Grant saw Captain Nathan Daniels approaching. Duane turned around as the captain stepped up to the door.

"Lydia and I will be right over to pick up her things, Captain," Duane said.

Daniels forced a smile. "Anytime is fine, Duane." He looked at Grant. "Lieutenant, we just received news that President Polk delivered a war message to Congress this morning. It doesn't look good. Colonel Marsh has called for an assembly of all men of the fort at four o'clock. There are a couple of corporals assigned to advise every man of the assembly, but I thought since I was close, I'd let you know."

Grant glanced at the clock on the wall. It was 3:35. "All right, sir. Thank you. I'll be there."

When the captain was gone, Lydia gripped Grant's hand, concern evident in her eyes. "Darling, what does this assembly mean?"

"Colonel Marsh wants to explain the status of the fort. There are certain steps to be taken when we know the president has delivered a war message to Congress. We will remain in an averred state of readiness to further prepare ourselves should war be declared. If that happens, we'll be put on alert."

"And that means?"

"Well . . . that any number of us could be sent to south Texas, or even to Mexico, to do battle with the Mexican army, and we must be ready to move out on a moment's notice."

"Oh, Grant, this is terrible. Our plans . . . the wedding —"

"I know. But we have to leave these things in God's hands . . . let Him work His will in our lives. Please. Keep your pretty little chin up and trust the Lord to take care of it all."

"He's right, Lydia," Duane said. "We

have to put our lives and our plans in the nail-pierced hands."

Lydia took a deep breath and let it out slowly. "You're right, I know. I just wish sometimes it wasn't so hard."

On Tuesday morning, May 12, 1846, President Polk made a grim announcement in Washington that war with Mexico was inevitable and unavoidable. All attempts at a peaceful settlement with the Mexican government had failed.

The next day, Congress overwhelmingly approved a declaration of war, which was called for by President Polk. The country was now officially at war with Mexico. General Zachary Taylor and his troops would be the first to move into Mexican territory. Other troops would follow as quickly as possible.

At military posts all over the twenty-eight states and many territories, the United States Army was put on alert.

At Fort McHenry, the troops and officers were assembled for a briefing of the situation and for assignments. Lieutenant Grant Smith was assigned to General Winfield Scott's battalion, and Scott informed him in a special meeting that the battalion would head southwest for

Mexico on Friday morning at dawn. Those officers who lived within a short distance of the fort would be allowed to ride home and tell their families good-bye, as long as they could be back by Thursday at 1:00 P.M.

Lieutenant Smith was given an army horse to ride, and he put the animal to a gallop as he headed for home. About three hours later, he rode into Montgomery Village. While trotting toward the Reynoldses' home, he was hailed by friends and questioned about the alert. He told them a battalion was leaving Fort McHenry at dawn on Friday, then hurried on, wanting to get to Lydia.

Grant dismounted in front of the house and saw Billy's face in the parlor window. The front door stood open, and he could hear Billy calling loudly to his sister that Grant was here.

Billy was first out the door. Grant hugged him, then saw Lydia behind her brother. There was apprehension in her eyes as she opened her arms to him, breathing his name. Lydia clung to the man she loved, her face partially buried against his chest, and his strong arms held her tight.

"We heard about the alert, darling.

What's happening at the fort?"

Grant leaned back so he could look into her eyes. "Sweetheart, I've been assigned to General Winfield Scott's battalion, Company C, under Captain Nathan Daniels. The entire battalion is pulling out and heading for Mexico at dawn on Friday."

The breath caught in Lydia's throat, and tears rushed to her eyes and spilled down her cheeks.

Grant cupped Lydia's chin in one hand and said softly, "Sweetheart, we have to trust the Lord in this. I know it will mean postponing the wedding, but probably not for long. This war shouldn't last but a few months at most. We have so much more firepower, and a much larger army than Santa Anna. It'll be over in short order."

Lydia drew another deep breath and wiped away her tears. "Darling, I'm sorry. I know I've got to keep my chin up. You're a soldier and duty calls. I must learn to live with that. And I must allow the Lord to give me the strength and faith I need to trust Him to keep you safe and to bring you back to me."

"That's my girl." Grant folded her in his arms once more. "I hate postponing the wedding, but we'll get through this and be married before the snow falls."

The Smiths and the Reynoldses were told of Grant's assignment to General Winfield Scott's battalion and of the plan to pull out for Mexico on Friday morning. Both families felt apprehension that Grant would be leading a unit of men into combat. Marjorie invited the Reynolds family and Pastor and Mrs. Britton to supper that evening. She wanted to have the pastor lead them in a special time of prayer for Grant's safety.

Late that evening, after the meal and the time of prayer for Grant, the engaged couple sat in the porch swing at the Reynolds house. The moon was full and cast a silver spray of light in the yard and on the porch.

The fragrant, warm air carried a heady aroma of May flowers. But the heavy-hearted couple were immune to the night's charming atmosphere as they held hands and talked of their future together, trying to keep their minds from the reality that tomorrow they must part.

Grant and Lydia whispered tender words of love and comfort to each other, making the most of their last evening together, not knowing how long they would be separated. Finally, at midnight, they walked to the front door. Grant gently took Lydia's face in his hands and placed soft kisses on her lips.

She fought to keep from breaking down as she told him good night, but once inside the house, she dashed to her room, closed the door, and flung herself, sobbing, onto the bed.

The next morning, Grant told his family good-bye and rode to the Reynolds house. After he said his good-byes to Duane, Beverly, and Billy, he and Lydia were left alone on the front porch.

"Lydia, we won't be able to write to each other while I'm in Mexico," Grant said as he held her in his arms, "but we can maintain a closeness by holding up each other in prayer."

"I know, darling. But I'm going to write you a letter every day anyhow. That, along with the prayer, will make me feel closer to you."

The army horse standing near the porch whinnied. Grant looked at the horse and said, "Okay, okay. In a minute." He turned back to Lydia. "I do have to get going, honey."

They kissed long and tenderly.

"Good-bye, Lydia. I love you."

A sob caught in her throat, but she fought it as she said, "Good-bye, darling. I love you."

"Our tender flame will never stop burning."

"Never."

Grant kissed her again, then wheeled about and walked briskly to the horse. He swung into the saddle and rode away without looking back.

Tears coursed down her cheeks as Lydia watched Grant until he was out of sight.

The next day, Lydia applied for a job she knew was open in a clothing store in nearby Germantown. She was hired immediately and began to work eight hours a day, six days a week.

True to her word, Lydia wrote Grant a letter each night. As the stack of letters grew, she kept it tied in a bundle with a blue ribbon.

She hung on every word that came from Washington about the Mexican War and read the reports in the newspapers. When she read of the many casualties among the U.S. Army, she couldn't help feeling a sense of dread. In the evenings, when her parents saw that she was burdened, they prayed with her, doing all they could to comfort and encourage her.

Lydia clung to her family and to Grant's family, but gained most of her strength from her private prayer time and reading her Bible.

She was glad to have her job. It helped to pass the time, as well as giving her mind something to dwell on besides war and death. The money from the job was a help too. Much of it was used to purchase items that one day she and Grant would have in their home. She put away each purchase, looking for the day when she and Grant would make their home together. And three evenings a week, she did volunteer work in Montgomery Village's small medical clinic.

Still, at times the load grew heavy. One Sunday morning, during the altar call, Lydia went forward and told the pastor that she just needed to kneel and pray in God's house. Pastor Britton had his wife join Lydia at the altar. Delia Britton listened to Lydia describe her fears, then prayed with her. Before they left the altar, Delia said, "Could we get together sometime soon and talk? I want to help you if I can."

"Of course," Lydia said. "I'm free tomorrow night. Could we talk then?"

"Tomorrow night would be fine."

Monday evening came, and Lydia and Delia sat on the edge of Lydia's bed.

"I don't pretend to know exactly how you feel," Delia said, "with the man you love off fighting a war, but I do know what God says in His Word, and I know that the God of peace is able to help you bear this burden.

"Here's one thing you need to think about: Since the early days of man's history on earth — I mean, for ages immemorial — men have gone off to war, and their women have stayed behind to keep the home fires burning. Those brave women kept a vigilant lookout for their loved ones to return.

"You must realize that you're not alone in your vigil. Thousands of American women are doing the same thing. Most of them are not Christians, but you are. You have something they don't. You have the Lord to lean on, and you have His Word to lean on."

Tears were trickling down Lydia's cheeks. "I've been sort of self-centered in this, haven't I, Mrs. Britton? Yes, I do have the Lord and His Word to lean on. I've been trying to do that, but I've also been wallowing in some self-pity."

"That's only natural," Delia said. "Now, let me suggest two things for you to do. First, it will help you immensely if you will memorize Psalm 91. Hide it in your heart so you can quote it, or parts of it, when your faith shows signs of weakening."

"All right. That sounds like a good thing to do."

"Also, you're busying yourself with your job at the store and your volunteer work at the clinic. This is good, and I commend you for it. But you still have some extra time left over each week, don't you?"

"Oh yes."

"How about teaching a Sunday school class? My husband was saying just a couple of days ago that he needs to split a class of six- to nine-year-old girls, and he's praying about a teacher to take the six- and seven-year-olds. You've substituted a few times when you were needed. How about a permanent class?"

A smile worked its way across Lydia's mouth. "I'd like that."

"Good! I'll tell my husband, and he'll put you to work in a hurry."

One week later, Lydia kissed her family good night and went to her room. She took out pencil and paper and began composing the day's letter to Grant:

June 7, 1846
Darling —
I can hardly see to write for the tears that fill my eyes. You understand my tears, I'm sure. This was to be the biggest day of my life, except for the day I opened my heart to Jesus. By this time tonight, I would have been Mrs. Grant Smith, if the war had not come along.

Please understand that I wish things could have happened as we planned, but I am not bitter. Our dear God in heaven could have prevented the war if He had pleased, but He has let it take place. Thus, we are hundreds of miles apart on what was to be our wedding night, and I don't know where you are or what you are facing.

As I told you in a previous letter, I am memorizing the Ninety-first Psalm, and it is helping me tremendously. I am victoriously dwelling in the secret place of the Most High, and sweetly abiding under the shadow of the Almighty. Between working, volunteering, and teaching, I am very busy, but I love each task.

I had to get over my self-pity, and with God's help, I believe I have. My faith is growing stronger and my precious walk with the Lord is even closer. Family and friends tell me I have my sunny disposition back.

Mrs. Britton has been a great help, as I wrote you before. She was so right when she said I am no different than thousands of other women who have gone before me, and thousands who at this time have their husbands or sweethearts in the war.

The Lord is helping me to bravely face each new day with renewed hope, and His matchless grace is alive and glowing in my heart. When I speak of your return, I never say *if* Grant comes home, but *when* Grant comes home. This seems to have helped women who come into the store, as well as those at the clinic and at church. I want to be an inspiration to everyone around me.

I love you, my darling Grant, with an endless, tender flame.

Yours forever,
Lydia

7

In the dry, rugged country of Mexico, General Winfield Scott had positioned his battalion some five miles east of the towering Sierra Madre Oriental Range, on a wide stream that was not named on his map. They were in the state of Tamaulipas, which they had reached in early October, after fighting the Mexican army all the way from the Rio Grande at Fort Texas to the advantage point they now occupied.

The Mexican troops had taken their toll on the American forces, but it was nothing like the casualties the Mexicans had suffered. In Mexico City, Santa Anna was working furiously to enlist more men to send against Scott's troops.

President Polk had sent more battalions from forts in both northern and southern states, and in New Mexico Territory. Some of them had been directed to join General Zachary Taylor on Mexican soil, where he and his troops were moving on Santa Anna's men due south of Laredo, in the Mexican state of Nuevo Leon. The others had been sent to join General Scott.

With these reinforcements came a letter from the president, informing Scott that he was now officially the commander of the entire United States Army in Mexico. The battle was his to lead, and Polk expected him to bring Santa Anna to his knees.

On October 22, a fierce battle had been fought with the Mexicans, both in the mountains and on the plains. The Mexicans had put up a good fight until early afternoon, then were forced to retreat.

General Scott watched his weary men file into camp late in the afternoon. A dozen or so wounded men were laid on the ground, and the medics went to work on them. The bodies of three soldiers killed that day were covered with blankets, and shallow graves were hastily dug near the river bank. Because Lieutenant Grant Smith had made it known that he was a Christian and was often seen with his Bible in hand, General Scott had appointed him battalion chaplain. As the men gathered at the burial site, Grant read Scripture, spoke a few words about the bravery of the men who had been killed, and closed in prayer.

Afterward, while half the men stood guard, the other half bathed in the stream.

As soon as the clean men put on their uniforms again, they stood guard while the rest of the men bathed. All were glad that summer was over in Mexico, and the oppressive heat had been replaced with cooler air and soft, refreshing breezes.

The men ate their supper in relative silence while the sun was lowering in the west. Then they laid out their bedrolls and fed the campfires, which fluttered in the wind sweeping down from the lofty mountains, with dead mesquite.

Lieutenant Grant Smith took his Bible out of a leather pouch. After reading a passage and letting its truths seep into his soul, he turned to the flyleaf, which had become his custom since beginning the march to Mexico in May. He angled the page toward the fire and smiled as the words warmed his heart.

To Grant, whom I deeply admire.
May this Bible be a lamp unto your feet
and a light unto your path.
                    Your friend forever,
                    Lydia

His smile broadened as he read words that were added later when he wasn't looking.

Darling, though I will always admire you and will forever be your friend, please change "admire" in your mind to LOVE and "friend" to

SWEETHEART!

Loneliness crept over Grant as he closed the Bible. He longed to hold his precious Lydia and whisper words of love to her.

As he was slipping the Bible into the leather pouch, he saw Corporal Lenny Proffitt coming toward him. Proffitt, a small, thin man of nineteen, was from Roanoke, Virginia, and had been assigned to Grant's unit. They had fought side by side, and when Proffitt told the lieutenant that he was a Christian, a friendship was born.

"Mind if I sit down, sir?" Lenny asked.

"Be my guest."

"It's this time of day that makes a fella miss his girl most, isn't it, sir?"

"Sure is. And I've got a feeling your Susie and my Lydia are missing us pretty bad about now too."

Swift footsteps were heard from the shadows, and a young soldier appeared by the light of the fire. "Lieutenant Smith, sir, one of the wounded men is dying. He's asking for you."

"I'll wait here for you, sir," Lenny said.

Grant leaped to his feet and reached for his Bible. "You do that, Corporal. And pray, will you?"

"Yes, sir."

Over an hour had passed when Lenny Proffitt, who was placing more mesquite on the fire, looked up to see Grant Smith enter the circle of light.

"I've been praying, sir. How did it go?"

"Praise the Lord, I was able to lead him to Jesus before he died."

"I'm glad for that, sir. Who was he?"

"Private Jess Fisher, from Pittsburgh. I was also able to lead one of the other wounded men to the Lord. He was listening while I was talking to Jess."

"Wonderful."

The two men talked some more about the young women who were waiting for them and about their families, and how they yearned for the war to be over so they could go home. After a while, Lenny said, "Well, sir, I guess I'd better turn in. More Mexicans to fight tomorrow."

Soon the fires all over the camp dwindled to red embers, and while the sentries remained alert, the rest of the men lay in their bedrolls. The night was silent except for the soft moan of the wind across the land and the sound of rippling water nearby. The soldiers slept with the light of the stars on their faces.

One day in early November, the battle-weary men returned to camp, which was now located several miles farther south, on the Santa Maria River. The Sierra Madres were still just west of them, and the coastal town of Tampico lay some twenty miles due east.

The battle had taken place toward Tampico and had been a fierce one. General Scott's goal was to occupy Tampico within a week. But the Mexicans were putting up a stiff fight. More graves were dug, and more wounded men were being attended by the medics. Lieutenant Grant Smith sat with the wounded men, trying to comfort them and lead them to Christ.

General Winfield Scott sat by a fire after supper, going over a map with six of his colonels. Just as they were finishing plans for the next day's battle, Scott looked up to see Captain Nathan Daniels draw near.

"Did you need to see me, Captain?" Scott asked.

"Whenever you have the time, sir."

"We can talk right now. The colonels

and I are through working on tomorrow's battle plan."

"Thank you, sir. I know you're busy. I'll only take a few minutes of your time."

As the officers melted away into the night, Scott smiled wearily and said, "My time is your time, Captain. What do you need to talk to me about?"

"About an act of courage I saw today, sir."

"One of our soldiers outdid himself on the battlefield, I take it?"

"Yes, sir."

"Let's sit over here by the fire, and you tell me all about it."

When both men were seated on the ground with the crackling fire between them, Daniels said, "Lieutenant Grant Smith is the man, sir. And when I tell you what he did, he's going to stand taller in your eyes, even as he does mine."

Daniels told Scott how Grant Smith had risked his life to take out three Mexicans who were sneaking through heavy brush and would have gunned down Daniels and one of his other lieutenants from behind. Smith had shielded them as much as possible with his own body while firing his revolver. He had taken the Mexican soldiers by surprise and dropped the first two before they could get off a shot, but the third Mexican fired at him. The bullet nicked the tip of Smith's left ear, but he was able to take out the man with his next shot.

General Scott shook his head. "Nicked his left ear, you say?"

"Yes, sir."

"Then Lieutenant Smith missed death, without question, by probably no more than an inch."

"That's right, sir."

"And he would have taken those enemy bullets to save your life if those Mexicans could've gotten off their shots."

"Yes, sir."

"You're right, Captain. The man most certainly does stand taller in my eyes than he did before. I will see to it that Lieutenant Smith is properly commended for his deed."

"I was hoping you would say that, General."

"It's the least I can do. And by making him an example, perhaps it will encourage more men to be just like him."

Daniels smiled. "And that would improve any army, sir."

Early the next morning, after briefing

119

and breakfast, General Winfield Scott called for a full assembly before sending the troops out to battle their way toward Tampico. As the troops gathered, the sun came over the eastern horizon.

General Scott stood before the throng of soldiers and called Captain Nathan Daniels to his side. Daniels told the troops of the act of bravery in yesterday's battle, leaving the hero unnamed. Daniels then asked Lieutenant Grant Smith to come to him. Reluctantly, Grant made his way through the throng and joined Daniels and Scott.

"Men!" Daniels said. "The valorous deed I just told you about was performed by this man, Lieutenant Grant Smith!"

There was a rousing cheer from the troops and officers.

Then General Scott told the assembled men that Grant was the supreme example of what a soldier in the United States Army ought to be. Then he saluted Grant and shook his hand, and again the troops cheered.

Grant was greatly relieved when the assembly was dismissed. As he mounted his horse to ride out to meet the enemy, he thought of Lydia and asked the Lord to strengthen and comfort her.

★ ★ ★

In Maryland, Lydia Reynolds continued to work at the store in Germantown, perform her volunteer work at the clinic, and teach her Sunday school class. Recently she had also joined the church choir.

One day in the third week of November, Lydia was in the stockroom at the back of the store when her employer stepped in and said, "Lydia, your pastor and his wife are in the store and want to see you."

"Oh. All right." She reentered the store and smiled when she saw the Brittons. "Nice to see you, Pastor . . . Mrs. Britton."

Delia embraced her and said, "Honey, I've told you . . . you can call me Delia."

"Maybe one of these days I'll be able to do it, but not yet."

The pastor had a folded newspaper in his hand. Opening it up, he said, "Lydia, have you seen today's edition of the *Baltimore Press*?"

"No, I haven't."

Britton gently placed it in her hands. "Take a look near the bottom of the page."

Lydia's eyes stopped on bold lines that read:

BRAVE LIEUTENANT SAVES LIVES OF SOLDIERS IN FIERCE BATTLE
See page 3 for story.

Lydia looked at Britton. "I have a feeling this brave lieutenant is someone I know."

The pastor grinned. "You might say that."

Lydia opened the paper and found the story written by war correspondent Jack Milan of Baltimore. Milan told of being on the very battlefield where Lieutenant Grant Smith of Montgomery Village had distinguished himself by saving the lives of Captain Nathan Daniels and Lieutenant Dale Matison.

Tears filled Lydia's eyes when she read of the commendation Grant had received from General Winfield Scott in front of the entire battalion. She lowered the newspaper and looked at the Brittons, her lower lip quivering.

"You're going to marry a hero," Delia said.

Lydia folded the paper as the tears started down her cheeks. "Grant has always been a hero in my book. Now the whole country can know it." She wiped her wet cheeks with a palm. "It's good to know that as of two weeks ago he was still alive.

I'm so proud of him."

"We are too," said the pastor. "And when he comes home, we'll have a great big welcome for our hero."

Duane Reynolds helped Beverly into her coat, while Billy did the same for Lydia.

"I'm sure everybody in town knows about it now, including the Smiths," Duane said. "Scott reads the *Press* from front to back every day, the same as I do."

"You'd almost think it was planned . . . our being invited to supper at the Smiths' on the very day the story about Grant came out in the paper," Beverly said. "We'll have plenty to talk about over the meal."

Billy opened the door. "They've got to be mighty proud of Grant."

"They couldn't be any more proud of him than I am," Lydia said.

Beverly looked around at her family. "Everybody bundled up good? Looks like it. All right, let's head out."

It was a brittle, cold night, and the stars were shining brightly as the Reynolds family trudged through a five-inch depth of snow. A biting wind picked up snow and ice crystals and flung them into their faces.

Naked, wind-whipped trees sang a creaking song, while beneath the Reynoldses' boots, the snow crunched and squeaked at every step.

Marjorie Smith was waiting just inside the door to greet them, and after they stomped snow from their boots, she quickly whisked them inside. Scott appeared and began helping the ladies with their wraps.

"You've seen the paper, I assume," Scott said.

"Sure have," Duane said, "and we haven't been able to think or talk about anything else since. That's some son you have. You have to be very proud."

"If there was a better word than *proud,* that's what we would be."

"The girls are busy in the kitchen, so I'll go join them," Marjorie said. "You folks go on into the parlor and thaw out by the fire."

"Lydia and I will be glad to help," Beverly said.

"Maybe next time. You go get your blood flowing again."

Scott led them into the parlor, where bright, dancing flames crackled and popped in the fireplace. The guests quickly moved toward it, holding out their palms and rubbing their hands together.

The parlor was softly aglow with kerosene lamps, and a serene silence enveloped the group gathered in the cozy room. The two families had long been close friends in the Lord but had drawn closer because of Grant and Lydia's love. Ever since Grant had been gone, they had gotten together often to gain comfort and strength from one another.

As always, Marjorie and her daughters had prepared a delicious meal, and everyone had a pleasant time around the table. When the meal was over and the kitchen cleaned up, everyone gathered in the parlor, where they held hands in a circle while Duane led in prayer. He thanked God that Grant was alive to receive the commendation from General Scott and asked Him to keep His mighty hand on Grant in the midst of battle.

When the Reynoldses were bundled up once again and ready for the walk home, Marjorie put one arm around Lydia and the other around Beverly, hugging them to herself. She looked around at the others and said, "I believe we all feel lighter in spirit for having been together. The old adage about 'a burden shared' has been proven in our hearts tonight."

★ ★ ★

Weeks passed, and soon it was almost Christmas. The ordinarily happy season was a lonely time for Lydia, yet she stayed busy and enjoyed helping her family prepare for the holiday. Between her job and other activities, she made time to shop for her parents and Billy and for each of the Smiths.

Christmas had always been a most special holiday in the Reynolds home. They made much of the wondrous virgin birth of Jesus Christ and His coming into the world to save sinners. And even though their hearts would be heavy because of Grant's absence, they would make this Christmas special too.

One frosty evening, the church choir went caroling about town. Lydia's heart soared with joy as she sang the hymns and songs that proclaimed the wonderful gift of God to the world — the promised Messiah and King.

Afterward the carolers gathered at the Reynolds home, along with Pastor and Mrs. Britton, for hot chocolate and homemade doughnuts. The carolers' cheeks were rosy, and their eyes sparkled as they tromped into the warm and brightly decorated kitchen.

Lydia took part in the gaiety, but Grant and the danger he was facing were never far from her thoughts. She was doing her very best to let the peace of God rule in her heart. She didn't want to put a damper on the holidays, though a part of her was hundreds of miles away in Mexico.

On the afternoon of December 24, Lydia gave a Christmas party in the church fellowship hall for the girls in her Sunday school class. She had bought a present for each girl and gaily wrapped it. Before gift-opening time, the girls played games, sang songs, and had refreshments.

Lydia enjoyed watching each child open her gift, but was surprised and touched when one by one, the girls produced beautifully wrapped gifts for her. Tears ran down her cheeks as she hugged and thanked each one.

When the party was over and the last child had been picked up by her parents, Lydia left the church and stepped out into the twilight. Her breath caught for a moment, then hung in the still, cold air as she saw the final light of day spread over the tree-laden hills in colors of purple and silver.

"Lord," she said, "no one but You could paint a picture like that. What a wonderful

God and Creator You are! I'm so glad I belong to You and that You belong to me. Thank You for all of Your blessings. Thank You that You who painted that picture and triumphed at Calvary hold my precious Grant in Your hand! Keep him safe from all harm, Lord. Bring him home to me soon."

The walk home was brisk and hurried as Lydia rushed to be with her family. Upon entering the house, she was met with the delightful aroma of potato and onion soup and cornbread — a family tradition on Christmas Eve ever since she could remember. She carried her presents into the parlor and piled them on the couch. As she took off her coat, she saw her father at the parlor door, his eyebrows raised.

"Where'd you get all those presents, honey?"

"My girls, Daddy. They really surprised me."

"Must mean they love you."

"I'd say so."

"Of course, not as much as Daddy loves you," he said, gathering her in his arms. Father and daughter held each other for a long moment; then he said, "Guess I'd better not detain you too long. Your mother heard you come in, and she'll be expecting you in the kitchen."

Lydia entered the kitchen and greeted her mother. "Sure smells good."

Beverly turned from the stove to smile at her. "Hi, honey. Have a nice party?"

"We did. And would you believe it — every one of those little girls gave me a present."

"Well, wasn't that nice? I'll have to take a look at them after supper."

Lydia kissed her mother's cheek, hugged her, and said, "I guess I'd better get the table set so we can eat when that soup is ready."

When supper was over and the kitchen cleaned up, it was time for another family tradition. Duane and Billy had gone into the woods that afternoon and cut down a Christmas tree. Now they brought it in from the back porch and placed it in the parlor in front of the big window. Together the family decorated the tree with strings of popcorn, red and green ribbons, and small candles. When it was done, they stepped back to admire their handiwork.

Then they brought in the presents and placed them under the tree. Lydia had wrapped presents for Grant, which made her feel as if he were a little closer. When the presents were all in place for opening the next morning, the Reynolds family enjoyed a big bowl of buttery popcorn and hot apple cider, with a cinnamon stick in each cup.

Soon all eyes began to droop. They hugged each other good night and headed upstairs for bed.

8

Lydia Reynolds was bone tired. Upon entering her room, she decided to wait until Christmas night to write Grant a letter. She donned her flannel nightgown, put out the lantern, and crawled wearily into bed.

For the next few minutes she talked to the Lord, then rolled onto her side, expecting to fall into slumber.

But sleep eluded her.

She rolled onto her other side, adjusted her pillow, and tried to turn off her mind, but her thoughts immediately went to Grant. She pictured the battle when he'd risked his life to save Captain Daniels and the lieutenant. How close had Grant actually come to getting killed?

She thought of tomorrow — Christmas Day — and tried to imagine what it would be like for Grant. He was so far from home. So far from his family. So far from the woman who loved him with all her heart and who so desperately wanted to be his wife.

Lydia pulled the sheet to her face and

wiped tears. She couldn't hold it in any longer and wept for several minutes. She threw the covers back and fumbled in the dark for a match to light the bedside lantern. She hastily put on her robe and slippers, went to her small desk, and took out her stationery. In every letter, since the story of his exceptional deed of valor had been published in the *Baltimore Press*, Lydia had told Grant how proud she was of him. She wrote it again in this one.

She went on to tell Grant of the Christmas party for the girls of her Sunday school class, and described her family's Christmas tree and how beautiful the brightly wrapped gifts looked beneath it. She told him he could open his gifts when he came home.

The last few lines were filled with words of love, and how much she missed him and longed to be in his arms once more. She closed with "Darling, the tender flame still burns."

Lydia folded the sheet of paper and added it to the stack of letters she had already written, then retied the blue ribbon around them and placed the bundle in a drawer.

She suddenly realized how cold the room was. She doused both lanterns, crawled beneath the quilts, and pulled them up under her chin. When her shivering stopped, she was still wide awake.

"Lord, I really need to get some rest. You said in Psalm 127:2 that You give Your beloved sleep. I claim it right now." She rolled onto her side, and the Lord kept His word.

Christmas Day was snowy and cold, but the parlor was cozy as the Reynolds family opened gifts. The time was sweet and enjoyable, except for the few minutes Lydia broke down and wept when she picked up the presents with Grant's name on them and held them close to her heart.

All in all, the Reynoldses enjoyed a lovely, quiet day, rejoicing in the birth of God's only begotten Son. Although their thoughts were never far from Grant, there was a deep-seated peace in their hearts.

January 1847 came, and the war with Mexico was still hot and heavy. The United States Army now held Tampico and was bearing down on the next coastal city — Poza Rica. Once Poza Rica was occupied, General Winfield Scott would move his army further south to Xalapa, then on to Vera Cruz. Once these cities were occupied, Scott would be in a position to move west on Mexico City.

General Zachary Taylor and his reinforced troops were moving farther south, with orders from Scott to do everything they could to be in a position to help Scott move on Mexico City when he was ready. He was sure the capture of the capital city would end the war.

The months rolled by. General Scott and his army captured Poza Rica in early May, then Xalapa in mid-August.

After some thirty American soldiers were buried near the camp just outside of Xalapa, Captain Nathan Daniels appeared at General Scott's tent. Scott was finishing a letter to General Taylor as he sat at the crude desk he carried with him in an army wagon.

"Yes, Captain?" Scott said, looking up as he finished signing the letter.

"Sir, I need a few minutes to tell you of another commendation that needs to be given by you."

"All right. Let me get this letter on its way, then we'll talk."

Scott sealed the envelope and got the attention of an army courier who was with a group of soldiers a few yards away. The courier would ride hard for two days to deliver the letter to General Taylor. When the pounding hooves of the courier's horse faded, Scott said, "All right, Captain. Who's our hero this time?"

"You know him well, sir. Lieutenant Grant Smith."

Scott's bushy eyebrows arched. "Again?"

"Yes, sir. The Mexicans had a cannon trained on a group of men and would have killed them if Lieutenant Smith hadn't dashed in and taken out the artillerymen. He had to run across an open field while bullets were flying everywhere. With no thought for his own safety, he made a dash across the field and saved his men from annihilation. Then, of all things, he found the cannon loaded and ready to fire, so he turned it on the Mexicans across the field, yanked the lanyard, and took out a whole nest of them."

A smile tugged at the corners of the general's mouth. "Some soldier, that one."

"You wanted to see me, sir?" Lieutenant Grant Smith saluted General Scott, who was sitting by his campfire alone. Night had fallen, and a pale moon was rising.

"Yes, Lieutenant. Come, sit down."

When Grant was seated on the opposite side of the small fire, the general smiled. "Lieutenant, I was told about the cannon incident that took place today."

Grant blinked. "Yes, sir."

"I want you to know that I am proud to have a man of your caliber serving under me."

"Thank you, sir."

"You are aware that dispatches have come to me periodically from Washington over the past few months."

"Yes, sir."

"Of course you know that I have kept President Polk abreast of our losses and of the reinforcements I've had sent from different forts. In a dispatch from the president last month, he spoke of the officers we've lost in battle and of the need to replace them. He gave me the authority to make promotions on the field. Actually, the president stated in the dispatch that he was giving me this authority for two reasons. The first reason is obvious. The second reason is so that when men distinguish themselves in battle and deserve promotion, I can take care of it right here on the field. When the rest of the soldiers see a valorous man promoted, it encourages them to distinguish themselves when the opportunity arises."

Grant's heart was in his throat. "That makes sense, sir."

"Therefore, Lieutenant Smith, I am hereby promoting you to the rank of captain."

Grant swallowed hard. "Yes, sir. Thank you, sir."

The general rose to his feet, and Grant followed suit.

"Tomorrow morning I will make your promotion known to all the men, Captain," Scott said. "However, before you retire for the night, there is someone who wants to interview you."

"Pardon me, sir?"

"You've met correspondent Jack Milan, haven't you?"

"Yes, sir."

"And, of course, you're aware of the story he wrote for the newspapers back home about your deed of valor last November."

"No, sir."

Scott grinned. "Well, son, everybody back home knows you're a hero. I'm sure your parents and that girl you left behind are very proud of you."

"Well, I hope so, sir."

"Captain Daniels has Jack Milan at his

tent, ready to interview you, son. They both know that when you show up there, you will have your new rank. I'll have captain's insignias for your uniform in the morning. Now, go answer some questions for Jack."

It was Tuesday, September 7. Beverly and Lydia were in the kitchen preparing supper when they heard the front door open and Duane call out, "I'm home!"

Beverly smiled at her daughter, whose hands were covered with flour as she kneaded bread. "I'll go meet your father. You can hug him later."

Beverly met her husband and noticed he was carrying his usual copy of the *Baltimore Press*. However, what she saw on his face was highly unusual.

"Duane, what's the matter?" she cried, hastening toward him. "Why are you crying?"

"These are proud tears, honey."

"What do you mean?"

"Where are the kids?"

"Billy's cleaning the barn. Lydia's in the kitchen, making bread."

"I have something to show all three of you. I'll go bring Billy in. You keep Lydia in the kitchen."

Moments later father and son entered the kitchen, and Lydia rushed to hug her father. "What's the big secret, Daddy?"

Duane handed her the newspaper. "You read it to us, honey. He's going to be your husband."

Lydia fought to keep her composure when she read aloud the story on page 3 by war correspondent Jack Milan. She choked up when she read of the courageous deed involving the cannon, and that Grant had been promoted to the rank of captain as a result of his heroism. The words blurred, and she stopped to wipe the tears away before continuing to read. After the story came the interview. This had the whole family crying, as Lydia choked it out a few words at a time.

Grant had boldly given praise to the Lord Jesus for helping him save the lives of other men in battle. He told of his fiancée, Lydia Reynolds, in Montgomery Village, Maryland, and said, "Lydia, if you should read this article, I want you to know that the tender flame still burns."

Lydia could not continue reading, she was crying so hard. She handed the paper to her father as both Beverly and Billy put their arms around her.

Duane silently read what was left of the

interview, and said, "It . . . ah . . . it closes off with Grant wishing you a happy birthday, Lydia. And he greets his family, us, his pastor and wife, and all his friends in Montgomery Village."

The Reynolds family sat down to eat, but the emotion brought on by the article had stolen their appetites.

On September 5, General Scott's army captured the city of Vera Cruz. As he had prearranged with Washington, reinforcements were waiting offshore, and upon signal that the city was in American hands, they came in.

General Scott called an assembly of all his men and briefed them on his plan to capture the capital city and President Santa Anna. Once Mexico City was conquered, he reminded them, the victory would be theirs.

Each captain then met with his company to welcome the new men and fill them in on their jobs when they went into combat. Captain Grant Smith was commander of Company F, and while he was addressing his men, his eyes kept going to the face of one soldier who looked familiar to him. After the meeting was dismissed, Grant went to the man, who wore a corporal's stripes, and said, "Soldier, have we met before?"

The corporal's face lost color. "We have, Captain," he said, saluting. "My name is Corporal Gerald George." He raised his upper lip and showed him a crooked tooth. "You knocked this loose for me."

"Gerald George! One of the boys who gave Lydia a hard time."

"Yes, sir. But not after you whipped up on both of us."

"I'm trying to remember . . . Kendall! Frederick Kendall! That was the other boy's name, wasn't it? You both moved away from Montgomery Village not long after our little tussle."

"Yes, sir. Freddie's family moved to Wisconsin just before my family moved to Shelbyville, Indiana. I haven't heard from him since. I joined the army at Fort Wayne a couple of years ago."

"Good to see you, Gerald," Grant said, extending his hand. "And welcome to the war. We'll have a real fight on our hands when we get to Mexico City. I'm glad to have you in my company."

"I'm honored, Captain. Ah, sir . . ."

"Yes?"

"Lydia Reynolds. Do you know if she's married?"

"She's not. But she's engaged to a soldier who's going to marry her as soon as this war is over."

"Oh, really? Is he from Montgomery Village?"

"Sure is."

"Do I know him?"

Grant chuckled. "You're looking at him."

"Wha— ? You? Lydia's going to marry you?"

"She'd better! She's wearing my engagement ring."

"Well, what do you know! I knew she had a sizable crush on you, but I didn't know you developed one on her."

"That and a whole lot more."

At dawn the next day, General Winfield Scott led his beefed-up army west into the high country toward Mexico City. As the days passed they met much opposition and fought many battles. Each battle was a victory for the United States Army, and Scott kept his men marching relentlessly toward the capital city.

On the evening of September 9, Scott camped his men on the east bank of the Rio de la Compani, near the city of Puebla. It was a forested area high in the mountains, less than sixty miles from Mexico City.

The general had just finished eating his supper when one of his scouts rode in to tell him there was a large Mexican force camped about a half mile west of the river. Scott knew there was no way he could get his men, animals, artillery, and equipment safely across the river in the dark. The enemy no doubt knew they were here and would move up to intercept them. They would have to fight the Mexicans on the riverbanks tomorrow morning.

A heavy rain fell during the night, muddying the river and running its depth to about five feet. The sky was cloudy at dawn, but the rain had stopped.

Scott positioned his artillery among the trees that lined the river. Spaced between the cannons, and flanking them for a quarter mile on both sides along the bank, were infantrymen on their bellies and on their knees, ready to open fire on command. Scott also had placed men in the trees who were watching for the Mexicans as dull light came over the land. One of the men saw the enemy artillery and infantry in their positions across the river and signaled a man on the ground, who quickly ran to General Scott, stationed a few yards from the river behind some large boulders.

The general gave the command to commence fire, and immediately the roar of battery filled the morning air, followed by the shriek of shells and the rattle of musketry.

Shells struck trees along the banks on both sides, shattering them and hurling deadly fragments in every direction.

On horseback, the captains rode up and down the ranks of their companies, shouting encouragement to keep their men steady in the teeth of the fight, and to help them maintain the ranks even as men fell wounded or dead.

The day wore on. It was about an hour past noon when Corporal Gerald George lay on his belly between two other men, pouring gunpowder into his musket. Through the drifting smoke he caught a glimpse of Captain Smith on his horse, threading among the trees just behind the firing line, shouting commands and words of encouragement to his men.

Upstream, the Mexicans were crossing the swift, muddy river with their muskets held above their heads. Mexican cannons continued to blast away at the Americans to give cover to the infantry crossing the river.

Smith saw that his company was closest to the crossing point. He dug his heels into the horse's sides and galloped toward the men at the end of the line, shouting as loud as he could that they were needed upstream to intercept the Mexicans crossing the river.

Suddenly Smith's horse took an enemy bullet, let out a high-pitched cry, and stumbled at full gallop down the riverbank. Smith was trying to get out of the saddle when a bullet struck him in the chest. Both rider and horse plunged into the river and disappeared.

Gerald George jumped up and ran in that direction. Other men of Company F were rising to their feet, intending to dive into the river as soon as their captain surfaced and bring him to safety.

But there was no sign of horse or rider.

The Mexicans cut loose fiercely, and every man who was on his feet had to flatten himself in a hurry.

"There's his horse!" a sergeant shouted to George.

The animal had risen to the surface some forty yards downstream and was floating on its side. But there was no sign of Captain Smith.

Corporal George dropped his musket and dashed along the bank behind the line. When he reached the end of the firing line, he dived into the murky river. Mexican bullets chopped water all around him.

A lieutenant took over in Grant Smith's place and rode his horse along the lines, shouting commands and encouragement.

Suddenly someone shouted, "It's Corporal George!"

Downstream a hundred yards, a mud-caked Gerald George stumbled his way up the steep bank. A private left his spot in the firing line and ran as hard as he could to George.

"Gerald, you all right?"

George gasped for breath. "Yeah. I'm fine. But . . . but I couldn't find the captain. The water's too muddy." George fought back the tears and looked toward the raging battle. "We've got to get back into the fight, Dave."

Corporal and private ran to the line, amid whining bullets, and resumed their places. Cannons roared. Muskets popped, and the blue-white smoke weighed down the air. Shouts and yells along the river made the heavens ring.

When his horse was crumpling beneath him, Grant Smith knew he and the animal were going down the riverbank and into the muddy water. Reacting instinctively, he pulled his feet from the stirrups. Only the right one came free. Then Grant's chest felt as if someone had hit it with a sledge-hammer.

Suddenly he was under the water with the horse taking him all the way to the bottom. He held his breath and opened his eyes, closing them instantly when he realized the water was too muddy to see anything. The pain in his chest was horrible.

Grant's left foot was still stuck in the stirrup, but at least the horse had ended up on its right side. Grant's lungs felt as if they would burst as he fought the twisted stirrup. Finally he was free!

He swam for the closest bank as the swift current carried him downstream. The pain in his lungs was now almost as excruciating as the wound in his upper chest.

Suddenly his hands touched branches above his head. By the hand of God, he had reached the bank beneath heavy brush. Grant clung to the branches with his right hand, stuck his head out of the water, and gulped air. His ears unplugged quickly, and the sounds of battle filled them. He blinked at the muddy film that covered his eyes and saw that he was on the wrong side of the river.

He looked at the wound in the upper left

side of his chest, which was bleeding profusely. The ball must still be in him. He was sure he would feel pain in his back if the lead ball had gone completely through.

Gritting his teeth, he pulled himself closer to the bank and peered through the brush. The fighting was fierce as both sides peppered each other with artillery and muskets. He strained to see upstream where he had sent his men to intercept the Mexicans crossing the river. But the pall of smoke over the battle blocked his view.

Weakness came over Grant, accompanied by severe dizziness. He summoned what strength he had left and inched his way up the bank on his belly, through dense brush. When he was out of the water, he looked toward the battle but still couldn't see anything.

It took all the strength he could muster to rip the left sleeve from his shirt, but he finally had it off. His head was spinning as he folded the sleeve, slipped it under his shirt, and pressed it against the wound.

Everything began to whirl around him, and his vision darkened. The last thing Grant was aware of before the black curtain descended was the sound of booming guns.

9

When Grant Smith regained consciousness, he remembered clearly what had happened before he passed out. The pain was still there in his chest where the bullet had entered, but he could not hear the sounds of battle.

He blinked against the grimy sediment clinging to his eyes and strained to hear artillery and muskets and the shouts of fighting men. But there was only the rippling sound of river and the breeze whistling through the heavy brush where he lay.

Grant raised his right hand to his eyes to rub the mud away. When he opened them again, he noted that the sun had moved a long way across the sky since his climb out of the river.

He raised his head to look at the wound. Blood had soaked through the folded sleeve and spread on the front of his shirt, but it was dried. He breathed a sigh of relief.

When his head started to spin again he lay back on the grassy bank, and the dizziness eased. A huge cloud was coming out of the west, its shadow creeping over him like a shade drawn against the lowering sun. The breeze whispered through the brush and touched his face. A slight chill ran through him.

Grant rolled onto his stomach and tried to ignore the spinning in his head as he inched his way farther up the bank until the brush thinned some.

A tinkling metallic sound met his ears from across the river, and he saw several soldiers in United States Army uniforms. Two men were working on the harness of the horses that pulled General Winfield Scott's supply wagon. He swung his gaze to see where the Mexicans were positioned, but there was no activity at all. Suddenly Grant saw General Scott and Captain Nathan Daniels guiding their horses along the edge of the river, near the wagon. General Scott called out, "All right, men! Let's move across the river! Mexico City is next!"

Grant struggled to get to his feet. When he made it to his knees, he saw the long line of men, horses, cannons, and wagons, moving down the bank and into the river. He took a deep breath to call out, and suddenly the black curtain descended on him again. A gust of breath was all he could get out. He fell backward into the brush.

When Grant came to, it was night. There were countless twinkling stars in the black, moonless sky overhead. Silence reigned except for the night wind soughing in the trees and dense brush, and the soft gurgle of the river.

He was cold and shaking.

He crawled to the top of the riverbank, and when his head began to spin again, he lay on his back and let the wind refresh him. After a few minutes, he eased himself to a sitting position. He drew his knees up under him, painstakingly rose to his feet, and stood on shaky legs.

When his head was clear again, he walked haltingly along the bank toward the place his battalion had headed across the river. He shuffled along the rough terrain in the dim light from the stars. Suddenly he stumbled over something and fell to the ground. Groping with his hands, he found the face of a dead soldier. He squinted through the semidarkness ahead of him and saw a number of dark forms on the ground. He was sure they were Mexican soldiers.

A sharp pain lanced through his wound as Grant forced himself once again to his feet. He stood swaying for a moment, and then his knees gave way and he felt himself falling.

When Grant opened his eyes, he could hear voices. Although he was lying face-down beside a dead Mexican soldier, he could tell the sun was shining out of a clear sky. As he homed in on the voices, he realized they were male, and they were speaking Spanish.

Suddenly a hand gripped his shoulder and rolled him onto his back. He found himself staring into the dark, mustached face of a Mexican soldier who shouted something to the others moving among the dead men.

Soon more soldiers were gathered around him, conversing rapidly. One of them knelt and took a look under Grant's makeshift bandage. He raised his eyebrows and said something to the others.

Grant was praying silently when he heard slow hoofbeats and the creak of wagon wheels. When the wagon rolled to a halt, four of the Mexican soldiers picked him up and laid him in the wagon with several corpses.

"Do any of you speak English?" he asked, looking from face to face.

They shook their heads.

"I want to know what you're going to do with me. Get me somebody who speaks English!"

One of them said something, but Grant had no idea what. He lay helplessly, watching as they carried more dead soldiers to the wagon and laid them next to him.

A short while later, after they had closed the tailgate on the wagon, a man who wore an officer's uniform drew up beside the wagon and looked down at Grant. He noted the captain's insignias on the shoulders of Grant's shirt and said, "What is your name, Captain?"

"My name is Grant Smith, sir."

"I am General Hernando Vasquez, Captain. You have been seriously wounded. We are going to take you to a doctor, who will remove the ball from your chest and take care of you."

"I appreciate that, General. Then what?"

"As soon as you are able to travel, we will transport you into the mountains southwest of here, where you will be put in a prison camp with other Americans we have captured."

"And how long will I be kept there?"

Vasquez smiled for the first time. "For

the rest of your life."

"The rest of my life?"

"Sí. We fear we are about to lose this war, but by keeping some American prisoners, we will not feel that we were totally defeated. Your president, your military people, and your families back home will never know what happened to you. We will allow you to live out your natural lives in our prison camp, but all the while, your people will think you are dead. Please allow us some satisfaction in this war."

On September 15, 1847, news came to Montgomery Village — as well as the rest of the United States — that General Winfield Scott's battalion, and the regiment of soldiers with General Zachary Taylor, had converged just outside Mexico City the previous day, and together had captured it. Antonio López de Santa Anna was now a prisoner of the United States Army. The fighting was over, and the soldiers who had survived the war were going home.

News of the war's end came to the Reynolds home in early afternoon, when Beverly and Lydia were working in the sewing room at the rear of the house. They heard neighbors shouting exultantly and dashed outside to see what the excitement was about. Men and women were waving newspapers and whooping the news that General Winfield Scott and his army had captured Mexico City and Santa Anna. The Mexican army had laid down its arms. The war was over! Their fighting men were coming home!

When Lydia heard it, she burst into tears and wrapped her arms around her mother, saying between sobs, "He's coming home! My darling Grant is coming home!"

As Beverly held her daughter and wept with her, she saw Duane and Billy hurrying down the street. The Reynolds family stood in their front yard, rejoicing and hugging each other, and soon they were joined by Scott and Marjorie Smith and their girls.

When the initial exultation had subsided, Duane and Beverly invited the Smiths in to pray together and give thanks to the Lord that soon Grant would be home. They gathered in a circle in the parlor and each person prayed aloud. When the last amen was said, everyone was weeping for joy.

On Sunday afternoon, October 10, a heavy sky lay over Montgomery Village, and a steady rain poured down. Even though the weather was dreary, there was no dreariness in the Reynolds house, where the Smiths had been invited to Sunday dinner.

Their excitement was almost palpable as the two families sat down to a delicious meal of roast chicken and all the trimmings. They had learned that morning from Pastor John Britton, as he made the announcements from the pulpit, that he had been in Baltimore the day before and had overheard some officers from Fort McHenry discussing the return of the victorious army. General Winfield Scott and the men of Fort McHenry were stretched out in a long line across Kentucky and Virginia. They were traveling in small units and would be arriving one after the other for the next three or four days.

To make sure he had heard correctly, Britton had asked the soldiers about it. The officers explained that the troops had not all left Mexico on the same day; therefore they would be arriving at Fort McHenry a few hundred at a time. Some could arrive as soon as the next day. There would be more arriving each day. The last of the soldiers would probably be there by Wednesday.

As raindrops pelted the windows, the

sole subject of conversation around the dinner table was Grant's return.

Two riders halted their horses in front of the Scott Smith home. Their hats were pulled low and they wore brown slickers with special markings to identify them as soldiers of the United States Army. Together they mounted the porch steps.

They waited for a long moment after knocking on the door, then knocked again. When there was no response, one of them said, "Let's try the back door. Maybe they're somewhere in the rear of the house."

When there was no response, they stepped off the back porch and headed toward their horses.

"Hey, soldiers!"

Through the rain they saw a middle-aged man standing on his back porch. "Yes, sir?" said one of them.

"You fellas looking for the Smiths?"

"We are, sir."

"They're eating dinner with the Reynolds family, who live one block east and two blocks south."

"Thank you, sir," said one man. "Do you know the number on the house?"

"No, but it's the second house from the

corner on the west side. It's the only house in the block with a big oak tree smack in the middle of the front yard."

"Appreciate the information, sir. Thank you."

The neighbor smiled. "Thought for a second there that one of you might be Captain Grant Smith. He's due home pretty soon. You fellas know him?"

"Ah, no, sir. But we've heard a lot of good things about him."

The neighbor grinned and nodded. "Well, anyway, you'll find his parents and his sisters at the Reynolds house."

The soldiers thanked him again, made their way to the front of the house, and mounted their horses. One of them commented that he was glad the rain was easing some.

Dinner was over at the Reynolds house and everyone had moved to the parlor. As Lydia talked about her plans to welcome Grant upon his arrival, movement out front caught Theresa Smith's eye. She strained to see through the window, and her pulse quickened when she saw two men in army colors and insignias dismounting near the big oak tree. She jumped out of her chair and ran toward the door, shouting, "It's Grant! It's Grant! Oh, he's home! He's home!"

Everyone rushed up behind Theresa as she jerked the door open, saying, "Grant, you're home! You're —"

A great disappointment swept over the group when they saw the dripping faces of two uniformed strangers, who looked nervous and ill-at-ease.

Duane moved past Theresa and said, "I'm Duane Reynolds, gentlemen. May I help you?"

"I am Lieutenant Wesley Albright, sir. And this is Lieutenant Clayton Lewis. We're looking for Mr. and Mrs. Scott Smith. We were told by one of their neighbors that they were here."

"Yes, they are. Please come in."

The soldiers removed their wet hats and dripping slickers before moving through the door. Scott and Marjorie stepped forward and introduced themselves.

Lieutenant Albright cleared his throat nervously. "Mr. and Mrs. Smith, could we talk to you in private, please?"

Scott frowned. "Is this about our son? Is this about Grant?"

"Yes, sir, it is."

"We're all family here," Scott said. "This young lady here is Lydia Reynolds. She and Grant are going to be married as soon as he gets home from Mexico. Whatever this is about can be told to all of us."

"Could we go into the parlor so all of you can sit down?" Lieutenant Lewis said in a soft tone.

Marjorie's hands were trembling. "What is it? Please tell me! Has something happened to our son?"

"We'd really like all of you to sit down, ma'am," Albright said.

When everyone was seated, the two officers remained on their feet, standing shoulder to shoulder. Albright cleared his throat again and said, "Mr. and Mrs. Smith, we have been sent here from army headquarters in Washington. It is — it is our sad duty to inform you that your son, Captain Grant Smith, was killed in action on September 10."

A collective gasp rose; then the group sat in stunned silence.

Albright continued. "He was in the battle at the Rio de la Compani in southern Mexico. He was shot while gallantly leading his company, and we are told that he distinguished himself in combat the entire time he was in Mexico."

Lydia didn't even feel her parents' arms encircle her as she hunched forward and put her face in her hands. Billy was on his knees in front of his sister but didn't know what to do or say.

Marjorie Smith let out a shaky whimper and closed her eyes. Scott's arm gathered her to him. Sharon and Theresa rushed to their parents and fell on their knees in front of them, sobbing.

As Marjorie rocked to and fro, she wailed, "No! No, there has to be some mistake! My son cannot be dead! I won't allow it! God won't allow it! Please . . . please tell me it's a mistake!"

Scott held her tightly and tried to give comfort to his daughters as well.

Tears coursed down Beverly Reynolds's cheeks as she kept a tight grip on Lydia, who continued to hunch forward, her face buried in her hands. Tears dripped between her fingers.

Marjorie's wails were wordless now as she hugged herself and rocked back and forth.

"Billy . . ."

The eighteen-year-old looked up at his father. "Yes, Dad?"

"Run and get Pastor Britton, will you, please?"

When Billy was gone, Scott looked at the soldiers and said, "What about my son's body? Did they bury him in Mexico?"

"I'm sure they must have, sir," Albright said. "No one said anything to the contrary when we were given the message of his death and told to bring it to you."

"You understand, Mr. Smith," Lewis said, "there wouldn't be any way of bringing home the bodies of our men who were killed in Mexico. The common practice is to bury them as quickly as possible right on or near the battlefield."

"Of course," Scott said, nodding. "I should have known better than to ask. I'm not thinking too clearly right now."

"Mr. Smith, we have to head back for Washington now. We want to say to you, to Mrs. Smith, to your daughters, and to Captain Smith's fiancée and her family . . . you have our heartfelt condolences."

Scott whispered for his daughters to stay with their mother and rose to his feet. Duane also stood and said, "I'll get your hats and slickers, gentlemen."

When the army messengers had stepped out onto the porch, they once again spoke their sorrow for the loss of Captain Smith, then strode through the falling rain to their horses. They mounted, saluted the house, and rode away.

Lydia stared at the closed door through

which the messengers had just departed. Tears streaked her face and there was a faraway look in her eyes as she said, "Grant was killed on my birthday."

Pastor John Britton sat in the Reynoldses' parlor and did all he could to comfort the grieving families.

"Pastor, help me to understand," Lydia said with trembling lips. "Why did the Lord let Grant and me fall in love? Why did He make it appear that we were so right for each other, then let Grant be killed? He's the great almighty God. He could have protected Grant's life and brought him home to me. Wouldn't it have been better not to let us fall in love in the first place?"

Britton rubbed the back of his neck, looked at the floor, then raised his eyes to hers. "Lydia, I can't answer for God. He doesn't need me to explain why He brings things or allows them to come into our lives. But I can let Him speak for Himself."

Britton picked up his Bible and began flipping pages near the middle. He stopped in the Psalms, flipped a couple more pages, and said, "Lydia, here's what God says about your questions. Psalm 18:30. Let me read it to you: 'As for God, his way is perfect: the word of the LORD is tried: he is a buckler to all those that trust in him.' It's those first seven words that I want you to grasp, Lydia. 'As for God, his way is perfect.' "

"Mother showed me that verse several years ago, Pastor. I believed that God . . . that He had given me Grant as part of His perfect work in my life."

"I know," Britton said. "It hasn't turned out as you and Grant had planned, Lydia. This is where faith comes in. As you well know, the Bible says we are saved by faith, and after we are saved, we walk by faith. You must trust the Lord in this, believing that, 'As for God, his way is perfect.' The great and wise God of heaven has a perfect plan for your life. You must allow Him to work it out."

Lydia closed her eyes for a moment, then looked at the pastor and said, "I am trying to let the truth of that verse come home to my heart, Pastor. But right now, the pain of my loss is tearing me up inside. Please . . . pray for me. I don't want to do wrong before the Lord. I need strength from Him to get me through this."

"I understand, Lydia, and so does the God whose way is perfect. You'll see His perfect hand in all of this one day."

★ ★ ★

It was early afternoon on Wednesday. Lydia was in the sewing room, working on a dress, trying to keep her mind occupied as much as possible. Her mother had gone to Gaithersburg with a lady from church.

Lydia's attention was drawn from her sewing when she heard a knock at the front door. Laying needle, thread, and thimble aside, she hurried to the front of the house and opened the door to find three soldiers standing there. One of them, wearing corporal's stripes, seemed vaguely familiar.

"Yes, gentlemen?"

"Lydia," the corporal said, "you might remember me. We went to school together years ago. I am Gerald George. Do you remember me?"

"I thought you looked familiar. Yes, I remember you. Is there something I can do for you and your friends?"

"We've come to do something for you. We know you've already been told about . . . about Captain Smith. We fought under him, Lydia. We'd like to tell you some things about him, if you have time."

"Of course. Please come in."

When the three soldiers were inside, Gerald said, "Excuse me, Lydia. I'm a little nervous. I forgot to introduce you to these men. This is Lieutenant Dale Matison, and this is Private Dave Stanley."

Lydia greeted both men, then looked at Matison and said, "I read your name in the *Baltimore Press*, Lieutenant. Grant saved your life, along with that of Captain Nathan Daniels."

"Yes, ma'am. And he also led me to the Lord a few days afterward. I not only owe my life to him, I owe him for my salvation."

Tears misted Lydia's eyes. "I'm glad to know that."

"We just returned to Fort McHenry yesterday, ma'am," Matison said. "We wanted to come and see you, hoping that in some small way, our visit could bring you comfort."

"Please come into the parlor and sit down," she said, pulling a lace handkerchief from the cuff of her sleeve. She dabbed at her eyes as she led them into the parlor.

The soldiers eased into overstuffed chairs, and Lydia sat on the edge of a small hardback chair and nervously twisted the handkerchief in her hands.

"We were there when Captain Smith was hit, ma'am," Matison said. "We saw the whole thing. Would it help you to hear about it, or would you rather not?"

Lydia took a deep breath. "I know it won't be easy for me, but I want to hear about it."

Tears sprang to Lydia's eyes when she heard the account, and she lowered her head and silently prayed for God's grace. The soldiers sat still, each with his gaze riveted to the floor.

After a few moments, Lydia said, "Gentlemen, I'm glad I could hear it from eyewitnesses. Now I will not have to go on wondering just how it was. Did . . . did they ever find his body?"

"No," Gerald said. "We had many men who were shot and swallowed up by rivers, and their bodies we never found. That's war."

Lydia nodded, biting her lips.

All three told her that Grant spoke often of her and of how much he longed for the war to be over so he could go home and make her his bride.

A bittersweet smile crossed Lydia's face. "Gentlemen, I want to thank you for taking the time to come and see me. You've been a source of strength, and I'm sure this will help me to be able to go on. I mean it. Thank you."

As Lydia led them toward the door, she

said, "Gerald, I'm glad you're not the mean bully you used to be."

He grinned, pointed out his crooked front tooth, and said, "I think I started down the right path shortly after Grant — Captain Smith knocked this loose for me. I owe him a lot. You do remember that day?"

"Yes, I do."

"We all owe the captain a lot, ma'am," Dave Stanley said. "His memory will live on in our hearts."

When the three men had gone, Lydia closed the door and leaned her back against it. She took a deep breath, then slowly reentered the parlor. She sat on the couch, closed her eyes, and let every word the men had spoken run back through her mind.

She bowed her head and thanked the Lord for sending them here. She wasn't even sure why their visit was so helpful, but their words had relieved her sorrow, and the heavy ache in her heart was lightened.

That night, while lying under the covers in the darkness, Lydia whispered, "Grant, I know you're in heaven and can't hear me, but I still have to talk to you. It's like the letters I wrote, knowing you would never see them. I . . . I just want to say, darling, that the tender flame will always live in my heart."

High in Mexico's southern mountains, Grant Smith and six fellow soldiers languished in the Mexican prison camp. There had been nine prisoners to begin with, but shortly after the fighting was over, two of the wounded had died.

The doctor who had taken the lead ball from Grant's chest had done a reasonably good job, and Grant was healing steadily.

As time passed, Grant quoted Scripture to the other prisoners, and eventually all six men opened their hearts to Jesus. Grant and his companions prayed daily that the Lord would help them find a way to escape. They also prayed for their families. Four of the seven men were married, and the other two, like Grant, were engaged.

10

As the months passed, Grant was often in Lydia's thoughts, but she stayed so busy there was little time to concentrate on her grief. She continued to work at the clothing store in Germantown and still did volunteer work three nights a week at the medical clinic in Montgomery Village. She also filled her time with service at church — singing solos, singing in the choir, and teaching a girls' Sunday school class.

One Sunday in June, Lydia sang a solo in the morning service, just before the message. When she finished, amens rang out through the auditorium. After the service, Lydia was standing near the platform, talking to the parents of a couple of the girls in her Sunday school class. When they moved away, she turned to leave and found herself facing a handsome young stranger.

"Miss Reynolds, I'm Dr. Clay Price. I realize that you don't know me, but I just wanted to tell you how very much your song blessed my heart."

Lydia's face tinted slightly. "Why, thank

you, Dr. Price. It's very kind of you to say so. Is this your first Sunday here at the church?"

"Yes. I just graduated from medical school in May, and I'm doing my internship at Montgomery County Hospital in Rockville."

"How did you happen to come here to church this morning, Doctor?"

"I heard about it from a patient who's visited here a few times. She told me Pastor Britton preaches the Word with power and always exalts the Lord Jesus Christ and makes the gospel clear and plain. She also said that souls are being saved here, and the church is growing. That's the kind of church I grew up in, and the kind I'm looking for."

Lydia smiled. "Looks like you found it."

"I sure did. Well, Miss Reynolds, I'd better be going. Nice to meet you. And let me say again . . . your song was a tremendous blessing."

Dr. Price spoke again to Lydia when he returned to Sunday services the next week. The following Sunday, and the one after that, they talked again. On his fourth Sunday at the church, Clay Price walked the aisle at invitation time to put his membership in the church. After the service he spoke with several people, wanting to get acquainted, but he made sure that Lydia didn't get away without spending a few minutes with him.

Both Lydia's and Grant's parents noticed that the young physician had eyes for Lydia, and that his amiable ways made her smile more than she had since Grant left to fight in the war.

On the second Sunday in July, Clay found a private moment in front of the church to talk to Lydia, and he asked her if there was a young man in her life. She told him of her engagement to Captain Grant Smith, who had been killed in the Mexican War. Clay was very sympathetic, but he asked if he could call on her.

Lydia hesitated for a long moment, then said yes.

Time moved on. Though Lydia still carried loving memories of Grant, she found Clay Price to be very good to her. Slowly, ever so slowly, the ache in Lydia's heart subsided. She was seeing Clay often, and every day the pain of losing Grant lessened and a sweet comfort and peace filled her heart where once there had been only loneliness and despair.

True to His Word, God made Psalm 147:3 a reality in Lydia's shattered life as daily she claimed the precious verse: "He healeth the broken in heart, and bindeth up their wounds."

On a dinner date in August, Clay took Lydia to a restaurant in Rockville. While they were eating, he brought up Lydia's volunteer work at the Montgomery Village clinic and told her of a need in the hospital for nurse's aides. With her experience, she could qualify as a nurse's aide. The pay would be more than what she was paid at the clothing store.

After praying about it and discussing it with her parents, Lydia decided to take the nurse's aide job.

Lydia was especially drawn to the children's ward. When the doctors and nurses saw how adept she was with the little ones, she was assigned often to that ward. She spent many hours there, comforting children, calming their fears, and reading to them.

Many times when they were on the same shift, Clay would take a moment to stop in and watch Lydia with the children. On one occasion, when she was holding two children on her lap and in spite of their ailments they were laughing happily, he told her that someday she would make a wonderful mother.

The months rolled by. One cold, snowy morning in November, Lydia made her way up the snow-covered hospital steps and passed through the main door. She greeted two doctors in the hall and stopped at the nurses' station to see what her duties would be that day. To her delight, she was assigned another shift in the children's ward.

She hung up her coat and hat in a small closet just inside the ward and could see the nurse in charge, standing over a tiny crib, holding a bowl and spoon.

Nadine Sellers looked up at the sound of footsteps. "Good morning, Lydia. We have a new little patient here. Come and meet Celia."

As Lydia hovered over the baby — who was not quite a year old — she learned from Nadine that Celia had pneumonia and would require much care and attention. Lydia leaned close, murmuring comforting words to the feverish and fretful little girl, then went to the woodstove in the center of the room to warm her hands.

"Lydia," Nadine said, "I'd like for you to

bathe her in tepid water. Let's see if you can get her fever down."

"All right." Lydia rubbed her hands together. "I think my hands are warm enough now to touch her without giving her a shock."

Nadine chuckled. "I'll be back in a while."

Lydia went to a nearby cupboard and took out a small tub. She poured cold water from a pail and mixed it with hot water from a pot on the stove until the temperature was just right. She undressed Celia and carefully lowered her into the water. The baby wailed, which started a deep, wracking cough.

Lydia looked around for a nurse, but none was in sight. She kept the baby in the water in spite of the coughing and used a cup to continually pour water over her little body. All the while she talked to the baby in a calm, soothing voice.

Soon the coughing stopped, and Celia no longer cried. When the water began to lose its mild warmth, Lydia lifted the baby out and wrapped her in a warm flannel cloth. After drying her and putting a diaper on her, she slipped a soft gown over the baby's head and wrapped her in a pink blanket, then sat down in a rocking chair.

"It's all right, sweetheart," Lydia said as she held the fussy baby close to her breast and began rocking. "You feel cooler now, and that's very important."

Lydia rocked in a slow but steady rhythm and hummed to the baby, gently patting her back. Soon Celia stopped her fussing. She relaxed, grew calm, and her little eyelids began to droop. Lydia kissed the downy little head and continued to rock as the baby drifted into a much-needed and healing sleep.

Lydia thought of the family she and Grant had planned. They had talked of having at least three or four children. She looked down at the sleeping baby and suddenly a strong, almost overpowering motherly instinct welled up in her. Her lower lip quivered, and tears filled her eyes. *Grant is gone and can never be the father of my children. Yet God has left me here to fulfill His purpose. This I must do as He leads me step by step.*

Grant Smith and his American companions continued to pray that the Lord would deliver them from their captors. Twice within the month of August, Mexican prisoners had tried to escape, but they had been shot down and killed before they could get over the high stockade fence.

In November, two prisoners managed to get over the fence but were hunted down and caught less than an hour later. They were brought back to the prison, where they were tortured and executed.

The prison facility was well built and well manned. The Mexican authorities boasted that it was impossible to escape. Though a few men had gotten outside the walls, not one had made it to freedom.

Grant and his fellow American prisoners agreed that whenever they made the attempt, it would have to be foolproof. And to a man they agreed they would rather die attempting to escape than to languish in the prison with its poor food, cold and drafty shacks, and ill treatment from the guards.

By January 1849, Lydia realized that she felt love for Clay Price, but she wrestled with it, holding it at bay, still clinging to the memory of the man she had loved since she was a girl. When she felt herself yearning to be with Clay, guilt would take its place, and she wondered if she could ever let go of Grant.

By spring, Clay told Lydia that he was in love with her and wanted to marry her.

Even so, he was careful not to push her.

Billy was now in college at Yale University. Without his presence in their home, Duane and Beverly began attaching themselves to Clay. He enjoyed meals in the Reynolds home two or three times a week.

Lydia talked about the situation many times with her parents. She even went to Scott and Marjorie Smith and to Pastor and Mrs. Britton to seek their counsel. All encouraged her to open her heart to Clay.

Lydia stayed on her knees until the wee hours one night in mid-May. She wept and prayed, asking God to give her peace about accepting Clay's marriage proposal. Just before dawn, Lydia received the peace she had prayed for, and she allowed the love she had been holding at bay to slip into her open and ready heart.

Clay came for supper that evening. Afterward, he and Lydia sat on the front porch, and he proposed again, telling Lydia he loved her with all his heart. This time she told him she was in love with him, and she accepted his proposal.

Clay's internship would be completed in June 1850. They would be married this August, then move west and establish Clay's practice in the frontier town of Sacramento. They agreed that the wedding would be a small and intimate gathering, with only family and close friends in attendance.

August 11 was a beautiful day for a wedding, and Lydia was a beautiful bride. She had chosen a pale pink dress made of fine linen with a round neck and pleated collar of creamy lace. Atop her glossy curls, a hat of the same hue as her dress framed her face and accented the lovely glow of her cheeks.

The ceremony was sweet and very simple as Clay and Lydia pledged their vows to one another. There wasn't a dry eye when Pastor John Britton pronounced them husband and wife.

As was Beverly's way, the reception in the Reynoldses' backyard was beautifully done. While most of the guests ate and talked in small groups, Marjorie Smith sat alone. When Lydia saw her, she excused herself from her groom.

Grant's mother rose to her feet when she saw Lydia coming. They embraced, and Lydia said, "Marjorie, you've told me how happy you are for me, but I know you have to be hurting. This day is what Grant and I had planned and longed for."

A smile graced Marjorie's countenance.

"Lydia, dear, our son's greatest desire was for your happiness. Please honor that desire. Go into your new life with our best wishes and blessings. Be very, very happy . . . and God go with you." She leaned toward Lydia and kissed her cheek. "I love you, Lydia."

They embraced once more, then Lydia turned and walked back toward the festivities. She touched the place where Marjorie had kissed her cheek and whispered, "Thank you, Grant, for wanting me to be happy. Good-bye, my tender flame." A bright smile lit her face as her eyes met Clay's.

During the next joyful year, Clay and Lydia talked and prayed about their upcoming venture to Sacramento. One day, Clay surprised her by saying he had been reading about the frontier and the wagon trains that were going west by the dozens, and that he had a growing impression that the Lord wanted them to go to Oregon City instead of Sacramento. Lydia agreed to pray with him about it, and after a couple of weeks, they both had peace about going there.

In the first week of June 1850, Clay and Lydia said a tearful farewell to Duane and

Beverly Reynolds, the Smiths, the Brittons, and their many friends. Though they were both eager to go, Lydia was a little fearful. But knowing this was God's will, she put her trust in Him, and confidently put her hand in Clay's as they left Montgomery Village behind.

The young couple, so full of hopes and dreams, set their faces toward Oregon.

On a Saturday evening in early December, Beverly Reynolds was preparing supper while Duane was at the barn, replacing hinges on the doors. As she laid out two place settings on the table, her heart felt heavy. Billy was still at Yale. A letter had come from him a few days earlier . . . the same day the first letter from Oregon came from Lydia.

It had taken the Prices three months to get to Oregon City, and it took the letter that announced their arrival another three months to reach her parents.

Beverly sent up a prayer of thanks that her children were in God's will and went on preparing the meal. A knock at the front door interrupted her thoughts. She pushed a skillet to the side of the stove and left the kitchen, wiping her hands on her apron.

As soon as she opened the door, Beverly froze. Then her arms and legs went limp, and her heart pounded wildly. "Grant!"

The familiar face and form, looking thinner than she had ever seen him, swam before her eyes, and her legs gave way. Grant Smith lunged through the door and caught her before she fell to the floor; then he helped her to the couch in the parlor.

"Are you all right?"

"I'll be fine in a moment. It's just that . . ."

"I know. You thought I was dead."

"Yes, I can't believe this. It's like . . . it's like seeing you back from the dead."

"Believe me, I'm not a ghost. Is . . . is Lydia here?"

"Ah . . . no. But Duane is out back. Let me go and —"

"I'm right here, honey," came a shaky voice from the doorway.

Grant turned to see a white-faced Duane Reynolds, his hand pressed against the door frame for support. "Grant? How on earth — ?"

"It's a long story, sir. I'm sorry to jolt you and Mrs. Reynolds like this, but I wanted to see Lydia."

Duane walked to Grant, shaking his head in wonder, and wrapped his arms around the young man. "I can't believe this! I just can't believe this!"

"How is Lydia?" Grant asked.

Duane and Beverly looked at each other helplessly, then Duane said, "She was fine the last we heard from her, Grant."

"Well . . . where is she?"

"She lives out west now," Duane said.

"Oh?"

"Grant, Lydia's married."

Grant Smith looked as if he'd been stabbed in the chest.

"Please sit down, and we'll explain it to you."

Duane and Beverly told Grant about the two lieutenants who had come from Washington to inform his parents that he had been killed. They told him how hard the news had hit Lydia, and how she had grieved for so long.

"Who did she marry?" Grant asked.

"His name is Dr. Clay Price," Duane said. "Lydia didn't marry him until almost two years after you were declared dead."

"Is her husband a medical doctor?"

"Yes. They moved out west. They live in —"

"Please, sir. It's better that I don't know where Lydia's living. Please understand. I still love her and . . . well, now that she's married, I must ask the Lord to take that love out of my heart. It's best that I don't know where she is."

"I understand, son. And I appreciate your attitude."

"Yes," Beverly said. "And I want you to know that before she married Clay, Lydia shared with me that she would never forget you."

"That helps," Grant said, trying to smile.

"You've lost weight," Duane said.

"Yes, sir. Poor prison food."

"Prison?" Beverly said. "You've been in prison?"

Grant nodded, then explained the events that led to his capture. He told them of the six fellow soldiers who were in prison with him and explained how all seven of them had finally escaped. It took them better than a month to make it back to Fort McHenry. They were immediately given a hero's welcome at the fort and told to go home for two weeks before reporting back.

Grant rose to his feet and said, "It's good to see both of you again. I haven't seen my parents yet. I need to get home."

"You mean you came here first?" Duane said.

"I wanted to see Lydia, sir. You understand."

Duane ran his fingers through his hair. "Well, I know it's going to be a shock to your parents when you show up on their doorstep, but are they ever going to be happy!"

Grant embraced Lydia's parents and they followed him to the door. Before Grant stepped onto the porch, he looked into their eyes and said, "I think it would be best if, when you correspond with Lydia, you don't tell her I'm still alive. No sense in upsetting her with that kind of news. I'll be staying in the army and working in forts around the country. The Lord will help me to build a new life. Would you please not tell her?"

Both of Lydia's parents agreed.

11

Grant's parents were eating supper when he knocked. After the first shock of seeing their son standing before them alive, they joyously welcomed him home.

While Grant ate his mother's cooking, he told his parents about his wounding, capture, and imprisonment. Scott and Marjorie listened as their son told of his escape along with his six fellow prisoners. After reporting in at Fort McHenry, he had come directly to Montgomery Village.

The Smiths were relieved when Grant said he knew about Lydia. When he told them he didn't want to know where Lydia and her husband were living and that he'd asked Lydia's parents not to let her know that he was still alive, Scott and Marjorie agreed that it was best to leave well enough alone.

Marjorie told Grant that both his sisters were married now and living in other states. When Grant had finally been caught up on all the family news, he told his parents he could spend a couple of weeks with them before reporting back to Fort McHenry. Marjorie teased that she could fatten him up some in that much time.

That night, in his own room once again, Grant lay awake in the dark. "Lord, I don't understand. I can't blame Lydia for marrying this Clay Price when she thought I was dead. But You didn't have to let me get shot and spend all that time in a rotten Mexican prison. The one and only woman I've ever loved is now another man's wife because I didn't make it home from the war like thousands of other men did. Why, God? Why?"

The next morning, Grant went to the church. When Pastor Britton was over the initial jolt of finding Grant alive and had learned what had happened to him, the young war hero said, "Pastor, I really need your help. It appears that the Lord has failed me."

The pastor looked at Grant with compassion. "You're referring to the fact that Lydia married someone else while you were locked up in prison?"

"Yes, sir. God could've kept it from happening. He could've let me come home and marry Lydia. Why didn't He?"

"I detect bitterness in your tone, Grant. The one thing you should never do is get bitter toward God." Pastor Britton picked up his Bible from the desk. "You say you want help . . ."

"Yes, sir."

"I don't have a magic formula that will make you understand why things happened as they did, but God Himself has the answer. You'll have to take Him at His Word, by faith. If you're willing to do that, you'll walk out that door in a little while with victory over this puzzle in your heart. Are you willing?"

Grant looked down for a moment, then said, "Yes, I am."

Britton opened his Bible to Psalm 18 and turned it so Grant could see it. "Read me verse 30."

" 'As for God, his way is perfect: the word of the LORD is tried: he is a buckler to all those that trust in him.' "

"When the army reported you dead, Grant, I used this verse to help Lydia. Believe me, she was crushed by the news. It says in this verse that the Word of the Lord is tried. Have you ever known His Word to fail? To be wrong or untrustworthy?"

"No, sir."

"All right. The verse also says that the Lord Himself is a buckler to all those who trust in Him. Trust in this context is the same thing as faith. Right?"

"Yes, sir."

"You said you were willing to take God at His Word by faith . . ."

"I did."

"All right, look again at the first seven words in the verse. What do they say?"

" 'As for God, his way is perfect.' "

"His Word is tried, Grant. It has never been wrong. Isn't that true?"

"Yes."

"Your heart is shattered, and your life is in a shambles right now. True?"

"Yes."

"You need a buckler."

"I need a buckler."

"Do you need a buckler who never does wrong? One who can be trusted to always do right?"

"Yes, sir."

"Then trust your Lord God in this deep disappointment and heartache. Believe Him. He says His way is perfect. Is it perfect, Grant?"

Grant turned his gaze to the floor.

"Well?" Britton said.

"It has to be, Pastor."

"Then this seeming tragedy in your life was directed by your Lord."

"Yes, sir."

"I know you don't understand why God brought it about this way, and the Lord knows you don't. What He wants from you now is to trust Him and believe that what He has done is right for you and Lydia . . . and perfect. Is the One who died on the cross for you worthy of your trust?"

Tears filled Grant's eyes and began spilling down his cheeks. "Yes, Pastor. He is worthy of it, and I was wrong to feel bitterness toward Him."

"Grant, you're not the first child of God to let bitterness toward Him get a grip on you. You're made of mortal flesh, like the rest of us."

"But I shouldn't have accused Him in my thoughts of doing wrong, Pastor. I want to ask Him to forgive me."

Britton left his chair and said, "Let's pray together. You go first."

The two men knelt side by side, and Grant poured out his heart to the Lord, asking to be forgiven for his bitterness and lack of faith. He asked the Lord to help him grasp the full truth of the words, "As for God, his way is perfect." And he asked God to give him a happy life without Lydia, because He was the only one who could do it.

Captain Grant Smith settled down to

army life at Fort McHenry. He found a good church nearby and became a member. All six of the men he had led to Christ in the Mexican prison were active in the same church.

Shortly thereafter, the army assigned a new commandant to the fort — Colonel Steven Baker. Colonel Baker, his wife, son, and daughter were Christians and joined the same church where Grant was a member. Not long after that, Grant and the colonel's daughter, Carrie, began seeing each other.

As Grant and Carrie spent time together, they found themselves falling in love. Grant proposed marriage, and after a proper courtship, they were married in March of 1852.

In June of the following year, Carrie gave birth to a baby girl they named Jessica. In August 1854, son Daniel was born, and another son, David, was born in November 1856.

It was a beautiful spring day in 1860. Carrie Smith was hanging clothes on the line behind her house on the grounds of Fort McHenry. She was taking one of five-year-old Daniel's shirts out of the laundry basket when she saw her husband coming around the corner of the house.

The sun glistened off Carrie's jet-black hair. She smiled at Grant and said, "Hello, darling. I didn't expect you home till this afternoon."

"I've been in a meeting with your daddy and some big brass from Washington," Grant said, kissing her on the cheek. "And I've got some news."

"Good news or bad?"

Grant smiled. "Well, a mixture, I guess. It will take us a long way from your parents and mine, but we'll get to see some new country."

Carrie placed Daniel's shirt on the line and fastened it with clothespins. "You're being transferred to another fort?"

"That's right. To Fort Union, New Mexico."

"New Mexico! Really?" There was a gleam in Carrie's eyes. "Honey, I've always had a secret desire to go out West. Of course I'll miss our families, but orders are orders. If the army needs their best man at Fort Union, then so be it."

Grant folded her in his arms, kissed her soundly, and said, "You're the perfect soldier's wife, sweetheart. Thank you for being so understanding."

"Well, I'm a soldier's daughter, too, you

know. That sort of prepared me to be a soldier's wife." She paused, then said, "What brought on the transfer?"

"They're having continual trouble from the Indians out there, and Colonel Arthur Ballard, Fort Union's commandant, put in a request to army headquarters for more troops and for a combat-experienced major to serve in the fort."

Carrie cocked her head to the side. "But you're a captain."

"Well, part of the good news is that I'm not going to be a captain much longer. I'm being promoted to major before we leave, and we're leaving in exactly three weeks."

Carrie wrapped her arms around his neck. "Oh, I'm so proud of you! I can't wait to tell the children!"

When the older Smith children came home from school, they learned of the change coming in their lives and of their father's promotion. The new adventure of living in the West had them excited.

Three weeks later the Smiths traveled from Maryland with various army units until they reached St. Louis. There they joined an army wagon train hauling weapons, ammunition, and supplies to two forts in New Mexico, one of them being

Fort Union. A heavily armed escort of cavalry met up with them when they reached the southeast corner of Kansas. They were now entering hostile Indian country.

The journey was difficult but exciting, and though they often saw Indians riding at a distance, there were no attacks. Grant told his family this was because of their cavalry escort.

The Smiths arrived at Fort Union on a blistering hot day in late August 1860. They were welcomed by Colonel Arthur Ballard and his wife, and all the other men, women, and children of the fort. Grant, Carrie, and their children were especially happy to meet army chaplain Brett Cornell, his wife Martha, and their children — twelve-year-old Joshua and nine-year-old Mary Ann.

Two days after their arrival, the Smiths attended the Sunday chapel services and loved Chaplain Cornell's preaching. They learned from other Christians that Cornell had been there only a few months, but already many souls had been saved, both from his preaching and from his personal interaction with people.

That week, Grant began leading patrols out of the fort. Carrie, like the other officers' wives, watched them ride out, praying for God's hand to keep her husband safe and to bring him home to her.

In the weeks that followed, Grant was involved in battles with Apaches, Hopis, and Navajos. Some of the soldiers were brought back wounded. Others were brought back draped over the backs of their horses. Each time, Carrie thanked the Lord that Grant had gone through the battles untouched.

The Smiths and the Cornells became fast friends and spent much time together.

One day after school, Jessica Smith and little brother Daniel were walking across the compound toward the section where the officers' houses were located.

Daniel's hair was like that of his brother. It was yellow as cornsilk and quite unruly. Both boys, like their father, had pale blue eyes.

Seven-year-old Jessica usually wore her glossy black hair in pigtails, and straight bangs framed her chocolate brown eyes with their long, dark lashes. And like her mother, Jessica had well-sculptured features and smooth, creamy skin.

Her permanent front teeth had come in and seemed a little large, but Carrie had assured her that soon they would fit her face just fine. Anyone who looked at her could tell that one day she was going to be a striking young woman. She had a sweet gamine smile and was filled with mischievous charm. Since birth, she had been the apple of her daddy's eye.

Daniel also had a mischievous streak, but to his sister, at times it was anything but charming.

They were about halfway across the compound when Daniel pointed toward the fort stables. "There comes your boyfriend, Jessica."

Big sister's eyes flashed fire. "Daniel Jay Smith, don't you say a word about you know what! Do you hear me?"

Daniel grinned. "What's it worth to you?"

Joshua Cornell had put his horse to a trot.

"We'll talk about it later," Jessica said. "Just don't you say anything!"

"Hi, kids!" said Joshua, drawing rein. "Want to go for a ride, Jessica?"

"I can't this time. Mama has some housework for me to do when I get home. Maybe tomorrow."

"All right. I'll check with you then. Bye." Joshua put the horse to a trot again and aimed for the fort gate. His father allowed him to ride outside the fort as long as he stayed close to the walls at all times.

As brother and sister walked toward home, Daniel said, "Well, I didn't blab that you're in love with him. What do I get?"

"I'll make your bed for you in the morning, all right?"

A wide grin spread over the boy's face. "Great! I hate to make my bed! Thanks, sis!"

News arrived from Washington, D.C., of trouble between the Northern states and the Southern states. There was a battle going on in Congress over states' rights and the issue of slavery, and the state politicians were in heated debate. At the same time, a national election had just been held, and Republican Abraham Lincoln was elected president of the United States. Though Lincoln was not an abolitionist, it was known before the election that he regarded slavery as an evil and opposed its extension. This in itself had the Southern states upset.

These hot topics were the talk of the fort.

To South Carolina, Lincoln's election was a signal for secession, and the state pulled out of the Union in December. By Inauguration Day, March 4, 1861, six more states had seceded, and along with South Carolina, they formed the Confederate States of America.

While the soldiers of Fort Union continued to fight Indians, a steady stream of news concerning the problems between the Union and the Confederacy came to the fort.

Ten days after President Lincoln's inauguration, Colonel Ballard called a meeting of everyone in the fort and told them it looked as though there was going to be a war between the North and the South.

The very next month, on April 14, Ballard called another meeting to announce that the War between the States had started two days before at Fort Sumter, South Carolina. The South had fired the first shot.

As the Civil War grew intense, President Lincoln called for volunteers to fight the Southerners. He also ordered the commandants of Union forts in the western territories to send troops to Virginia, where most of the fighting was taking place.

Colonel Ballard gave up half of his troops to the Union cause.

By the end of 1861, the people of Fort Union learned that the Civil War was coming in their direction. Many of the Indians had joined with the Confederate troops who were coming into New Mexico Territory by direct order of the Confederate president, Jefferson Davis.

As things began to look worse for the Union forts in the West, Major John M. Chivington formed a band of fighting men called the Colorado Volunteers. There were skirmishes in several places across Colorado and New Mexico, and by the end of February 1862, the fighting had become fierce.

In mid-March, the federal authorities in Washington wired a message to Colonel Ballard, directing him to send Major Grant Smith to Glorieta Pass in New Mexico with a unit of two hundred men. The pass was sixty miles southwest of Fort Union, at the southern tip of the Sangre de Cristo Range in the Rocky Mountain cordillera. The Confederates were also sending troops toward the pass. Whichever army controlled the pass would control the Intermountain West.

Grant's orders were to join forces with Major Chivington and the Colorado Volunteers, who were at that moment on a fast ride from Denver to the pass. The Union forces must beat the Rebels to the spot, defeat them in the impending battle, and maintain control of the pass.

Major Grant Smith and his men stood ready to leave the fort at sunrise on Thursday, March 20. Cannons on wheels had been hitched to ammunition and supply wagons, which were pulled by mules. Horses were saddled and stood in ranks of ten for the sixty-mile journey.

It was a difficult moment when the wives and children of the officers gathered for good-byes. Chaplain Brett Cornell prayed with the men; then the officers said good-bye to their families while the enlisted men looked on and thought of their own families back home.

Carrie Smith gave Daniel a gentle push toward his daddy. When both her brothers had hugged their father's neck, Jessica moved to her father, tears in her eyes, and said, "I'll be praying for you, Daddy."

Grant folded her in his arms and held her tight. "You do that, honey, and Daddy will be back before you know it. I love you."

Jessica sniffed. "I love you, too."

Carrie had seen her husband off to battle many times, yet each time he left, it became a little more difficult. But Grant was in God's hands, and she had absolute confidence that God's will would be done. With an inner calm, she moved close to her husband as Jessica stepped aside.

Carrie's eyes flooded with tears, and she reached up a slender hand to caress Grant's cheek, looking deeply into his eyes. Grant clasped her hand and brought it to his mouth, placing a light kiss on her palm. He then folded her in his arms and kissed her tenderly.

"I'll be back, sweetheart."

Carrie nodded. "Of course you will. I love you, darling."

"And I love you. With all my heart."

Carrie wiped tears from her eyes and took a step backward to stand between Jessica and Daniel. David positioned himself in front of her, a small fist clinging to her skirt.

Grant pivoted, mounted his horse, and his voice reverberated across the compound as he shouted, "All right, men . . . mount up!"

As Grant, flanked by a corporal carrying a Union flag, led his cavalry unit toward the open gate, he turned in the saddle one last time and let his eyes roam over his family.

The wives and children followed the column as far as the open gate.

While tears streamed down Jessica's cheeks, Joshua Cornell slipped up beside her and put an arm around her shoulder. She looked up through her tears to see who it was, and managed to smile as he said, "It'll be all right, Jessica. Your daddy will be back before you know it."

Soon the distant riders were only a small cluster of dots on the horizon, but the tight-knit group at the gate did not turn away until the men had vanished from view.

On the last day of March, the two sentries in the Fort Union tower were watching the red-gold sun sink behind the rugged horizon. Four units had gone out on patrol that morning and had returned within the last half hour.

Private Harry Combs squinted at the horizon. "Bill, you see that?"

Corporal Bill Watts reached for the one pair of binoculars in the tower. "Do you think it could be them?"

"You tell me."

"Looks like only about a couple dozen men," Bill said as he gazed through the binoculars. "I sure hope there are more men than that, out of two hundred, coming back."

After several more minutes, Watts said, "It's Major Smith's unit, all right. I don't see the major, but I recognize Captain Scudder out front. And . . . ah . . . yes, that's Lieutenant Brimble next to him. There's a wagon at the rear. It's got wounded men in it. I can see a jumble of uniforms back there, and both medics are attending them."

"I'll go let Colonel Ballard know," Combs said.

"Better stop off and alert Dr. Chandler. Looks like he's going to have his hands full."

Word spread quickly through the fort that some of Major Smith's men were returning from the battle. Within minutes everyone in the fort was at the wide-open gate, watching the weary-looking men as they drew near.

Carrie and her children were near the front of the crowd, and Jessica said, "Mama, Daddy's not with them."

"Maybe he had to stay behind with the other men, honey," Carrie said, trying to keep her voice from shaking.

Colonel Ballard, flanked by a few other officers, moved out to meet them. Captain Fred Scudder dismounted, saluted the colonel, and said, "We won the battle at

Glorieta Pass, sir. What few Rebels were left have gone on the run. We left a hundred thirty-eight men to help Major Chivington occupy the pass . . . buried thirty-two. We've got eleven wounded men in the wagon. I'll give you a detailed report in your office."

"Major Smith stayed at Glorieta?" Ballard said.

"No, sir. He's in the wagon. Got his leg shot up pretty bad. Our medics have done a marvelous job bandaging him and the rest of the wounded."

When Carrie heard that, she dashed past the mounted men to the wagon. Grant lay at the tailgate, his eyes closed.

One of the medics said, "He's unconscious, Mrs. Smith. Took shrapnel from a Rebel cannonball in his left thigh."

"Will he be all right?"

"I can't really say, ma'am. Dr. Chandler will be able to tell you once he looks at him. We took the shrapnel out, but it damaged bone. That's all I can tell you."

The colonel's authoritative voice said, "Doc's preparing for these men in the infirmary right now. Let's get them there."

12

Chaplain Brett Cornell and his wife, Martha, sat in a small waiting room adjacent to the infirmary with Carrie Smith and Florence Roberts, wife of Lieutenant Dean Roberts. Dr. Clifford Chandler had already explained to the two women that he and his assistant would work on the officers and enlisted men according to the seriousness of their wounds. In this situation, military rank had no precedence.

About six o'clock that evening, Dr. Chandler entered the waiting room and broke the news to Florence that her husband had died on the operating table. The Cornells and Carrie did what they could to comfort the woman; then Martha took Florence and her children to their apartment in the officers' quarters.

It was almost nine o'clock when a weary Dr. Chandler came to the waiting room, drying his hands on a towel. "Mrs. Smith, your husband lost some more blood, but he's going to pull through all right. It took better than two hours of surgery to clean the bone fragments out of the wound, repair what damage I could, and sew him up."

Carrie breathed a sigh of relief and hugged her children close. "Praise the Lord, Daddy's going to be all right."

Dr. Chandler hunkered down in front of Carrie. "I must tell you, ma'am, that the shrapnel cut deep into the thigh bone, just above the knee, and did permanent damage. Major Smith will be on crutches for at least three months. I think he may have to walk with a cane. I could be wrong, and I hope I am, but even if he gets past the cane stage, he'll walk with a prominent limp for the rest of his life."

"But how will he continue his military career with an impediment like that?"

"He won't, ma'am. His military career is over. It will be my duty to inform Colonel Ballard that Major Smith can no longer fulfill his duties. If he tried to do so, the leg could give out on him at any time. In combat it could cost the major his life . . . and maybe the lives of other soldiers. He must never lead a cavalry unit into battle again. In fact, he won't even be able to get on a horse for a long time."

Tears filled Carrie's eyes and spilled down her cheeks.

Jessica looked up. "What will Daddy do, Mama? The army is his whole life."

"Your daddy is a resourceful man, honey. He'll find something else to do." She looked at the doctor. "I assume Grant doesn't know this yet."

"No. He's still under the chloroform. I suggest that you and your children go home and get a good night's rest. He's going to be under for a while. Can you bring the children and come back in the morning? Say . . . eight o'clock?"

"Certainly. Jessica and Daniel can be late for school."

"Good. I'd like you to be with him when he hears the news." He added to Cornell, "It would be good if you could be here too, Chaplain."

Brett nodded. "You can count on it, Doctor."

At eight o'clock the next morning, Carrie and her children entered the small room where Grant lay on a cot. The chaplain and the doctor looked on while the major's family embraced him. Then, while Carrie held Grant's hand, Dr. Chandler carefully explained the seriousness of the wound.

Grant looked up at Carrie and said,

"Well, I guess that's it, then. Not exactly what I'd hoped to hear, but God knew all along. I think the best thing for us to do is go to Montgomery Village. I know a lot of people in the area, and I'm sure someone will give this crippled man a job."

"If that's what you feel is best, then that's what we'll do, darling."

"You'll need to stay here at the fort till you completely recuperate from the surgery, Major," Dr. Chandler said. "You mustn't travel for at least three months. It would be best to wait until you're off the crutches and using a cane."

"You're the doctor."

"We'll sure miss the Smith family around here," Brett Cornell said, "but the Lord's will be done. Let's pray, Major, thanking the Lord that you're still alive and that you didn't lose your leg."

Grant smiled. "Things could always be worse, couldn't they, Chaplain? The Lord is so good to us."

On that same first day of April 1862, at Montgomery Village, Maryland, Duane Reynolds came home from work and found Beverly in the kitchen. After a tender kiss, Beverly said, "We got a letter today from Lydia."

"Did she say she still loves her old father as much as ever?"

"Well, not in those exact words, but the love is there in the letter." A shadow passed over Beverly's eyes as she said, "There's something else in the letter that you need to know about."

"Something bad?"

"Well, she and Clay are taking it pretty well, and trusting the Lord in it."

"What is it?"

"Do you want to read the letter, or should I just tell you?"

"Tell me."

"Remember that I told you that in my last letter to her I asked if there might be a baby on the way?"

"Yes."

"There is no baby on the way . . . and there never will be. They found out that Lydia can't bear children. Some problem she was probably born with that cannot be corrected, even with surgery, Clay says."

"That's hard. But you say they're taking it pretty good?"

"Lydia said they have peace about it because they know God's hand is in it. She quoted Psalm 18:30, 'As for God, his way is perfect.'"

"That verse has been a real source of

strength to Lydia ever since you first pointed it out to her."

"Yes, it has. She says in the letter that in addition to working in the office as Clay's assistant five days a week, and on top of teaching her girls' Sunday school class and singing in the choir, she's teaching children's Bible clubs on Saturdays in Oregon City and surrounding communities. When she learned she could never have children of her own, she went to Pastor Farrington and told him she wanted to be involved with children as much as possible. Pastor Farrington was delighted and agreed to make the Bible clubs a ministry of the church. So now the pastor's wife, Madeline, and a couple of other women are helping her with the clubs."

Duane shook his head. "That's some girl God gave us, honey."

"Don't I know it. By the way, Clay wrote another little note with her letter, telling us how valuable she is to his practice."

"He's mentioned a couple of times how much his patients love her, especially the children."

Beverly paused for a moment, then said, "She certainly has a way with children. They can't help but love her."

"Lydia's had some real bumps in life,

but she always seems to rise above them."

"Oh, that reminds me . . . Marjorie and I were talking about Grant when she stopped by this morning. She had a letter from Carrie last week. They seem to be very happy at Fort Union. Grant loves his army life, and the rest of the family does too. Marjorie brought up the old agreement we made with Grant years ago not to tell Lydia he's alive. She and Scott still think that's the best way."

"I agree. Leave well enough alone. Let Lydia go on with her life as Clay Price's wife, and let the past stay in the past."

"Marjorie and I are having tea tomorrow afternoon at her house. I'll tell her we feel just as they do about it."

Josh Cornell hoisted Jessica Smith into the saddle on his gray stallion. He lifted the reins, whose tips touched the ground, and stroked the horse's long face. "All right, Stormy, let's take the prettiest girl in the fort for a ride." Josh, of course, was unaware of the thrill he always sent through Jessica when he called her the prettiest girl in the fort. She loved him more than ever, but so far she had been able to bribe her little brother to keep him from letting the cat out of the bag.

Josh led Stormy outside the gate and swung up behind Jessica, sitting just behind the saddle. He put his arms around the younger girl to hold the reins.

It was late April, and the desert had blossomed with cactus flowers of various colors — red and gold cane chollas, dark green chokecherry shrubs, and the bright yellow catclaw acacia.

Jessica loved every minute as they rode Stormy at a slow walk under the gaze of the sentries in the tower. Josh was her hero, and she delighted in his presence . . . especially when she was this close to him.

When they reached the first corner of the stockade wall, Josh let his eyes roam over the colorful desert, the Sangre de Cristo range in the distance to the west, and the azure sky with puffy white clouds drifting beneath the sun. A huge hawk rode the air waves overhead.

"Just think of all this beauty around us, Jessica," he said, awe evident in his voice. "And so many people think it came from some mysterious explosion."

"That really is silly, isn't it? It's a lot easier to believe that God created it by His mighty hand."

"Only a fool believes there is no God

and that the universe came into being by accident."

They rode without speaking until they had turned the next corner, then Josh said, "Jessica, since we're good friends, I'd like to share something with you. The Lord has been dealing with me about being a preacher."

She turned in the saddle to look him in the eye. "Really, Josh?"

"I'm certain of it."

"I think that's wonderful!"

Her exuberant approval brought a smile to his lips. "I hope I can be a preacher as good as Dad."

"Your father is an excellent preacher, Josh, and I'm sure you'll be as good as he is."

"It'll take some doing."

"Yes, but since the same God is calling you to preach who called your father, He can give you the same talents and abilities. I think it's wonderful that you're going to be a preacher."

"I thought you would; that's why I was sort of eager to tell you."

"Are there any other preachers in your family?"

"Not unless they're distant relatives we don't know about."

"Not even a grandfather, great-grandfather, someone like that?"

"Huh-uh. My grandfather on my dad's side was in the lumber business in Vermont. He's dead now. My grandmother's still alive, but her health isn't good. My grandfather on my mother's side was a fisherman in Maine. He and my grandmother are both dead."

The sentries smiled down on the children as they completed their first trip around the perimeter of the fort wall and started another.

When they reached the first corner again, Josh said, "I sure am going to miss you and your family when you leave the fort."

"I — we will miss your family too."

"Maybe we'll meet again someday."

"I hope so."

By the first of July, Grant had recuperated enough to lay aside his crutches and walk with a cane. He made arrangements with the army, through Colonel Ballard, to provide his family an escort as far as Independence, Missouri, where they would cross the Missouri River out of hostile Indian territory. They planned to leave Fort Union on July 16.

On Wednesday, July 9, Jessica was at the front door of the Smith house watching her father limp toward the family wagon with the help of his cane. A corporal had hitched up the team and now sat on the wagon seat.

"Corporal," Grant said, "go ahead and take the wagon outside the gate. You can leave it there and go on about your business. I'll be leaving for the trading post in a few minutes."

"But wouldn't you rather I left it here, sir? So you wouldn't have to walk clear to the gate?"

"That's the point. I've got to strengthen this bad leg, and walking is the best way to do it. Thanks for your help, corporal. Tell the sentries I'll be there shortly." As Grant limped back toward the house, he smiled at Jessica and said, "I have a feeling somebody wants to ride with me to the trading post."

Jessica grinned. "Would it be all right, Daddy? Daniel and David are playing games with their friends over by the stables. My work's all caught up. Could I please go with you?"

"Sure, honey. I'll kiss your mother goodbye and be right back."

"I'll wait right here."

Jessica turned back to see Josh on Stormy, trotting across the compound toward her.

"Hi," said Josh, reining in. "Want to go for a ride?"

"I'd love to, but I'm going with Daddy to the trading post. He has to pick up some supplies for our trip. We're about to leave."

"How about tomorrow?"

"Sure, I'll ride with you tomorrow."

Jessica felt a stab of pain in her heart as she watched Stormy carry Josh toward the fort gate. She wished the Cornells were moving to Maryland too.

She looked back through the open door of her family's quarters, expecting to see her father tapping his way with his cane. When several minutes had passed, Jessica went inside and walked toward the kitchen, where she could hear her parents' voices. She found her mother standing over the kitchen table. Her father lay on his back, using a screwdriver on one of the table legs.

"Are you about ready to go, Daddy?"

"Be a few minutes, honey." He grunted as he tightened a screw. "Why don't you go on out and get in the wagon? Tell the sentries I told you to wait for me there. I'll be along in a few minutes."

"All right." She kissed her mother's cheek and headed for the front door. She skipped across the compound, greeting people along the way. When she reached the gate, it was closed.

"You going with your father to the trading post?" Private Harry Combs called down from the sentry tower.

"Yes. Daddy'll be along in a few minutes. He told me I can go ahead and get in the wagon."

Private Combs came down the stairs and opened the gate wide enough for them to pass through. He ushered Jessica to the waiting wagon and lifted her onto the seat. The horses swished their tails at pesky flies.

Jessica thanked him, and Combs went back inside the fort. A few moments later, her attention was drawn to Josh galloping his horse around the nearest corner of the stockade fence. Her smile broadened as horse and rider slowed and drew up beside the wagon.

"You going to drive to the trading post by yourself, Jessica?"

She giggled. "No, silly! Daddy will be here in a minute."

Stormy blew and stomped a hoof, impatient to get on with his run. "Looks like I'd better get back to my riding before Stormy gets upset at me." With that, Josh put Stormy to a gallop and soon rounded the far corner of the stockade fence. He waved to her just before he disappeared.

Time seemed to drag while Jessica waited for her father. She turned slightly on the wagon seat and let her gaze roam over the desert toward the west, admiring the distant peaks of the Sangre de Cristo Range. She noticed movement a few yards to the rear of the wagon, and her back went rigid when she saw a diamondback rattlesnake slither from under a small pile of rocks. She could see the black, bulging eyes and flitting tongue.

"Private Combs! Corporal Watts!" she called, turning back toward the tower.

"What is it, Jessica?"

"I . . . I'm in trouble down here. There's a rattlesnake crawling toward the wagon!"

"Stay right were you are!" Combs shouted. "Don't move!"

Jessica heard the rapid footsteps on the tower stairs. She leaned over the side of the wagon and watched the snake slither underneath, then between the team. When one of the horses swished its tail and stomped a hoof, the rattler hissed and quickly drew itself into a tight coil, its head high and weaving.

Jessica watched, spellbound, as the snake's rattle became a blur against the reddish earth, and the whirring sound grew louder.

The startled horses whinnied shrilly, danced about for a few seconds, then bolted when the snake struck one of them.

The lurch of the wagon almost caused Jessica to fall over the back of the seat, but she managed to hang on as it bounced and fishtailed over the rugged, uneven ground.

Josh Cornell was some two hundred yards from the gate, leisurely trotting Stormy around in a wide circle, when he saw the bounding wagon and a great dust cloud behind. Josh gouged Stormy's sides with his heels and put the horse to a full gallop.

Grant Smith was making his way toward the gate when he saw both sentries thunder down the stairs of the tower, muskets in hand. He quickened his pace as they charged through the gate, leaving it partially open. Before Grant could see what was going on, he heard the muskets roar, one right after the other.

He hurried as fast as his bad leg would let him, his heart thudding at the sound of shouting soldiers behind him, coming on the run.

When he pushed open the gate, he saw clouds of blue-white gunsmoke floating away on the air. The two sentries were standing over a dead rattlesnake, but their eyes were watching a dust cloud to the southwest.

"What happened?" Grant gasped.

"This snake spooked the horses, sir," Watts said. "Jessica called to us, telling us the snake was crawling under the wagon. Before we could get down here, the horses bolted."

Suddenly Josh Cornell appeared on his galloping horse, heading for the runaway wagon. He was steadily gaining, but even if he reached Jessica in time, could he get her out of the wagon?

Colonel Ballard arrived on the scene, having heard the gunshots, and Watts told him the situation. All eyes stayed riveted on the wagon and the pursuing rider. Ballard ordered three men to get their horses and get out there.

"Please, dear God," Grant whispered. "Please help Josh. Please bring my little girl back to me safe and sound!"

★ ★ ★

Flecks of foam from the horses' mouths struck Jessica in the face as she clung to the seat. She was too frightened even to scream. Suddenly she saw a gaping hole in the desert floor, looming up ahead. The horses were charging full speed toward a fifty-foot-deep gully. And then, seemingly from out of nowhere, Josh appeared beside the wagon on his galloping steed.

"Jessica!" Josh shouted above the thunder of hooves and rattle of wagon. "I'm coming in close! Move to the edge of the seat! When I come in, let me put my arm around you! Once I have a grip on you, grab my arm and hang on!"

Jessica glanced forward and saw the sharp rim of the gully dead ahead.

"Here I come, Jessica!" Josh cried. "Get ready!"

He veered Stormy dangerously close to the side of the wagon, his arm reaching for Jessica's small body, then shouted, "Now, Jessica!"

She leaned toward him and felt his arm encircle her. For a split second, as she left the wagon seat, Jessica felt as if she were slipping from his grasp. She dug fingernails into his arm and hung on. Josh pulled the small girl to his side.

As Josh slowed Stormy, the wagon pulled away. Within seconds, Josh had brought the horse to a smooth halt. He and Jessica watched the galloping team go over the edge of the gully, their hooves pawing the air. The horses' shrill cries echoed from the deep gully for a few seconds, then broke off with the sound of the crash.

A breathless Jessica was now clinging to Josh's neck, and he swung her up in front of him. Three uniformed riders thundered toward them, then slowed and came to a stop.

"Looks like you got her off that wagon just in time, Josh," Lieutenant Osgood said.

Josh let out a heavy sigh. "Yes, sir. The Lord was with us."

"That was some kind of riding, young man," Sergeant Deemer said. "It took a lot of courage to do what you did."

Josh managed a thin smile but didn't reply.

Carrie and Grant Smith were wiping away tears of relief and joy as Josh and Lieutenant Osgood drew rein. Carrie rushed to Stormy's side with Grant just a pace behind. Josh lowered the girl into her mother's arms, and as Grant joined them, there was a moment of praise to the Lord.

Colonel Ballard lauded Josh for his courage and quick thinking. He congratulated Chaplain and Mrs. Cornell for having such a fine son. Everyone in the crowd voiced their agreement, breaking into applause when Jessica shyly planted a kiss on Josh's cheek.

The Smiths completed an uneventful journey to Independence, Missouri, where the army escort bid them good-bye. Three weeks later they arrived in Montgomery Village, Maryland, and were welcomed by family and a great number of Grant's old friends.

Grant took a job at the bank in Germantown, and Carrie and the children were befriended by all, especially the pastor and congregation of the Montgomery Village church. The Smiths bought a lovely home and settled down to a quiet life. No one brought up Lydia Price in conversations with Grant, not even Duane and Beverly Reynolds.

Jessica and Josh exchanged letters for about a year; then little by little the correspondence dropped off. Though there were no more letters from Josh, he was often in Jessica's mind. She would always have a soft spot in her heart for Joshua Cornell.

In early 1864, Chaplain Brett Cornell developed an incurable problem with his voice and had to retire as chaplain of Fort Union. His mother had died the previous November and left him a sizable inheritance. He and Martha felt the Lord was directing them to travel farther west and go into the lumber business, since Brett had been raised in it and knew the business well. After reading about the growing Pacific coast frontier, they decided on booming Oregon City, Oregon.

There were tearful good-byes at Fort Union when the Cornells pulled out and headed for the Pacific Northwest.

13

In April 1865, the Civil War came to an end. Only days afterward, the nation was stunned when President Abraham Lincoln died from an assassin's bullet.

At Montgomery Village, Maryland, a new family moved into town in May of that year. John and Betty Moore and their twelve-year-old daughter, Brenda, were devoted Christians and quickly became active in the Montgomery Village church. Jessica Smith and Brenda Moore became friends, and as time passed they grew closer and closer, each calling the other her best friend.

Jessica and Brenda graduated from high school in May 1871, and the following month Jessica turned eighteen. She had blossomed into a lovely young woman.

Jessica had told her best friend about Josh Cornell and the torch she'd carried for him when she was a young girl. She often thought about Josh, but she had no idea where he was. A couple of years after their correspondence dwindled and finally ceased, she had written Josh a letter. It was returned "addressee no longer at Fort Union."

One day in July, Jessica carried a glass of lemonade from the kitchen into her parents' bedroom. Carrie was dressed but was lying on the bed. She smiled at her daughter and sat up. "Thank you, honey. It is a rather hot day, isn't it?"

"Yes, and I think you should stay down for a while yet, Mama. Don't want you to overdo."

Carrie took a sip of the cool lemonade. "I can't just lie around all the time, Jessica. Even the doctor said I have to stay as active as possible."

"I know how you feel, Mama, but I don't want you trying to do the washing and ironing. I'll take care of it. I'll stay out of your way when it comes to the cooking, though. I know your favorite thing is to cook for us."

Carrie took another sip of lemonade and smiled. "No mother ever had a better daughter than you, honey."

Jessica's dark brown eyes glinted with humor as she said, "You'd get some argument on that if other mothers heard you say it."

There was a knock at the front door.

"That will be Brenda. Why don't you lie down, Mama?"

"I'd rather sit up in my chair," said Carrie, slipping off the bed.

Jessica helped her mother from the bed to the overstuffed chair by the window, then hurried to the front of the house and opened the door.

"Sorry to keep you waiting, Brenda. I was occupied with Mama. She's sitting in her room right now."

Brenda Moore smiled as she stepped inside. "How's your mother doing?"

"Better than last week. She's been up and dressed every day. Dr. Westland says patients with low-grade consumption should try to live as normally as possible. They just can't do all the things they would like to. If I'd let her, she'd still be doing the housecleaning, washing, and ironing."

Jessica noticed that Brenda was holding a portion of the *Baltimore Press* opened to the classified section. "Looking for a job?"

"No . . . a husband."

"A what?"

As they drew near the master bedroom, Brenda said, "I'll tell you about it after we

227

stop in here. I want to say hello to your mother."

Carrie smiled and greeted Brenda as the two young women entered her room.

"Hello, Mrs. Smith. I'm glad to see you sitting up. Jessica says you're feeling better than last week."

"Much better."

"I'm so glad. Our family prays for you every day."

"I appreciate that."

"Mom said to tell you she's coming to see you tomorrow."

"I'll look forward to it."

A few minutes later, the two young women entered Jessica's bright, sunlit room.

"All right, Miss Smarty," Jessica said. "What's this husband business?"

Brenda laughed. "Well, you asked me if I was looking for a job, and I told you I was looking for a husband. You think I'm kidding, but I'm not. Haven't we both been afraid we might end up as old maids?"

"Well, sort of, but —"

"I want to show you something."

Brenda unfolded the paper and pointed to a column headlined:

MAIL ORDER BRIDES WANTED

"Look at this," she said, running her finger down the page and stopping at an ad marked with an X.

"Brenda, don't tell me you're serious! You're not really thinking of answering one of those ads?"

"This ad was put in here by a twenty-three-year-old man who lives in Carson City, Nevada Territory. He's done well in gold mining and wants to get married."

"You can't just pack up and go out there and marry a man you don't even know! Why, he's probably a hard drinker like all the other men out there in those goldfields, and —"

"Wait a minute. Let me finish. This man's name is Gil Simmons. He gives a clear testimony right here of being a Christian, and is looking for a Christian wife who lives for Jesus."

"Brenda! You're not going to write him, are you?"

"Well, I'm seriously considering it. I've always had a fascination for the West. You've told me so much about New Mexico and how you would like to go back there, or maybe somewhere else in the West someday."

"All right, but not this way. You've never laid eyes on this Gil Simmons. How do you know what he's really like? You can't just pack up and —"

"Jessica!" said Brenda, throwing up her hands. "I've prayed about this. And I —"

"You couldn't have prayed about it very much. That's yesterday's paper. Brenda, you're playing with fire! I can't stand by and let you throw yourself away on a man you've never met."

Brenda laughed. "I love you for hovering over me like a mother hen, but let me explain what's on my mind."

"All right. I'm listening."

"I've prayed about this, and I feel the Lord would have me write to Gil Simmons and ask more about him. I'll put some tough questions in the letter and see how he answers."

Jessica shook her head. "I couldn't do it. I could never be a mail order bride. You go slow with this thing. Talk to your parents about it."

"I did. Last night. I showed them the ad and told them I had prayed over it and that I felt I should write and get more information about this man."

"And they said . . . ?"

"Papa said it can't hurt to write and find out more about him. Mama agreed. So that's what I'm going to do."

Jessica sighed. "Brenda, I know it's not pleasant to think that you might end up an old maid, but marrying the wrong man is worse than not being married at all."

"I know that. And I'm going to approach this very slowly. Mama and Papa will be with me all along, and if the Lord is in it, we'll know it."

Suppertime in the Smith home was always a lighthearted time. Carrie was an excellent cook. She thoroughly enjoyed preparing the food and gathering her family together around a meal after a long day apart.

As soon as Grant offered prayer over the food, Daniel and David began bombarding their father with questions that only lively teenage boys could come up with. Grant sent a smile to Carrie and patiently answered the boys' questions while he filled their plates. As soon as their food was before them, Daniel and David began wolfing down their supper.

"Really, boys," Jessica said, "you act like you're starving."

"It's not that," Daniel said. "It's just that Mama's cooking is so good!"

"Yeah!" David said. "When I grow up, I'm gonna marry a girl just like Mama, so all the rest of my life I can enjoy good cookin'!"

Carrie gave a smile and shrugged her shoulders. "What can I say?"

While the boys returned their attention to supper, Carrie said to Grant, "Darling, how were things at work today?"

"Quite satisfying. I was able to work out loans for two families who want to start businesses in Germantown. One is a dry goods company and the other is a hotel. Both are needed, and I believe they'll do well. They'll also make good accounts for the bank when they get on their feet."

"Wonderful. I know it has to give you a great deal of pleasure to help people like that."

"It does. I have to admit I still miss the military at times, but I praise the Lord for giving me a job I enjoy and one that's fulfilling for me."

"God has been so good to us," Carrie said.

Jessica glanced at her father. "Brenda was here today, Daddy."

Daniel handed Grant his empty plate and smiled contentedly as his dad gave him second helpings.

"She said Betty's coming to see me tomorrow," Carrie said.

"That's good. You two always have a good time together." He turned to Jessica. "Something special you were going to tell me about Brenda's visit today?"

Grant loaded David's plate, too, and handed it to him.

"Yes. I didn't tell Mama about it after Brenda left because I wanted to talk to both of you at the same time."

"What is it, dear?" Carrie asked.

Jessica laid her fork down and cleared her throat. "Well . . . you and Daddy know that when a woman reaches eighteen — as Brenda and I have — and she doesn't have any prospects for marriage, she begins to fear that she might become an old maid."

Grant let out a low chuckle. "What did I tell you just the other night, Carrie?"

"Daddy and I have actually been talking about this," Carrie said. "We're glad you've kept your head, honey, and haven't jumped at some of the young men you've dated when they have brought up marriage. Better by far to let the Lord bring that certain young man into your life in His own time and His own way. So . . . what about Brenda?"

"She's got me worried."

"How's that?"

"She's . . . well, she's looking into

becoming a mail order bride."

"A what?" Daniel said. "Brenda's gonna mail herself to some guy and marry him?"

"Not quite, son," Grant said. "Let's hear about it, Jessica."

"When she came to see me today, she had the classified advertisement section of yesterday's *Baltimore Press* with her. They have that column where men out west advertise for women to come and marry them.

"Well, Brenda showed me an ad from a man who lives in Nevada. He said in the ad that he's a Christian and wants a wife who's devoted to Jesus. He said he's done well in gold mining and can provide well for his mail order bride."

"And Brenda is going to reply to the ad?" Carrie asked.

"She says she'll throw some tough questions at him in her letter and see how he answers. She wants to make sure he's a genuine child of God."

Grant shook his head. "She's being awfully foolish."

"That's how I feel, Daddy. I told her I could never bring myself to become a mail order bride. But she says she's prayed about it and believes she should reply. Her parents say it can't hurt to write the man

234

and ask for more information about him."

"Downright foolish," Grant said. "She shouldn't jump the gun and get ahead of God. Seems to me the Lord has some young man in Maryland for Brenda to marry. She'd better be very careful."

"That's what I told her, Daddy."

"I agree she should be careful," Carrie said, "but on the other hand, I don't think we should limit God. He, of course, will not go against His Word and lead a child of His to marry an unsaved person, but who's to say the Lord couldn't bring Christians together through the mail?"

Grant frowned and shook his head.

"Nobody asked me, but I think Mama's right," Daniel said. "I think it'd be neat to have the Lord bring a couple together through the mail."

"Be different, anyhow," David said. "God could do it that way, couldn't He, Dad?"

"Well, son, I can't argue that He could. It would be quite rare, but like your mother said, we can't limit God. I just hope that if Brenda goes ahead with this, she does it slowly, carefully, and with a lot of prayer."

"I'm sure that will be her intention, Daddy," Jessica said, "but I hope her fear of becoming an old maid won't cause her to make a big mistake. I love Brenda so much, and I don't want to see her mess up her life."

"We'll have to pray for her," Carrie said. She lifted a hand to her brow and pressed her fingertips to her temple.

"Sweetheart, are you all right?" Grant said.

"I . . . I feel a bit tired."

Jessica shoved her chair back and said, "Mama, you go sit with Daddy in the parlor and rest. I'll take care of the table and clean up the kitchen."

"The boys can help you," Grant said.

"It's all right, Daddy. It's bath night for my darling brothers, and I wouldn't want them to miss that. I'll take care of cleaning up."

Carrie smiled at her daughter. "Thank you, Jessica. I'll take you up on it. Just for tonight, you understand."

"We'll see," Jessica said as she kissed her mother's cheek.

Jessica watched her mother as her father helped her to the parlor; she sent a prayer toward heaven for her mother's recovery.

The next afternoon, Brenda accompanied her mother when she came to visit

Carrie. While the mothers sat in the parlor and talked, the daughters went to Jessica's room.

"I did it, Jessica! I wrote the letter to Gil Simmons last night and mailed it this morning. It'll take at least a week to get to him, and if he responds, another week for me to hear back."

"I'm glad you said, 'If he responds.' He may receive lots of letters and pick out his bride before he even gets your letter."

"Yes, I'm prepared for that. I only want God's will in my life. I want the man He has chosen for me."

Jessica embraced her friend. "I love you, Brenda, and I've been praying you won't allow your fear of becoming an old maid to cloud your judgment. The Lord has His plan for both of our lives, and we must be patient and let Him work it out."

Brenda gave her friend a squeeze, then said, "I'm going to visit my Aunt Bertha over in Fairfax, Virginia, for a few days. She's my mother's older sister. Great Christian lady. Her husband died a few years back, and their only child died at age two."

"I'm glad she has you to help relieve some of the loneliness once in a while. How soon are you going?"

"Tomorrow. Would you like to go with me? I've told Aunt Bertha about you many times. When we wired back and forth about this visit, she said to tell you to come with me if you can."

"Oh, I'd love to go. But I can't leave Mama with the housework."

Brenda let a sly grin curve her mouth. "That's all taken care of."

"What?"

"Mom said that if you wanted to go, she would come over and take care of things over here."

"Oh, I can't ask her to do that."

"You don't have to. Mom's already volunteered. How about it? We won't stay more than four or five days, and we'd have a great time."

"Well, all right then."

It was early afternoon the next day when Brenda and Jessica alighted from the surrey they'd hired at the Fairfax depot to bring them to Aunt Bertha's house. The adorable white clapboard with bright, shiny green shutters sat in the middle of a garden of jewel-colored flowers. Through each gleaming window, white lace curtains moved gently in the breeze.

Before the girls reached the front steps,

the door opened and a smiling little lady who stood barely five feet tall stepped onto the porch. "Brenda! It's wonderful to see you!"

Brenda embraced her aunt, then introduced her best friend. Bertha gave Jessica a hug, and the girl inhaled the sweet scent of lavender.

Aunt Bertha had the kindest eyes Jessica had ever seen. They sparkled with merriment and were set in a round face of soft, milky skin and apricot-hued cheeks. She wore her snow white hair in a single long braid coiled at the back of her head.

"Well, come on in, young ladies," Bertha said, opening the door wide.

Jessica followed Brenda to the rear of the house and entered a tiny, immaculate bedroom decorated with frilly things. There were shelves lined with trinkets and figurines.

"You girls unpack, then come to the kitchen. I'll have some refreshments for you."

Jessica sent an inquiring glance to her friend.

Brenda giggled. "Might as well get used to it, Jess. Aunt Bertha will try to fatten us up while we're here."

In the days that followed, Bertha was

seldom still. She bustled from one thing to another, making sure her young guests were comfortable.

On Sunday morning, the girls rose extra early and dressed with special care for the church services. They insisted on helping Aunt Bertha with breakfast, and soon the three of them sat down to fried ham and eggs with hot biscuits and honey.

When they had eaten their fill, the girls washed and dried the dishes while Bertha started preparations for Sunday dinner. She wanted as much done as possible before they went to church.

While the cleanup was being done, Jessica watched Bertha, who was a lively bundle of energy. Jessica couldn't help but think of her mother and how much her illness had slowed her in the past several months. Determined to let nothing mar this pleasant day, Jessica dispelled the small frown from between her eyebrows and turned a sunny smile toward Aunt Bertha, saying, "Looks like Sunday dinner is going to be real good!"

The church was only a short distance from Aunt Bertha's house, and as the three women walked along, Brenda said, "I've told Jessica about Pastor Wilkins, Aunt Bertha. She's really looking forward to hearing him preach."

"She'll have to wait till tonight. We're having a guest speaker this morning."

"Oh, really? Who is it?"

"I can't recall. Pastor told us last Sunday, but I'm terrible at remembering names. Anyway, he's a young man who just graduated from Arlington Seminary. He was valedictorian of his class at graduation in May, and Pastor said he's quite the preacher. I'm sure we'll enjoy his message."

After Sunday school, Bertha led the way to her favorite pew, five rows from the front and directly in line with the pulpit. The piano and pump organ were playing a lilting gospel song.

Soon the choir was in place, and the music director came to the pulpit and began a rousing, lively song service with the choir and congregation standing. While they sang, two men entered from a side door and crossed the platform.

Brenda leaned close to Jessica. "The older man is Pastor Wilkins."

Jessica smiled. "I assumed as much."

Jessica looked more carefully at the young man and was puzzled that he looked familiar. She kept her eyes on him as he stood beside the pastor in front of the choir loft. Suddenly her heart lurched and she swallowed hard. She studied his face to be sure, then leaned close to her best friend and said, "Brenda, I know that young man!"

"You do? Who is he?"

"It's Josh, Brenda! Josh Cornell!"

14

Bertha pressed close to her niece and said, "She knows him? Who is he?"

"Someone she's known for a long time but hasn't seen in nine years, Auntie. We'll tell you more later."

Bertha nodded, and the song came to a close.

Pastor Wilkins went to the pulpit and prayed, then bid the congregation be seated. While the choir was singing a special number, Jessica kept her eyes on Josh.

Brenda saw the effect Josh's presence had on Jessica. She reached down, took hold of her friend's hand, and squeezed. Jessica gave her a fleeting glance and smiled.

After announcements and the offering, followed by more congregational singing, a ladies' trio sang the latest Fanny Crosby gospel song. Then Pastor Owen Wilkins stepped to the pulpit.

Wilkins told the crowd that he had heard their guest speaker preach to the students in chapel service at Arlington Seminary a few weeks earlier and was deeply impressed by him. He wanted his people to hear this dynamic young man. Introducing Joshua Cornell as one of the most promising graduates of Arlington Seminary, he invited him to the pulpit and then sat down.

Josh's manner was relaxed as he looked out over the large crowd and made some introductory remarks, then opened his Bible, announced the Scripture passage, and began his message.

While he preached, his gaze ran across Jessica several times, but there was no sign of recognition.

At the invitation to come forward, several people walked the aisle to be led to Jesus, and many Christians came to the altar to dedicate their lives to serve the Lord better.

When the service was over, Josh stood at the vestibule door with the pastor and his wife, greeting people and shaking their hands. Jessica got in the slow-moving line with Brenda and her aunt. The closer she drew to Josh, the more her heart pounded. She discreetly wiped her moist palms on her dress and breathed a prayer.

"Afraid he won't know you?" Brenda whispered to Jessica.

Jessica shrugged. "I was only nine years old when he last saw me. Brenda . . . will you do me a favor?"

"Sure."

"Since you know the pastor and his wife, would you introduce me to them so Josh can hear you? I want to see if he'll pick up on it."

"Be glad to."

Two or three agonizing minutes passed. Then Brenda stood before the pastor and his wife. They told her how nice it was to see her again and made some comments to Aunt Bertha about what a lovely niece she had.

Jessica watched Josh turn away slightly to listen to a man's question about a point in his sermon. Just as Brenda drew Jessica closer to the pastor and his wife for introductions, Josh turned to see who was next to greet. He heard Brenda say, "Pastor and Mrs. Wilkins, I would like for you to meet my very best friend in all the world, Jessica Smith."

Josh looked intently at Jessica, who was telling the Wilkinses how glad she was to meet them.

"Jessica! It's you!"

"Hello, Josh. It's been a long time."

A broad smile lit up his face. "Jessica, I

can hardly believe what I'm seeing! This beautiful young woman is my little friend from Fort Union!"

"It's me," she said, extending her hand.

Josh took it tenderly. "It's wonderful to see you. What brings you to Fairfax?"

Jessica introduced Brenda and Aunt Bertha to him, explaining that she still lived with her parents in Montgomery Village and that she and Brenda had come to visit Brenda's aunt, who was a member of the church.

"Well, somebody said it's a small world," Josh said. "I'm beginning to believe it. Jessica, it's so nice to see you."

"So you know this young lady, eh?" said the pastor.

"Yes. Our fathers were both stationed at Fort Union, New Mexico, years ago. We became very good friends."

"Actually, Pastor," Jessica said, "I owe my life to Josh."

"Oh? How's that?"

"I was in a wagon alone once, outside the fort. The team was spooked by a rattlesnake, and they bolted. Josh was on his horse nearby and saw what was happening. The terrified horses were charging toward a precipice, but Josh galloped his horse alongside the wagon and lifted me off only seconds before the team and wagon went over the edge. I was only nine years old at the time. He's been my hero ever since."

"I only did what needed to be done at the time."

"I'm sure glad you did or I wouldn't be here today."

"Girls," Aunt Bertha said, "we'd better get out of the way so these other people can shake hands with Pastor and Loretta."

Jessica glanced at the line behind her. "Oh my, yes."

"Jessica," Josh said, "don't leave, please. I'd like to have a few more minutes with you as soon as I'm through here."

Jessica looked toward Brenda and her aunt.

"That's fine, honey," Bertha said. "I'll go on home and get a fire built in the stove so we can cook dinner. Brenda can wait here and walk home with you."

When the handshaking was done, the Wilkinses and Brenda struck up a conversation, giving Josh and Jessica a few minutes together. They walked to a spot under a large oak tree out of earshot from the others.

"I just can't believe this, Jessica. Imagine running into you after all this time. And to see you so grown-up." Josh could hardly reconcile this young woman standing before him with the little girl whose teeth were too big for her face and whose black hair always hung in straight braids down her slim back. He stared at her silently, then shook his head as if to clear his vision of that child he had rescued from a violent death.

Jessica smiled. "What's going on in that head of yours, Josh?"

"I'm just stunned at how mature you are at eighteen. And my . . . how beautiful you are!"

"Thank you," Jessica said, blushing.

After asking about her family, Josh told about his family's move to Oregon City some years before, and that his father had used the money from his inheritance to start a lumber business. The business was doing exceptionally well.

Josh was going to leave tomorrow for Oregon City to work with his pastor, Lester Farrington, who was set to retire soon. When Pastor Farrington retired, Josh would become pastor of the church.

"That's wonderful," Jessica said. "I'm glad to see how the Lord is working things out so beautifully for you. You deserve the very best."

"I'm glad you feel that way, Jessica." He

paused, then said, "I don't have your address anymore. Would you give it to me again?" He took a pencil out of his coat pocket and opened his Bible. While Jessica gave the address to him, he wrote it on the flyleaf.

"I'll write you again sometime. I want to know how things are going for you and your family. You will write me back, won't you?"

"Why, of course, Josh. It will be nice to get a letter from you again."

"Well, I guess I'd better be going, Jessica. It sure is nice to see you. Maybe we'll bump into each other another time."

"Yes, it's been nice to see you again." As she spoke, Jessica extended her hand.

Josh clasped it and dipped his head. He grinned slightly as he looked at her from the tops of his eyes and said, "When we said good-bye at Fort Union, I got a hug. How about this time?"

The hug was a discreet one, but sufficient to show affection between the two old friends.

On Monday the girls sent a wire to Brenda's parents, telling them they would arrive at the Montgomery Village depot late Tuesday afternoon.

During the train ride back, Jessica's mind was filled with thoughts of Josh, yet her heart was heavy. Even though he had taken her address and said he would write sometime, she doubted he would. She glanced at her friend beside her and noted that Brenda's eyes were closed. She set her gaze out the window again.

Jessica was staring at milk cows in a pasture, with a white farmhouse, barn, and outbuildings as backdrop, when she felt her friend stir, then stretch and sit up straight. Smiling, Brenda said, "You may be taking in the countryside with your eyes, honey, but I know where your mind is."

Jessica looked at her and grinned. "Oh, you do, huh?"

"Mm-hmm. On Josh. Tell me I'm wrong."

Jessica shrugged. "You're right."

"He seems like a very nice man. Handsome, too. I can tell you're head-over-heels about him."

"Oh, you can, huh?"

"Mm-hmm. I sure hope something will develop between you."

Jessica sighed. "That would be wonderful, but Josh is going to be in Oregon, and yours truly is in Maryland. Pretty hard for something to develop with thousands of miles between us."

Brenda playfully tapped her friend on the shoulder. "God is able to bring people together no matter what the circumstances, if it's His will."

"Which brings up a like subject. Gil Simmons. You're pretty excited about hearing from him, aren't you?"

"I sure hope I hear back from him, but I'm not letting myself get too excited. He's probably received lots of replies to his ad." Brenda sighed wistfully, then said, "Maybe he's already got his mail order bride on her way west."

"Well, to quote a very famous friend of mine, 'God is able to bring people together no matter what the circumstances, if it's His will.'"

Brenda laughed, and Jessica joined her. They spent the rest of the journey enjoying each other's company as only best friends can.

When the train pulled into the Montgomery Village station, John and Betty Moore were there to meet them. Betty was happy to tell Jessica that Carrie was doing well and was preparing a special meal for her daughter's return.

When the Moore buggy pulled into the

Smiths' driveway, Grant, Daniel, and David were on the front porch waiting for her. Daniel rushed to help her from the buggy, and David picked up her small piece of luggage. Grant stayed on the porch, leaning on his cane, and thanked the Moores for bringing Jessica home.

When Jessica entered the house, the aroma coming from the kitchen made her mouth water. "I smell fried chicken!" she cried, hurrying ahead of her father and brothers toward the kitchen.

Carrie was at the stove, stirring gravy in a pan. She turned and smiled as Jessica came through the door. "Oh, there's my favorite daughter!"

Jessica embraced her. "And here's my favorite mother!"

During supper, Jessica told them all about her trip and the stay with Brenda's Aunt Bertha.

"John was telling me Sunday that the Fairfax church is a good one," Grant said, "and that Pastor Wilkins is a tremendous preacher. How'd you like the church, honey?"

"It's a wonderful church, Daddy. Pastor Wilkins preached Sunday night . . . and yes, he's a great preacher. You'll never guess in a million years who preached Sunday morning."

"Someone we know?"

"Yes!"

"Well, who?"

"A tremendous preacher."

"C'mon, sis," David said. "Who?"

"I know!" Daniel said. "The apostle Paul!"

"Well, not quite . . . but almost!"

"John the Baptist!"

"Close, but this preacher doesn't wear camel hair or eat locusts and wild honey."

"Is it someone this family knows personally?" Carrie asked.

"Mm-hmm. You might recall that he shared with me that God had called him to preach."

"Josh Cornell!" Grant said. "You saw Josh?"

"I did. He graduated with honors from a seminary in Arlington, Virginia, in May. Pastor Wilkins invited him to preach last Sunday morning. He's really good! Several people were saved at the invitation, and lots of Christians were at the altar getting things right with God."

"Well, bless his heart," Carrie said. "Did he know you?"

"Not at first, but when he heard Brenda

introduce me to Pastor and Mrs. Wilkins, he looked at me with his eyes bulging and said, 'Jessica! It's you!' "

She went on to tell her family about the Cornells being in the lumber business in Oregon, and that Josh was on his way to Oregon City to become assistant pastor in his church.

Daniel grinned impishly. "Are you still in love with him?"

"Some things are none of your business, little brother."

Daniel chuckled. "I just got my answer."

Jessica fixed him with eyes like dark pinpoints. "At least I'm not having to bow to your blackmail like when we lived at the fort."

"Yeah, but —"

"Daniel!" Grant said. "How your sister feels about Josh or any other man is none of your affair. If she wants to include you in on it, she'll do so. Otherwise, son, don't torment her about it."

The grin on Daniel's face melted like wax held to a flame. "Yes, sir. I was only funnin' her, Dad."

"I know that and Jessica knows that, but right now she's feeling like she's going to end up an old maid, and it's a serious thing for her."

"You're not going to be an old maid, Jessica," Daniel said. "You're a sweet person, and next to Mama, you're the most beautiful woman in all the world. God's going to give you a good man just like Dad for your husband."

Grant chuckled. "Oh, so now you smooth things over with flattery, Daniel."

Carrie smiled. "It's not flattery, honey. What Daniel just used was *diplomacy*."

"Well, he didn't say anything good about me," David complained.

"You know why, don't you, little brother?" Daniel said.

"No, why?"

Daniel looked impish again. "Because to say anything good about *you*, I'd have to lie!"

Grant laughed, and soon the whole family was laughing.

When the laughter subsided, Grant said, "I'm glad to hear that Josh followed through on his call to preach, and I think it's great that the Lord has already lined up a church for him to pastor. Oregon City, you say?"

"Mm-hmm," Jessica said.

"I hear that area is growing by leaps and bounds, with all those wagon trains going out there. Should be a good place to reap a harvest of souls for the Lord."

"I'm glad for Josh," Carrie said. "He's such a fine boy."

"Best thing about him is that he saved my sister's life," David said. "We'll always owe him a debt of gratitude for that."

Joshua Cornell had fallen asleep in the rocking, swaying coach as the train rolled across the southwestern tip of Pennsylvania. He awakened and looked out the window just as the train approached the trestle over the Ohio River.

He rubbed his eyes and looked down at the river and saw the afternoon sunlight dancing on its broad, rippling surface. The shadow of the trestle on the water, with its skeletal framework and the racing train atop it, made an interesting scene.

Josh's thoughts went to Jessica, as they had continuously since Sunday. Jessica had always been such a joy to be around as a child — so vibrant and full of life. That had not changed. Neither had her sweet spirit. Jessica was still a fine and dedicated Christian. And how strikingly beautiful she had become.

He took his valise from the overhead rack and pulled out a pencil and paper. An hour later, the letter was finished and in an envelope addressed to Jessica. When he reached Chicago in the morning, he would mail it to her.

Josh replaced the valise in the overhead rack, then sat down and eased back on the seat. He was excited about the ministry God had for him in Oregon City. While he pondered his future there, Jessica kept coming to mind.

A week from the day Jessica and Brenda had returned home from Fairfax, Jessica was in the backyard with a rug paddle in her hand, beating the dust from throw rugs draped over the clothesline. She turned to see her mother standing at the back door.

"Did you call me, Mama?"

Carrie lifted a white envelope and waved it. "Yes, honey. A letter here for you. It just came in the mail."

"Oh? Who's it from?"

"That man who's almost as good a preacher as Paul, and close to being as good as John the Baptist, but doesn't wear camel hair or eat locusts and wild honey."

Jessica's knees went watery. "Josh?"

"The one and only!"

She dropped the paddle and hurried to her mother. Her fingers shook as she took the letter and said, "I'll go to my room to read it."

When she was inside her room with the door closed, she tore open the envelope and unfolded the single sheet of paper. Her hands trembled as she began to read:

July 20, 1870

Dear Jessica,

I am on the train, headed toward Chicago, where I will change trains and head west. I couldn't wait any longer to write to you. I simply have to say that it was such a wonderful and pleasant surprise to see you in Fairfax. It brought back so many special memories of our years at Fort Union.

I know I said this on Sunday, but I have to say it again. What a beautiful and mature young lady you are for eighteen! You certainly have grown up since I last saw you in New Mexico. And Jessica, let me add that I am glad you haven't lost your sweetness. You are one very special young lady.

The only regret I have about our meeting Sunday is that it was so brief. I wish we could have had more time together. In one way, I feel we needed more time to get reacquainted. But in another way, it was like no time at all had passed since we were to-

gether last. You're still the sweet Christian girl that I remember . . . so warm in spirit and delightful to be with.

Please write to me at the address in the upper left-hand corner of the envelope. I want to know what's going on in your life. Also, please greet your parents and brothers for me, and tell them I wish I could have seen them, too.

I will look forward to hearing from you.

Love,
Josh

Tears coursed down Jessica's cheeks as she held the letter close to her heart.

That evening after supper, the Smith family gathered on the front porch to enjoy the cool of the evening. The lowering sun gave off a vibrant orange light. Jessica pulled Josh's letter out of her pocket, angled it toward the setting sun, and read it aloud. When she finished, everyone said how nice it was for her to renew her old friendship with Josh Cornell.

Jessica's gaze lingered on the word *love* above Josh's signature.

15

Jessica stayed up past her normal bedtime to write to Josh. It was a chatty three-page letter, describing her return trip home from Fairfax and things about her church. Just before her trip to Fairfax, she had been asked to be an assistant teacher in a girls' Sunday school class and was excited about the prospect.

She also told him about her mother's illness and the work she had taken on at home to alleviate her mother's load.

Although Jessica covered up her true feelings for Josh, she did tell him he would be in her prayers every day. She closed the letter by saying that she yearned to return to the West someday and see it all the way to the Pacific coast.

Joshua Cornell's heart quickened pace as the stagecoach topped the last hill before dropping down into Oregon City. He hadn't been home since last summer and was eager to see his family and friends. It was August 4, a typically hot summer day. Earlier that morning the stage had passed two wagon trains that wouldn't arrive in Oregon City for a couple of days yet.

Josh leaned from the coach window and looked up the busy street, focusing on the Wells Fargo office. He could see his parents and Mary Ann. When the stage ground to a halt, the Wells Fargo agent was there to open the door. Josh was the first passenger to step out.

Mary Ann rushed to him, wrapped her arms around him, and cried, "Oh, Josh, I've missed you so!"

Josh held her tightly and kissed her forehead. "I've missed you, too, sister."

Next to embrace him was a sniffling Martha, trying not to cry. Josh kissed her cheek and said, "How's the sweetest little mom in all the world?"

"Fine, now that you're home."

Father and son embraced, and in his husky, strained voice, Brett said, "Welcome home, son. I've sure missed you."

"I've missed you too, Dad."

"We wish we could've been there for your graduation, son," Martha said.

"That would've been nice, but it just couldn't be. How are Pastor and Mrs. Farrington?"

"Quite well. They're looking forward to seeing you."

Josh glanced at the family buggy parked on the street nearby. "I'll grab my luggage, and we'll be on our way. I can't wait to sleep in my good ol' bed tonight!"

Father and son loaded the luggage in the back of the buggy, then helped the ladies into the rear seat. Brett climbed onto the rider's side, saying, "You drive, Josh."

Josh started to climb in, then hesitated when he saw his mother's face. "Mom, what's wrong?"

Martha's lips quivered and she looked down at the buggy floor.

"What's going on? A few minutes ago you all seemed happy to see me, and now all three of you look like you'd lost your best friend."

"Get in and sit down, son," Brett said. "Believe me, all three of us are thrilled to have you home, but . . . well, we have some bad news."

Josh climbed into the buggy and took his seat. He set steady eyes on his father. "All right. What is it?"

"It's Dr. Clay Price. He died yesterday afternoon of heart failure. It hit him while he was working on a patient in his office, a lady you don't know — Sarah Dunne. She

262

and her husband moved here just a few months ago. Sarah called for Lydia, who was in the next room, but when Lydia got to him, he was dead."

Josh's face lost color. "Aw, no. Heart failure. He was only what . . . forty-seven?"

"Forty-eight," Martha said. "The whole town is in shock. Dr. Price had never had any symptoms of heart trouble at all. It was so sudden."

Tears sprang to Josh's eyes. "How's Lydia taking it?"

"Pretty hard," Brett said. "Pastor Farrington and Madeline are with her now. They stayed in the house with her last night."

Josh raised his head and wiped tears from his cheeks. "This has got to be tough for her. Those two people were so good to me, always going out of their way to encourage me. They helped me with my tuition every year, and many times they wrote and sent money for anything I might need. Sent me three hundred dollars as a graduation present. I owe them so much. I — well, he's in heaven now. I can't do anything to pay him back. But whatever that dear lady needs, if it's in my power to provide it, she's got it."

"Josh," Martha said, "Lydia knows you

were to arrive today. We were at her house earlier this morning. She asked if you would come see her as soon as possible."

Josh picked up the reins. "Right now is possible." As he pulled the buggy out into traffic, his dad put a hand on his arm.

"Son, let's do this," Brett said. "Lydia shouldn't have too many people in the house at once. Since we were there earlier, just drop Mary Ann and me off at the lumber mill. You can take Mom home, then go on over to Lydia's house."

"All right." Josh looked over his shoulder at his sister. "Mary Ann, I can't get used to the idea that you're out of school and working in the office at the mill. Seems like you should still be in first grade."

"We all have to grow up sometime," she said with a grin.

Josh turned at the next intersection and headed the buggy out of town eastward, toward the lumber mill.

"I'll tell all three of you about the graduation ceremonies later," Josh said, "but there's something I'd like to tell you right now. On my last Sunday before leaving for home, I preached at a church in Fairfax. After the service, I was shocked to see Jessica Smith. You remember Jessica . . . from Fort Union?"

"Of course," Brett said. "I imagine she's all grown up now."

"Is she ever! I'm telling you, I would never have known her. She's a beautiful young lady."

"That doesn't surprise me. She was a pretty girl when she was little."

"I assume she knew you," Martha said.

"Yes, she did."

"Are the Smiths living in Fairfax now?" Mary Ann asked.

"No, they're back in Montgomery Village."

"Why was Jessica at the church in Fairfax?"

"I'll tell you all about it tonight at supper."

Mary Ann leaned forward on her seat. "Did she say if she's engaged or has a steady beau?"

"No. But then we didn't have very long to talk."

They left the outskirts of town and soon were at the lumber mill. While Josh helped his mother into the front seat, some of the lumbermen passed by and welcomed him home. He flashed a smile and told them it was good to see them again.

Josh delivered his mother home, put the carriage in the barn and the horse in the small corral behind the house, and carried his luggage to his room. He kissed his mother's cheek and said he would be back shortly, then headed the two blocks down the street to the Price home.

He knocked on Lydia's door and heard muffled footsteps; then the door swung open. "Josh!" Lester Farrington exclaimed.

"Hello, Pastor!" Josh stepped through the door and embraced the older man. "It's good to see you."

Farrington gripped the younger man by the upper arms. "It's good to see you too, Josh. Everybody's been looking forward to your becoming my assistant."

"Not as much as I have. How's Lydia?"

"She's taking Clay's death pretty hard. But she's got a good grip on the Lord in it all. Or I should say the Lord has a good grip on her. Anyway, even though she's shaken to the core, she shows signs of the Lord's loving arms being around her. Come. She's expecting you."

The Price house was two stories, with several bedrooms upstairs and two downstairs. Josh followed the pastor down the hall from the vestibule, past the parlor and dining room to a small sitting room. They could hear Madeline Farrington's soft voice as the pastor pushed open the sitting room door.

"Oh, Lydia, it's Josh, all right," Madeline said. She rose to her feet and gripped Josh's hand. "It's so nice to see you, Josh."

"You too, Mrs. Farrington." Josh knelt in front of Lydia Price and took her hand. "I'm so sorry. My parents just told me what happened."

The sight of Josh brought fresh tears to Lydia's eyes. "Thank you for coming so soon to see me. I know you just got off the stage."

"I wouldn't be anywhere else right now. You and Dr. Price have been special blessings to me. So special that I can't even find the words to express it. I'm so sorry for what you are suffering."

"I won't say it hasn't been a shock, Josh. It has. And I'll feel it more in a day or two. But the Lord has given me peace in my heart. Our wonderful God doesn't make mistakes. Though Clay was still a young man — I have to say that because I'm almost forty-five — God had higher service for him. I miss him so much, but I can't wish him back. What a dull and dismal place this world would be now, after he's looked into the bright face of the Lord Jesus and had a glimpse of the glories of heaven."

"You're so right," Josh said. "We can't

wish him back, but we can look forward to the day when we meet him at heaven's gates."

"Yes. Oh yes! What a glorious day that will be!"

Madeline sat beside Lydia again and patted her arm.

Lydia touched Madeline's hand. "Josh, these two people have been such a strength to me. And so have your parents and Mary Ann."

"Lydia," Pastor Farrington said, "why don't you talk to Josh about . . . you know —"

"Oh yes. Of course. Josh, I asked Pastor just a few minutes ago if you could have a part in the funeral service. He said that would be fine with him, if you want to. It's set for tomorrow morning at ten o'clock."

"Why . . . yes. I would be glad to."

"How about giving the eulogy?" Farrington said. "And after that, you offer prayer, all right? Then I'll preach the message."

"I'll be glad to," Josh said. He said to Lydia, "You really honor me by letting me do this."

"I know Clay would want you to have a part in the service, Josh. He loved you very much. And so do I."

★ ★ ★

The funeral was held the next day, Friday, August 5. On Saturday morning, Lydia was eating breakfast with Sadie Bunch, an elderly widow from the church, who was staying with her for a few days. They were discussing the funeral and what a touching and comforting service Pastor Farrington and Josh Cornell had conducted, when there was a knock at the front door. Lydia went to answer it.

"Well, hello, Josh. Please come in. Have you had breakfast? Sadie and I are just getting a good start. There's plenty —"

"I've already eaten, thank you, ma'am. I'm sorry to have interrupted your breakfast. I'll come back later."

"No need for that. We both sort of slept in this morning, and we're getting a late start. Come on back to the kitchen. I can talk and eat at the same time."

"Well, all right. If you don't mind."

"Of course not. Come on."

Josh greeted Sadie warmly, asking how her health had been. Then he thanked her for staying with Lydia.

"I'm just glad to help and keep her company. I was widowed at just about her age, so I know what it's like."

Josh turned one of the kitchen chairs

backward and sat down.

"I'm glad to see you again so soon, Josh," Lydia said. "Can I do anything for you?"

"It's not what you can do for me, ma'am; it's what I'm going to do for you."

"Oh? And what might that be?"

"Lydia, you and Dr. Price have been awfully good to me. You helped with my tuition all the way through seminary and sent encouraging letters often. Those letters also had money in them. And you gave me a generous graduation gift."

Lydia smiled. "We did those things because we saw real potential in you, Josh. We wanted to have a part in your ministry. And just think, someday you'll be my pastor. We also did it because we love you."

Josh nodded. "Lydia, what I'm going to do for you is because I love you, too, and I love Dr. Price's memory. You have a big house and a large yard. I'm going to be here every Saturday morning — starting today — to take care of the place for you."

Tears filled Lydia's eyes. "Josh, I don't know what to say. I —"

"Just say you'll make up a list of things to be done each week. Of course, in the summer, there'll always be the lawn to cut and weeds to pull, but let me know what needs to be done all year long. Painting, squeaky door hinges, whatever. I'll take care of it for you."

"But what about your church work, Josh? You'll be assistant pastor as of tomorrow morning. You'll have your hands full with your new duties."

"I already talked to Pastor Farrington about it. I told him I thought I could take care of your place working Saturday mornings. He said that was fine, and if sometimes I need to work here on Saturday afternoons, that would be fine, too. So it's all set. Will you keep a list of work for me to do?"

Lydia looked at Sadie. "What am I going to do with him?"

"Seems to me like his mind's made up. I guess you'll just have to put him to work."

"Sound advice, Sadie," Josh said. "Any questions?" he asked Lydia.

"Yes, one. How will I ever be able to thank you?"

"The only thanks I want, Lydia, is to see you happy and well taken care of."

The next day, Joshua Cornell was installed as assistant pastor of the church.

271

His ordination was set for the next Sunday night.

On the following Monday, August 14, Josh received a letter from Jessica Smith. That evening in his room, he wrote a reply. In it, he cautiously asked if there was a young man in her life. He went on to tell her about his ordination service and thanked her for praying for his ministry. The rest of his letter was taken up with Carrie Smith's illness, and he assured Jessica he would tell his parents about it, and the family would be praying for Carrie daily.

He signed the letter *Love, Josh.*

On August 16, Jessica Smith was on her hands and knees in the kitchen, scrubbing the wooden floor with a brush. A bucket of hot, sudsy water was at her side. She heard a knock at the front door and started to get up, but her mother, who was in the parlor, called out, "I'll get it, Jessica!"

Jessica blew at a stray lock of hair on her forehead and continued to scrub. When she stopped to dip the brush in the bucket again, she heard a familiar voice talking to her mother.

Footsteps echoed in the hall as Jessica heard Brenda say, "You just sit down, Mrs.

Smith. I'll find her."

When Brenda entered the kitchen, Jessica noted an envelope in her hand. "What's that?"

"A letter."

Jessica dropped the brush in the bucket and rose to her feet. "From President Ulysses Simpson Grant? Or someone else?"

"Someone else!" Brenda said with a giggle. "It was last week that I got the letter from President Grant, wanting my expert advice on how to run the country."

"All right, Miss Smarty, who — Wait a minute, is it —"

"Uh-huh. Gil Simmons!"

"Well, what does he say?"

Brenda's eyes danced with excitement. "He says he's received several letters from young women in reply to his ads, but none of them intrigued him like mine. There are two full pages in here, giving all the details about himself. He's a genuine Christian, without a doubt. He teaches a Sunday school class and is active in his church's visitation program."

"This is sounding good," Jessica admitted. "What else?"

"Well, he's done well in gold mining, but he recently bought a gun and hardware store in Carson City because he says one day the gold will play out."

"Smart man."

"He sent a photograph of himself. Want to see it?"

"Of course."

Brenda pulled out a daguerreotype of a smiling Gil Simmons, standing at the mouth of a gold mine. She handed it to Jessica, who raised her eyebrows and said, "He's good-looking."

Brenda chuckled gleefully. "I know. And he wants me to send a picture of myself. So . . . what do you think?"

Jessica handed the picture back. "Well, I've already said I could never be a mail order bride, but Gil Simmons certainly sounds like a fine Christian man. If you should feel the Lord is in it and you go out there, does Gil expect you to marry him right away?"

"Oh no. He says in here that if, after more letters and much prayer on both our parts, we feel I should go to Carson City, he will put me up in a boardinghouse at his expense, and we can try a courtship. If, after an agreed amount of time, we feel the Lord is in it, we'll get married."

Jessica nodded her approval. "I like this man. Do you feel comfortable sending your picture and another letter?"

"Yes, I do. So what do you think?"

"I think you should write another letter and send your picture."

Brenda laughed. "Oh, I'm so glad! 'Cause I already wrote the letter, put in a photograph, and mailed it on the way over here!"

"You stinker! Why were you asking for my advice?"

"I just wanted to see what you'd say. Since the Lord has already given me peace in my heart about it, I went ahead with it."

Jessica moved to her friend and hugged her. "Brenda, if you go to Nevada, I'm going to miss you terribly!"

"Maybe you can come out for a visit. You keep saying that you love the West and want to see more of it."

"Yes," said Jessica, blinking at her tears. "Maybe someday I can come and visit you."

In late August, Josh received a second letter from Jessica. He read it in the privacy of his room that evening. She began by telling him that her mother's condition was not improving; she asked that he and his family continue praying for her. She told him that her best friend, Brenda Moore, whom he had met at the church in Fairfax, might be going west to Carson City, Nevada, to get married. A smile tugged at Josh's lips when he read about Brenda possibly becoming a mail order bride.

Just before closing off the letter, Jessica wrote: *You asked in your last letter if there was a young man in my life. I have dated several young men from the church, but there's no one special. I'm leaving it in God's hands. Whenever He is ready to bring that certain someone into my life, I'm ready. Please write again soon. Love, Jessica.*

After reading the letter twice more, Josh sat down at the desk in his room and penned a reply. He told her that Pastor Farrington's plan was to groom him for about a year, and if at that time he thought he was ready to be the pastor, Farrington would retire and step aside. Josh went on to say that he and his family were keeping her mother before the Lord every day and trusting that she would soon show improvement.

He then told Jessica of Oregon City's continual growth and that many souls were being saved and added to the church, which was keeping him quite busy as he took over more and more of the pastor's responsibilities.

At the end of the letter, Josh told her that God had that special man all picked out for her, and when it was His time, He would bring them together.

16

Early in the last week of August, Jessica Smith stood at the door of her parents' bedroom and observed her mother sleeping. She appeared to be getting worse. Each day, she seemed to tire more easily. Yet she insisted on being awakened in time to go to the kitchen and start supper. It was barely three o'clock now.

Jessica pulled the bedroom door closed and made her way through the house and out to the backyard. The garden was ripe and ready for picking. *Looks like I'll spend the next few days canning vegetables.*

As far back as Jessica could remember, her mother had been an energetic person, loving her home and family. Since the Smiths had moved to Montgomery Village, each spring Carrie had planted and grown a first-rate vegetable garden, as well as a beautiful, fragrant flower garden.

Jessica had watched her mother delight in gardening, from the planting to the harvesting and even beyond, as she prepared savory dishes from the fruits and produce.

Then as the summer days began to wane, Carrie had busied herself canning and drying the remainder of her crops.

This year — even with the disease evident in Carrie's body — Jessica had watched her mother pore over seed catalogs from various companies on the East Coast, making decisions about what fruits and vegetables she would plant.

Time turned back in Jessica's thoughts to last spring. It was a breezy morning in late April . . .

Carrie was at the kitchen table, making out her list of seeds and cuttings for her beloved garden. She looked up to see Jessica smiling at her.

"Got everything picked out, Mama?"

"Just about, honey." Carrie placed a limp hand to her tired eyes and rubbed them.

"Mama, you didn't sleep very well last night, did you?"

"Not really." Carrie glanced back at her catalogs. "I was up several times. Some nights I wake up and my breathing is labored. Sometimes I rest better sitting up in a comfortable chair, so I go into the parlor and sit. Before dawn, I go back and crawl in bed so your father won't know I've been up most of the night."

"I know, Mama."

"You do?"

"Daddy sleeps much deeper than I do."

"Please don't say anything to him."

"I won't, Mama, but maybe you should ask the doctor for something to help you sleep."

Carrie was studying one of the catalogs. After a moment, she said, "I will, if I don't start sleeping better."

"Promise?"

"Promise."

"All right," said Jessica, getting up from her chair. "I'll go out and sweep the front porch and the sidewalk. Be back in a little while."

When Jessica was out of the kitchen, Carrie put her head down on the table, resting it on her arm. "Lord," she said, giving in to her tears, "please give me strength."

When Jessica touched her shoulder, Carrie looked up, startled. "I . . . I thought you went out to sweep the porch and sidewalk."

"I started out, Mama, but I came back and stood over there by the door. I just couldn't leave you." Jessica leaned down and put her arms around her mother.

"Honey, I'll be fine. I'm just a little tired."

"Mama, you're more than just a little tired. Come on, now, be honest. Tell me what's making you cry like this."

Carrie took a hankie from her apron pocket and wiped away all traces of tears. She forced a smile to her lips and said, "I'm fine. Really, I am."

"How about some nice hot tea?"

As soon as the water came to a boil and Jessica had brewed the tea, she placed a steaming cup in front of her mother. Then she reached over and clasped her mother's thin hand in her own young, capable one.

"Mama," she said tenderly, "you were crying because you're not sure you have the strength to plant your gardens this year. That's it, isn't it?"

Carrie sat with her head bowed. Her lips began to tremble, and with tears shining in her once-bright eyes, she looked up through wet lashes at her daughter. There was a long silence; then as tears slipped down her pale cheeks, she said, "Jessica, I . . . I know I won't have the strength I need to plant and work my garden this year."

"Oh, Mama . . ."

Carrie sniffed and said softly, "I know

it's silly for me to carry on like this over my gardens, but they've always been such a joy for me, and through the dark, cold days of winter, I've always looked forward to planting and working them."

Jessica swallowed a sob that was trying to escape her tight throat. "Mama, you're not being silly. There's nothing wrong with you loving your flowers and your fruits and vegetables. Tell you what. I'll do the work, and you do the supervising. Pick out what you want planted, then guide me as I do it. I'll do the planting, weeding, watering, and harvesting. You make sure I'm doing it right, and together we'll have the best yield ever. All right?"

Carrie placed her hands tenderly on either side of Jessica's face. "Honey, that would make me very happy. Let's pick out the seeds together."

Mother and daughter bent their heads over the catalogs strewn on the table and eagerly made their plans.

Jessica let her gaze roam over the colorful, aromatic flower garden and the rich garden of fruits and vegetables. Truly, this year's gardens had been the best ever. Maybe her mother would be able to help a little with the canning. Enough, at least, that the project would be hers as well as Jessica's.

Two months passed. From the first of September to the first of November, Josh and Jessica continued to write to each other. It seemed to Jessica that ever since she had answered Josh's question about a young man in her life, something changed in his letters. But maybe she was reading into Josh's words what she was hoping to see.

Carrie was taking a nap, and Jessica was in the kitchen, cleaning up from lunch, when someone knocked on the front door. It was Brenda, in coat and cap. She was smiling from ear to ear.

"Come in out of the cold," Jessica said. "You look plenty happy today. Get another letter from Gil?"

"I sure did!"

"Well, take off your coat and come to the kitchen. I was just cleaning up after lunch."

"Is your mother down for her nap?"

"Mm-hmm, but she won't be able to hear us in the kitchen, so we won't disturb her rest."

When they were seated at the kitchen

table, Jessica said, "All right, Brenda, let's hear it."

"Gil's seventh letter came this morning. He wants me to come to Carson City with marriage in mind. Because of my latest letter to him, he was so sure I'd say yes that he enclosed the money for my railroad fare and other travel expenses. I'm leaving a week from today!"

"Just like that? Are you sure you're doing the right thing?"

"I have perfect peace about it. And from Gil's letters, he sounds like a man I could really love. My parents don't like the idea of my going so far away, but they feel it's God's will. I didn't tell you, but two weeks ago, Papa wrote a long letter to Gil, telling him what he expected of the man who married his daughter. The envelope that came this morning had a letter to Papa in it, too. Papa was very pleased at what Gil had to say. He thinks Gil will make a perfect son-in-law."

Jessica set steady eyes on her best friend. "Brenda, you sound like it's already settled . . . that you're just going to get off the train in Carson City and march with Gil right to the preacher and take your vows. Don't you think you'd best go slower?"

"It'll still be as Gil and I agreed early on,

Jessica, but we both have a pretty strong feeling that the Lord has chosen us for each other."

"Well, just be careful. As somebody put it, all that glitters is not gold. I really think you're going too fast with this and — Oh, Brenda, I'm sorry. Here I am, shooting off my mouth on something that's none of my business. Please forgive me."

"It's all right. I know it's because you love me and care about my life."

"No, it's more than that. I just realized what it is."

"What do you mean?"

"Yes, I do love you, Brenda, and I care about what you do with your life, but I've let something creep in that caused my big mouth to spout off."

"What's that?"

"It's called envy. Truth is, I'm envious of you. Here you are, about to climb aboard a train and go to the man you no doubt will marry. And here's ol' Jessica, wanting with everything that's in her to hear from the man she loves that he wants her to come and be his bride. Please forgive me, Brenda. I'm just selfish. I want an envelope in my hand with money in it for railroad fare and travel expenses. I want from Josh what you have from Gil."

"Now, you stop that kind of talk, Jessica Smith. If there's anything you're not, it's selfish! One of the reasons I love you so much is because you're so *un*selfish. It's going to be all right between you and Josh. I just know it. The Lord wouldn't let you love that man so much if He hadn't chosen him for you."

Jessica's eyes filled with tears. "Oh, Brenda, do you really believe that?"

"Yes, I do. You just keep loving Josh. In the Lord's perfect time, you're going to become Mrs. Reverend Joshua Cornell."

On a Tuesday in mid-November, the two best friends said a tearful good-bye, promising to keep in touch by mail.

On the following Saturday, Grant took Carrie to the family doctor while Jessica cleaned house and the boys cleaned up their rooms. The three siblings were in the kitchen discussing their mother's worsening condition when they heard the front door open and close. They hurried down the hall to their parents.

"So what did Dr. Freeman say, Daddy?" Jessica asked.

Grant smiled as he handed his cane to David and removed his hat and coat. "He has given us hope, honey."

"Well, tell us!"

"Let's go in the parlor and sit down. It involves a big change in our lives. Your mother and I want to explain it to you."

Daniel took hold of Carrie's arm, and David rushed to support her on the other side as they walked her to the parlor.

"Do you want to tell them, honey?" Grant said to Carrie.

"I'll give them the initial news, then let you take it from there." Her features were a bit gray, and there were dark circles around her eyes, yet her eyes held a new light. "Dr. Freeman strongly suggests that we move out West for my health's sake. He said it should be in a high, dry climate, preferably along the foothills of the Rocky Mountains in Colorado Territory. His choice for me would be in or near Denver. The altitude is over five thousand feet, and there's little humidity."

"Dr. Freeman said if your mother lived there, it would make her consumption much easier to withstand and give her a longer life."

"Grant, we have to be honest with the children."

"Well, honey, I —"

"We have to. They have a right to know."

All eyes turned to Grant. Finally he said,

"Dr. Freeman said the move to Colorado would give your mother a longer life unless it's already too late to make a difference. But since the high, dry altitude will make her consumption easier to withstand, I think it has to prolong her life."

"Yes, Dad," David said. "I think we should all agree to look at it like that."

"What about a job for you, Daddy?" Jessica said.

"Well, I've read quite a bit about Denver. It's really growing by leaps and bounds. The town already has four banks. I believe the Lord would have us do what's best for your mother, and let Him see to it that I get a good job."

Carrie's health seemed to improve with the prospect of the move to Colorado. She had more energy, and the light was back in her eyes that had grown so dull of late.

Grant wanted to travel while Carrie was feeling well, so the Smith family began preparations in earnest for the trip to Colorado. With winter coming on, they could run into severe weather across the plains of Kansas and eastern Colorado, so Grant arranged for them to travel with a company that transported various goods to the West. They would be in good company all the way to Denver.

Jessica wrote to Josh, telling him they were moving to Colorado, and why. It would be in or near Denver, the Mile High City. Their house had sold quickly and they would soon be on their way. Before closing off the letter, she told Josh that Brenda had gone to Carson City to become Gil Simmons's mail order bride.

The Grant Smith family arrived in Denver, Colorado Territory, in early February. They had endured two blizzards and a few lesser snowstorms on the way, but traveling with the supply wagon train, they had made it through with no mishaps.

They lived in their covered wagon for a few weeks until they were able to buy a house about a half mile south of town. Because of Grant's banking experience and a letter of recommendation from the bank in Germantown, he was able to land a good job within the first week.

As soon as they were in their house, Jessica wrote to Josh, giving him her new address.

As the weeks passed, Carrie seemed to improve even more, but their new doctor in Denver was watching her closely, and their new pastor had asked the church to hold her up in prayer.

March came to Oregon, carrying warmer breezes and rain mixed with snow. Brett Cornell now had a huge lumber camp in the Cascade Mountains, some forty miles east of Oregon City. With each new wagon train that had arrived in late autumn, he was able to find men who wanted jobs. The demand for lumber grew along with Oregon's population, and Brett was eager for the wagon trains to start arriving in the spring.

Since the church was not yet large enough to pay Josh a full salary, he worked three days a week for his father. Saturday mornings, of course, still belonged to Lydia Price.

One warm day in the first week of March, there was a gentle knock on the door of Brett's office.

"Yes?" he called.

The door opened, and Mary Ann said, "Daddy, Josh is here to see you."

"Send him in, honey."

Josh entered with the scent of fresh-cut wood in his clothes. He grinned as he said, "That sure is a pretty secretary you've got there, Mr. Cornell."

"And don't I know it," Brett said, chuckling. "She's almost as pretty as her mother!"

"I won't argue with that. Of course, when it comes to father and son in this family, the son is much better looking than the father."

"And I won't argue with that!"

"Dad, one of the men said you wanted to see me right away."

"Yes, son. Sit down. I suppose I could've waited till supper tonight to talk to you, but you get called away so often to fulfill your pastoral duties."

"I need a little breather anyhow. What is it?"

Brett leaned forward, placing his elbows on the desk. "I'm really feeling burdened for the souls of the lumbermen and their families out there at the lumber camp, son. I know you share that burden. It bothers me that those folks won't come into town to church."

"Well, Dad, every time I invite the men to bring their families, they say it's just too far. Thirty miles is quite a distance."

"Exactly. So I've come up with an idea, and I wanted to see what you think about it."

Josh grinned. "I'm all ears."

17

Brett Cornell eased back in his chair. "Here's what I've been thinking, son. Since it's too far for those folks to come to the church to hear the gospel, let's take the gospel to them . . . have preaching services right at the camp. And I'd like for you to do the preaching. I figure to have the services Sunday afternoon. You could make it out there in short order on horseback and be back in town for the evening service at the church."

A wide smile captured Josh's face. "Now you're talking my language, Dad. I'll talk to Pastor Farrington. I'm sure he'll go along with it, but I want his permission and his blessing."

"Well, if you can talk to the pastor yet today, and he's for it, I'd like you to ride out to the camp and talk to the men and their families. If we get even a few who'll attend, we'll start as soon as possible."

"You're telling me that I have the rest of the day off so I can work on this?"

"That's what I'm telling you. I'm thrilled

with the prospect of this, and now it's up to you to get the wheels rolling."

"I'm halfway to the pastor's study right now!"

Pastor Lester Farrington was so excited about Josh preaching at the lumber camp that he told him he would talk to his song leader, Jim Curtis, and encourage him to go along and lead the singing. Maybe he could get a couple of the young men who played musical instruments to join them.

Josh rode back to the Cornell Lumber Camp and began asking the men and their wives if they would attend preaching services at the camp on Sunday afternoons. Many showed interest and said they would come. That evening, Brett and Josh met with Pastor Farrington and Jim Curtis, and it was quickly settled that they would begin services the next Sunday afternoon.

The week passed quickly, and on Sunday at three o'clock, Brett was there with Josh, Jim, and two young musicians. Cliff Wright played a guitar, and Barry Stout played an accordion. More than half of the camp's lumbermen and their families were in attendance.

After the opening singing, Josh preached a clear gospel message, and when he gave an invitation, two lumbermen and their wives responded.

After the service, Brett and the gospel team rode their horses toward Oregon City, rejoicing all the way. There was rejoicing also in the church service that evening when Pastor Farrington told of the souls saved that afternoon at the lumber camp.

At the end of the work day on Monday, Martha Cornell was in the kitchen when her husband, son, and daughter came in. Mary Ann hugged her mother and kissed her cheek.

Brett edged himself ahead of Josh and said, "I'm next, son."

Josh grinned and playfully pushed his dad.

"Oh, Josh!" Martha said. "A letter came today from Jessica. I put it on your dresser."

"Great! They must've gotten settled in Colorado."

"Mm-hmm. There's a Denver address on the envelope."

Josh glanced at the food on the stove. "Do I have time to go up and read it?"

"I think so, as long as you don't tarry while you drool over it."

"Drool over it?"

"You know what she means, son," Brett said.

"You're not fooling anybody, Josh," Mary Ann said. "Your long friendship with Jessica is developing into something else."

"Be honest with us, son," Brett said. "Your sister's right, isn't she?"

Josh's face tinted. "Well . . . I . . . she's turned out to be some kind of young lady, I'll say that."

Martha nodded. "Some kind of young lady who's captured your heart."

"Well, right now I'm trying to read my own heart on this. And even if I should decide I'm in love with Jessica, that won't mean she's in love with me. I think she looks at me as no more than a very good friend."

"I have an inkling that Jessica feels more for you than she's letting on," Martha said.

"Based on what, Mom?"

"A woman's intuition."

"Don't ever discount that, son," Brett said. "Women's intuition is a powerful force."

"Jessica may very well be waiting for you to declare yourself," Martha said.

"You really think so?"

"I do. Now go on and read her letter.

Supper will be ready in a few minutes."

Later, as the Cornell family was eating supper, Martha said, "So are the Smiths settled in Denver?"

"Sounds like it. They had to live in their covered wagon for a while until they were able to buy a house. They're living in the country about a half mile out of town. Major — Mr. Smith got a good job in a Denver bank."

"And how is Mrs. Smith?" Mary Ann asked.

"Jessica said she withstood the trip quite well and is feeling some better."

"That's wonderful," Martha said. "I hope this move will improve her health substantially."

"Jessica seems to think it will." Josh loaded his fork with chicken and dumplings and started to take a bite. Then he paused and said, "Remember my telling you about Jessica's friend going to Nevada as a mail order bride? I've kind of joked about the mail order bride idea with Jessica. Well, she told me there are two couples in their church who found each other that way."

"God works in many ways to bring about His will in people's lives," Brett said.

Martha nodded. "I can see the Lord providing Christian mail order brides for the many lonely Christian men who've come west to make their fortunes. Of course they'd have to be very careful and prayerful in choosing their mates. But then, that's important even when courtship is not done by mail."

Mary Ann sighed. "I just wish I had someone to pray about marrying."

Martha reached across the table and patted her daughter's hand. "Honey, God will bring that someone into your life when the time is right. You have to be patient and wait on the Lord."

"It's hard, Mother. It seems like all the other girls in the church are getting engaged and getting married. Sure, I have my share of dates, but I don't even have a steady beau."

"You will, sis," Josh said, "and one day you'll marry some dashing young man. But no matter who he is, in my mind he'll never be quite good enough."

Mary Ann smiled. "Big brother, you say the nicest things sometimes."

In the privacy of his room that evening, Josh wrote to Jessica, telling her all about the Sunday afternoon services at the Cornell Lumber Camp, and that four souls had already been saved. He asked her to pray that many more would come to the Lord.

When it came time to close off the letter, Josh pondered his mother's words earlier that evening. Finally, he wrote: *Jessica, I miss you more each time I receive a letter from you. I find myself living for the day I can see you again. Love always, Josh.*

The following Sunday afternoon, Josh preached at the lumber camp, making salvation plain and clear as he pointed to the Lord Jesus Christ as the one and only way to heaven. When he gave the invitation, no one responded, but a small group of men gathered around him after the service, asking questions. Josh answered their questions, using his Bible, and with compassion he pressed the men to repent of their sin and open their hearts to Jesus.

In the group were two single men, Neil Stratton and Bob Lynch, both in their early twenties. When the other men had walked away, those two remained to talk with Josh.

Lynch said, "Doesn't the Bible say that after the people in hell burn for a certain period of time, they'll have another chance to be saved?"

Josh shook his head. "No, it doesn't, Bob. There's no such thing as a second chance to be saved after you die. In the last chapter of the Bible, when the white throne judgment is past and all Christ-rejecters are in the lake of fire and all the saved are in heaven with the Lord, God's Word says, 'He that is unjust, let him be unjust still: and he which is filthy, let him be filthy still.' If you die without being justified before God by the blood of Christ, you will be unjust forever. It can't be changed. That's why I said in my sermon that it's dangerous to put off salvation. Nobody knows when they're going to die."

Both men let Josh's words sink in, then looked at each other.

"Next Sunday, right?" Bob said. "A little time to think on it."

"Fellas, listen to me. What's there to think about? You both know you're lost, don't you?"

Both men nodded.

"You believe that Jesus is the only way of salvation, don't you?"

They nodded again.

"Then why put it off? What's to think about?"

Neil wiped a hand over his mouth. "It's . . . it's just a pretty big step to take, Josh.

We gotta think on it."

"But what if you die while you're thinking on it?"

Neither made a reply.

"I'll tell you what will happen," said Josh. "You'll spend eternity in hell wishing you had done the right thing while you could. Proverbs 27:1 says, 'Boast not thyself of tomorrow; for thou knowest not what a day may bring forth.' You don't even know if you'll see another sunrise, much less that you'll be here next Sunday."

"Like we said . . . we'll think on it this week," Neil said. "Thanks for answering the questions for us."

Josh's heart was heavy for the two young men as he watched them walk away. When they had gone some thirty yards, they looked back. Bob waved and said, "Work us up another good sermon, Josh. We'll see you next Sunday!"

The following Tuesday morning, some twenty lumbermen left the Cornell camp with axes and saws in hand, and made their way eastward toward higher ground. The surrounding forests of towering spruce, douglas fir, ponderosa pine, and birch stretched upward toward the jagged peaks of the Cascade Range.

The spruce on the lower slopes of the Cascades gave way to deep gorges lined with misty-green alder that crept up the steep slopes for great distances, then disappeared into pallid rock ledges and shale saddles. Shadowed canyons gaped alongside the rocky ridges.

Brett Cornell's foreman, Luke Kimble, paired the men off. Kimble had been through the designated area the day before and had marked the trees to be cut down. Before sending the men forth to begin their work, he reminded them to stay alert at all times.

As the group of lumbermen headed up a steep ridge where they would separate and start their work, some of the men who had been in Sunday's service brought up Josh Cornell's sermon. The men who had not been in the service listened quietly.

"I like Josh a lot, so don't misunderstand me," one man said, "but he's awfully narrow-minded about how people go to heaven."

"That's what I've been thinking," another said. "Seems to me a man's goin' to heaven if he's sincere in his religion, no matter what name it has on it. Josh cut a pretty thin line sayin' that Jesus Christ is the only way."

"One thing you guys gotta admit, though," Bob Lynch said. "What Josh preached he showed us right out of the Bible. It clearly says that Jesus Christ is the only way of salvation."

"So if you believed what Josh preached, Bob," said another man, "why didn't you go forward and get saved?"

"Well, I'm thinking about it."

"And I'm thinking about it too," Neil Stratton said.

Casey Harmon, who was walking close to Lynch and Stratton, said, "Tell you what, guys. As far as I'm concerned, this Bible stuff is all a bunch of fanaticism. I wasn't in the service on Sunday, but I've heard those hellfire-and-brimstone, Bible-thumping preachers plenty in my time. They're nothing but a bunch of fanatics. I don't want anything to do with them."

Jed Andrews, who had been assigned to work with Harmon, said, "Well, I was in the service, Casey, and Josh doesn't sound like a fanatic to me. He laid it on the line, plain and clear. What I heard made sense, but I'm not going over the edge yet. I'm only twenty-one. I've got a lot of living to do, and I don't want the Lord or anybody else getting in my way. Not until I've sown some wild oats, anyway."

"There you go, Jed," said another man. "Them's my sentiments exactly. Fella ought to live it up while he's young, then worry about heaven and hell and that stuff when he gets old."

Soon the lumbermen were hard at work, chopping and sawing to bring down the marked trees. The sound of axes and saws filled the forest.

Neil Stratton and Bob Lynch had their tree down after some four hours and were using their axes to cut off limbs. Just above them to the northeast, Jake Weathers and Eldon McGrady were still sawing a giant pine. Finally their two-man saw bit through the last remaining fibers to the notch, and the tree began making a cracking sound. They stopped sawing when the giant pine began to tilt.

McGrady shouted, "Timber!"

Something had gone wrong with the notching job. The tree was falling at an angle to the southwest. Directly in its path, Stratton and Lynch were still swinging their axes, and neither heard McGrady's shout.

Stratton and Lynch stopped chopping at the same moment and suddenly heard the warning cries. But the giant of the forest was nearly on top of them when they looked up. One second of terror, and then they were crushed beneath the falling pine.

Jake Weathers and Eldon McGrady were the only two lumbermen who did not attend the funeral services at the church in Oregon City on Thursday morning. They were too sick at heart to put in an appearance.

Josh preached the funeral message with love and compassion. He told of how Neil and Bob had talked to him about salvation after the service on Sunday afternoon, and how he had urged them to receive Christ. Josh then preached the gospel and gave an invitation. One lumberman and two women came to the altar to be led to Christ.

The plain wooden coffins were transported to the local cemetery for a graveside service, where Pastor Farrington gave a brief message. When the service was over, Mary Ann came up to her brother and said, "Josh, you did a wonderful job. Your message was very touching, and I'm so glad those three people came to the Lord."

"Thank you, sis."

Casey Harmon's voice cut through the air. "Aw, c'mon, Jed! You don't want that

Jesus stuff! You're not gonna do that!"

"Oh, yes I do, and oh, yes I am!" Jed Andrews turned away from Casey and stepped toward Josh and Mary Ann. "Can I talk to you, Josh?" he said.

"Of course."

Mary Ann excused herself and went to join her parents.

Jed's voice held a tremor as he said, "Josh, I can't go on any longer this way. What happened to Neil and Bob could just as easily have happened to me. I'm not ready to die. Just Tuesday I told Casey about the sermon you preached at the camp and that what you said made sense. But I said I'd wait till I was old to take care of this salvation business. Well, Josh, I realize I may not live to be old. I want to be saved now."

"Wonderful!" said Josh, opening his Bible. "You've heard me read from Scripture that Jesus Christ came into this world for one basic purpose, and that was to shed His precious blood for sinners like you and me. You've heard me read that Jesus arose from the grave and is alive today and will save any repentant sinner who puts his or her trust in Him for salvation."

"Yes."

"And you believe that?"

"Yes, I do."

"Now let me read you something from the book of 1 John, chapter 4: 'In this was manifested the love of God toward us, because that God sent his only begotten Son into the world, that we might live through him.' Do you see that if you are going to live eternally with God in heaven, that eternal life can come only through Jesus Christ? Not through religious rites or good works . . . only through Jesus?"

"Yes, sir. I see that. And I believe it."

"Then are you willing to call on Jesus right now, in repentance of your sin, and ask Him to cleanse your sins with His blood and save your soul?"

Tears were in Jed's eyes. "Yes, I am."

Josh put his arm around Jed's shoulder and guided him in prayer as he called on the Lord to save him. When they finished praying, Josh and Jed looked up to find Casey standing close by.

Jed rushed to his friend and cried, "Casey, I'm saved, I'm saved! I'm going to heaven when I die!"

"Well, Jed, if that makes you happy, so be it. It's just not for me."

Josh took a few steps in Casey's direction. "Is dying for you, Casey?"

"What do you mean?"

"I mean, are you going to die?"

"Well, sure. Someday. Everybody dies."

"Some much sooner than they expect, like Neil and Bob. Could happen to you too."

"Well . . . yeah."

"So if Jesus Christ is not for you, Casey, hell is. The God who gave you life and existence also gave His Son to save you from hell. Without Jesus, all you have beyond your last breath is to suffer the wrath of God in an eternal hell."

Casey wiped a hand across his mouth. "Josh, you're the boss's son, and I don't want to insult you, but I want no part of this fanaticism."

"Don't worry about insulting the boss's son, Casey. You'd better worry, though, about insulting God's Son."

Josh stepped closer and laid a hand on Casey's shoulder. "I'm going to be praying for you. I want to see you saved before it's too late."

Casey looked him straight in the eye, started to say something, then changed his mind. "I . . . I appreciate that you care, Josh. It's just that I don't see it like you do."

Josh smiled. "I'll be praying that you will."

18

Jessica Smith rushed to her room, carrying two letters that had just come in the mail. Her heart warmed to see Josh Cornell's return address, but she decided to save it until she had read Brenda's letter. She knew before she opened it that Brenda and Gil had married, for the name on the return address was Brenda Simmons.

Brenda loved her new church. She had become a member just before she and Gil were married, and now she was helping Gil with his Sunday school class by being class secretary and going with him on visitation calls. She had married God's man for her, and the letter was filled with the happiness she and Gil had found.

As Jessica folded the letter and placed it back in the envelope, she whispered, "Thank You, Lord, for making Brenda so happy. Thank You for bringing her and Gil together."

She laid aside the letter and carefully opened the envelope from Josh. Her fingers trembled as she unfolded the letter. It began: *My dearest Jessica* . . . He had never used *dearest* before. It made her heart pick up pace.

Josh told her about Bob Lynch and Neil Stratton, and of the souls that were saved on the day of the funeral. He used almost a full page to give Jed Andrews's story, then asked her to pray for Casey Harmon.

Josh told Jessica that the church was growing steadily and just last week had been able to raise his salary some. And the Cornell Lumber Company was prospering; the whole Cornell family was superbly happy.

Well, Jessica, he wrote, *I guess I should say the whole Cornell family is superbly happy except me. I'm happy in my church work, yes. I'm happy doing the preaching at the camp and in my work at the lumber mill. But there is one sad aspect to my life. I miss the sweetest girl I have ever known. I miss her very much. Know who she is? I won't give you a name, but her initials are Jessica Smith. Love always, Josh.*

Tears filled Jessica's eyes, and a smile lit up her face. She pressed the pages close to her heart and whispered, "Oh, Josh, you've come so close. If you're in love with me, please say it. Please. I need so very much to hear it!"

After supper, when Jessica and her parents were in the parlor, she read them the letter. When she finished, she said, "Mama . . . Daddy . . . I so want to write back and tell Josh that I'm in love with him, and that I want to spend the rest of my life with him."

"You must let him say it first, dear," Carrie said. "If it's in Josh's heart, it will come out."

"That's right," Grant said. "All you can do at this point is pray."

"I'm doing a whole lot of that, Daddy."

"Maybe you should casually mention to Josh the young men in our church who are showing interest in you," Carrie said. "Might make him realize that if he's in love with you, he'd better let you know."

Jessica chuckled. "All right. I'll just mention that some of them are asking me out for dinner and that kind of thing."

"It might be a good idea for you to start accepting those invitations," Carrie said. "Johnny, Hal, Dan, and Earl are all nice young men."

"I suppose you're right, Mama. They are very nice. I'll accept the next invitation, but all I can do is be kind to them. There's room for only one person in my heart."

★ ★ ★

Josh Cornell faithfully worked at Lydia Price's home on Saturday mornings, and the rest of the week he stayed busy with his church work and the three days he labored at the mill. But no matter what he was doing, Jessica continually came to mind. The truth of it had been gradual in coming, but by late March, Josh knew that what he felt for Jessica was much more than the friendship they had shared as children.

The last two letters from Jessica had disturbed him. She had not mentioned dating anyone until then, but in her last two letters, she had mentioned going on dates with four different boys. He decided he should wait no longer.

Late that evening, Josh sat in his room to compose the letter. First he prayed, asking the Lord to help him word it just right and to not let Jessica fall for any of the men she was dating.

In the letter, Josh told Jessica that ever since they first met at Fort Union, he had felt a friendship love for her, and that as the years passed, the love grew stronger. He said that ever since the day they saw each other in Fairfax, the friendship love had been changing to another kind . . . and growing deeper. He told her plainly that he was in love with her and he hoped that she might possibly feel the same way toward him. He could wait no longer to find out.

Jessica, he wrote, *there's never been anybody but you for me, and there never will be. I'm asking you now, from the depths of my heart, will you honor me by becoming my wife? Will you marry me? If your answer is yes, I will send the money for your travel expenses. You have often mentioned your best friend, Brenda Moore — now Simmons — and how happy she is married to Gil. Just think, my proposal comes to you through the mail. If you accept my proposal, that will make you my mail order bride!*

The next day, Pastor Farrington knocked at the door of Josh's small office at the church.

"Hello, Pastor," Josh said. "Something I can do for you?"

"I'd like to talk to you in my office if you can spare the time right now."

"Sure. I was just working on my sermon for next Sunday afternoon."

When both men were seated in the pastor's office, Farrington said, "I want to commend you, Josh, for the marvelous job you're doing as my assistant. I'm hearing many good things from the people."

"I'm glad you and they are pleased with my work, sir."

"I am especially pleased with the way you've managed the counseling jobs I've given you. You've handled them quite well, and you will find this experience invaluable when you're the pastor here. This leads me to what I want to talk to you about."

"Yes, sir?"

"You've probably noticed that I haven't had you doing any marriage counseling."

"Yes, sir. I just assumed it was because I'm not married."

"Right. Which brings us to the next item of business. We're getting closer to the day when I'll be stepping aside and you'll become pastor. I really think to be as effective as you can be, you need to have a wife. We need to pray for God to give you the young woman He has chosen for you . . . and soon."

Josh leaned forward on the chair. "Well, Pastor, this may happen within a few weeks."

Farrington's eyes widened. "How can this be? I haven't seen you with a young lady."

"That's because she lives some fourteen hundred miles from here. I told you once about Major Grant Smith and his family, who meant so much to me when Dad was chaplain at Fort Union."

"Yes, I remember."

"Well, sir, let me tell you about their daughter, Jessica." Josh told the pastor the whole story, from the time he was twelve and Jessica was seven, up until the present moment, including the letter he had mailed to her just that morning.

Farrington stroked his jaw. "Josh, I'm glad to hear this. Seems to me this calls for a two-man prayer meeting right now. Let's take it to the Lord and ask Him to reveal His will to both you and Jessica."

Two days after sending the letter, Josh trotted his horse into the lumber camp and reined in at the tool shack where foreman Luke Kimble stood.

"Morning, Luke." Josh swung his leg over the horse's back to dismount. "Dad said you had a little shortage of manpower today."

"Mack Potter wrenched his back yesterday and can't swing an ax or work a saw. I sent word to your pappy late yesterday afternoon that I needed a man to fill in for him. Didn't know he'd send you."

"I guess Dad's scraping the bottom of

the barrel, but here I am."

"You'll be working with Herman Jacobs. He's already up at the cutting site." He pointed toward the west. "They're only about three hundred yards straight up toward that rock that looks like a church steeple."

"All right. I'll just leave my horse here and walk on up."

Josh started up the steep slope and came upon a crew of men loading cut and trimmed timber onto wagons to be taken to the mill in town. Jed Andrews and Casey Harmon were working side by side. A half dozen other men stood nearby.

"You heading up to the cutting area, Josh?" Casey said.

"I'm substituting for Mack Potter. Luke said he's got a sore back." Josh continued on up the slope.

"That's what we hear. Take care up there."

Josh raised a hand in acknowledgment and kept walking.

When Josh was out of earshot, Casey said, "I really like that guy, Jed, even though he's a preacher."

Jed laughed. "Even preachers can be likable."

One by one, the crew looped ropes on

the ends of the huge logs, lifted them with a hand-cranked crane on wheels, and placed them on ox-drawn wagons. They used steel bars about five feet in length to position the logs at the bottom of the stack so they could be picked up by the crane. After a while, a log about a third of the way up the stack angled itself slightly crossways when one of the bottom logs was rolled from the stack.

"Hold it!" one of the men called. "Log jam!"

"I'll get it," Jed said.

Jed maneuvered his way cautiously up the stack while the other men waited and watched. When he reached the spot, Jed slipped the end of his pry bar into a strategic spot and slowly gave it pressure to straighten the angled log. He had it almost in place when his right foot slipped.

The log dislodged and rolled down the stack. Jed jumped out of the way, but the next log behind it slid, and suddenly there was an avalanche of logs rolling and tumbling down, sounding like thunder.

By the time the jumbled logs came to a halt, Jed was pinned from the chest down between two logs. His teeth were clenched in pain as he tried to get a breath. He was barely able to breathe for the weight against his chest.

"Jed!" Casey cried. "Hang on! We'll get you out!"

By this time, Luke Kimble was on the scene, calling out orders and warning the men to be cautious and not set off another avalanche. While the men worked to free him, Jed labored to breathe.

"Casey, if . . . if I don't make it, tell Josh — thank him . . . for leading me to the Lord. Tell him I — tell him I'll meet him . . . in heaven."

Tears shimmered across Casey's vision and slid down his face. "Jed! Don't die, Jed! You're my best friend. Please don't die!"

Josh Cornell was swinging his ax, timing his blows alternately with Herman Jacobs's as they chopped a wedge-shaped notch in the trunk of a pine tree. Suddenly Josh noticed a man running up the steep slope toward him and calling his name.

"It's Casey," Josh said. "I think something's happened."

"Josh!" Casey called, panting as he drew up. "Jed . . . Jed's been caught in a log slide!"

"Is he — ?"

"He's still alive. At least he was when I

left to come and get you. Luke and the men are trying to get him out. He's pinned from the chest down."

Josh darted down the slope, weaving between trees, with Casey and Herman behind him.

When they reached the spot, the men were carefully laying Jed on the ground. Josh breathed a sigh of relief when he saw Jed clenching his teeth and blinking his eyes. Josh knelt beside Jed, then looked at Luke Kimble.

"No way to know how much damage is done, Josh, till we get him to Doc Fraser."

"Get a wagon ready," Josh said. "I'll take him."

"I'll go with you," Casey said, "if it's all right with Luke."

Kimble nodded, then told a couple of men to bring a wagon.

Josh leaned close to the injured man. "You'll be all right, Jed. We'll get you to Doc Fraser."

Jed swallowed hard and met Josh's gaze. "I . . . can breathe now. It hurts, but up there between those logs, I thought I was going to have the life squeezed out of me."

"You just rest easy. Don't try to talk. It'll be a bumpy ride, but we'll get you to town as soon as possible. Casey will ride in the back of the wagon with you and keep you as comfortable as he can."

At the clinic, which had once been owned by Dr. Clay Price, Josh and Casey sat in the waiting room while Dr. Emmett Fraser and his nurse tended Jed. Josh had his head bowed and was silently praying that the Lord would spare Jed's life. When he finished praying, he looked up to see Casey staring at the floor, hands clasped, face pale.

"God won't let Jed die, will he, Josh?"

"I'm certainly praying that He won't. Like Dr. Fraser said, there could be serious internal damage. We'll know a lot more when he's finished examining him."

Casey stared at the floor again and mumbled something unintelligible.

"What did you say?"

Casey cleared his throat. Tears were swimming in his eyes. "I said it could've been me crushed between those logs. I've climbed many a log stack and used a bar to straighten up a wayward log. I've never had my foot slip like Jed's did. It could've been me, Josh. If it had been, and I had died —" His voice choked as the tears streamed down his cheeks.

"Yes, it could have been you, Casey,"

Josh said quietly. "And?"

"If . . . if it had been me, and I had died, I'd be in hell now."

"Jed told me you said you weren't sure that you believed there's a hell. Apparently you've changed your mind."

Casey drew in a deep breath. "Yeah, I've changed my mind. Jesus wouldn't have gone to the cross and suffered like He did if there was no hell to save us from. Jed helped me understand that."

"That's exactly right. And you admit that you would be in hell right now if it had been you crushed in the logs and you had died?"

"Yes. I don't want to go to hell."

"There's only one way to miss it."

"I know."

"And that is?"

"I have to repent of my unbelief, repent of my sin, and ask Jesus to come into my heart and save me."

"That'll make you one of us fanatics. Do you understand that, Casey?"

"Yes, I understand. And that's what I want, Josh. I want to be one of those born-again fanatics who loves Jesus like you do . . . and like Jed. I don't want to wait another minute!"

After Josh led Casey to the Lord, he told

him they should pray together for Jed. Josh led them as they prayed, but when he said amen, Casey prayed aloud too, fumbling a bit with his words but asking the Lord to spare his friend.

The door opened and portly Dr. Fraser entered the waiting room. "Your friend is quite bruised up from his chest to his toes, but I find no indication of internal injuries. He's got three cracked ribs, but those will heal in a short time."

"Doctor!" Casey said. "You mean he's not going to die?"

"No. He's going to be just fine."

Casey looked toward heaven and said, "Thank You, Lord Jesus! Thank you!"

"This young man sounds like a fanatic to me," Fraser said with a smile.

Josh chuckled. "Yes, Doctor, he just became one. Could we see Jed?"

"Sure."

"I'd like to take this fanatic in there and let him tell Jed what just happened to him."

The morning sun was glowing over the plains as Daniel and David Smith embraced their mother. Her condition had deteriorated, and she was sitting in an overstuffed chair in the parlor. Grant had taken the morning off from his job at the bank to drive Carrie into town for a doctor's appointment.

"I'll be fine, boys," she said. "You head for school before you're late."

Jessica looked at her mother, noting the dark circles that shadowed her eyes. "Now, Mama, if Dr. Stafford says you shouldn't try to cook breakfast and supper for a while, you mind him. I can take care of it until you're feeling better."

"We'll see."

"We sure will," Grant said. "If Dr. Stafford tells you to rest more, Jessica and I will see that you do it, even if we have to hog-tie you to that bed!"

Carrie smiled.

Thirty minutes later, Jessica stood at the front door of the house and watched her parents' buggy turn onto the road. She blinked at the sudden tears in her eyes and quickly closed the door, then went to her room. She fell to her knees beside her bed and prayed, "Dear Lord, I beg of You, please make Mama well. She's the most wonderful mother in all the world, Lord, and I thank You for letting me be her daughter. You know how much I love her and need her. Please make her well. And Lord . . . about Josh. You know how much

I love him. If it's not in Your plan for Josh and me to be married, then You'll have to work a miracle in my heart. I really need to hear from You on this, Lord Jesus. Amen."

19

For a while after their move to Colorado, Carrie Smith had experienced renewed strength and vitality. But in the past few weeks, the symptoms of her illness had been becoming more pronounced by the day.

Grant and Carrie concentrated on the positive as they drove to the doctor's office. There was a deep and abiding love between them, and Grant would do anything to make her life as happy and fulfilled as possible, however long that life might be.

Grant sat in the waiting room while Dr. Peter Stafford made his examination of Carrie, with a nurse at his side. Carrie had lost weight since her last appointment. Her face had an ashen hue except for the rosy spots on her cheeks due to the fever.

She studied the doctor's eyes as he listened to her lungs with his stethoscope. When the nurse took the thermometer from her mouth, Carrie said, "Doctor, I want you to be honest with me. Please don't try to spare me. I want to know the truth about my —" Her words were cut off by a sudden, hacking cough. When the coughing ceased, Carrie lowered her hand from her mouth. "I want to know the truth about my condition."

Stafford looked at the nurse for the temperature reading.

"101, Doctor."

The doctor turned to Carrie, a serious look on his face. "Mrs. Smith, it is true that you're not improving as I had hoped, and as your doctor in Maryland had hoped when he sent you to Colorado. But we mustn't despair. I can give you some stronger cough medicine, and if you'll get more rest, I can be somewhat optimistic."

"More rest. All I'm doing now, Doctor, is cooking breakfast and supper for my family. The rest of the day, I do nothing but lie in bed or sit in a chair while I watch Jessica do all the housework. She and Grant do the grocery shopping. Must I even stop cooking?"

"You've told me before that Jessica helps you do the cooking, but that you carry the main load yourself."

"Yes."

"Can you continue to cook the two meals?"

Carrie closed her eyes. "No. Not like I

have been. It's down to Jessica doing about half of it."

"Mrs. Smith, as your physician, I'm telling you that you must leave all the cooking to Jessica. Without total rest, your condition will get worse. You asked me not to beat around the bush, right?"

"Yes."

"Then I won't. Until we can get you much improved, you are not to do any of the cooking. Do you understand?"

Carrie stared at him silently, a pained look in her eyes.

"And please obey my orders about staying in the house during inclement weather. If you should catch a cold, it would be extremely dangerous for you. Now, while Nurse Johnson helps you button up, I'll go tell your husband what I've just told you."

Grant and Carrie drove to the general store to pick up a few groceries and supplies while in town.

"Want to stay out here or go in with me?" Grant asked.

"I'll go in with you," she replied, giving him a fragile smile.

When they returned to the buggy, Grant placed the boxes of groceries and supplies in the back, then helped Carrie onto the seat.

"Next stop, the post office," he said. "Then we'll head for home. Are you all right?"

"Just a little tired. Dr. Stafford's nurse gave me a dose of salicylic acid before I left the examining room. I can tell it's helping to bring my fever down, but it's making me feel a bit weak. I'll be fine."

Moments later, they pulled up in front of the post office. Carrie waited in the buggy, watching people move about on the street. Soon Grant emerged from the log building and laid the mail on the backseat.

"Jessica will be happy. There's a letter from Josh."

She smiled. "I hope there's something positive in it."

"Mr. Smith!" It was young Rollie Demers, the Western Union delivery boy, aboard his horse. "I was about to ride out to your house, sir. I have a telegram for Miss Jessica from Oregon City, Oregon. Are you headed home?"

"We sure are. We can take it to Jessica."

For lunch Jessica had prepared barley beef soup, which was simmering on the stove. She was cutting thick slices of hot bread when she saw the family buggy pass by the kitchen window. In a few minutes, her parents came through the back door. Grant had a steadying arm around Carrie.

"What did Dr. Stafford say?" Jessica asked.

"Your mother is to get more rest, honey. Doc said she's not to cook any meals till she's much better. He gave her some stronger cough medicine and said if she'll obey his orders and get more rest, he expects that she'll get better."

"Well, Mama, that settles who cooks the meals, doesn't it?"

Carried managed a smile. "Only temporarily."

"Fine. When you get better, we'll see about it. Soup's on. Do you want to eat here at the table, Mama?"

Carrie placed fingertips to her temples. "I'm pretty tired right now. I'll have Daddy help me to the bedroom. You can bring lunch to me there. That soup and hot bread sure do smell good."

"I'll have it on a tray shortly," Jessica said.

"As soon as I get your mother in bed, I'll come back and bring the groceries and things in from the buggy."

"All right, Daddy."

When Grant and Carrie entered their bedroom, he said, "Sit here on the edge of the bed, honey."

Grant removed Carrie's shoes, swung her thin legs up onto the bed, placed fluffy pillows at the headboard, and propped her up against them.

"Aren't you going to give her the letter and the telegram?" Carrie asked.

"I'll wait till lunch is over. Otherwise she'll be dashing off to her room to read them, and lunch will get cold. I've got to get to the bank as soon as I can."

A moment later, Jessica came in carrying a tray. Steam was lifting off the soup and butter was melting into a thick slice of bread.

"Sure smells good," Carrie said.

"I hope I've done justice to it."

"You're already twice the cook I am."

"She's good, honey," said Grant with a chuckle, "but not that good!"

While Jessica filled their bowls with soup, Grant carried in the boxes from the buggy and set them on the cupboard.

"I'll put everything away, Daddy. Come on and eat your lunch. I know you need to get to the bank."

When they were finished eating, Jessica started to wash the dishes. Grant took a final sip of coffee, rose from the table, and set the cup beside her.

"Got a little something for you in the buggy. Be right back."

When Grant returned, Jessica's hands were deep in hot soapy water. He waved the white and yellow envelopes in front of her, a mischievous grin on his face. "From Josh."

Jessica squealed. "Daddy! Why did you wait till now to give it to me?"

"Because I wanted my lunch!" He extended the two envelopes toward her. "There's a telegram here, too."

She eyed the yellow Western Union envelope, which was on top, while drying her hands on a dish towel. "The telegram's from Josh?"

"I would think so. It's from Oregon City. The Western Union messenger was on his way to deliver it when he saw us in town."

Jessica's fingers trembled as she took the envelopes from his hand. "Which one should I read first?"

"Well, since he no doubt wrote the letter first, I'd say you should read it before you read the telegram."

Eyes dancing, she said, "See you when you get home from work."

"Well, tell you what. Mama and I are more than a little bit interested in what

Josh has to say, so I'll go look in on her. Come and tell us what he says, will you?"

"All right." Jessica ran out of the kitchen.

Grant watched his daughter disappear through the door. A wistful smile curved his lips and a sigh escaped him. He gave himself a mental shake, then left the kitchen and entered the bedroom and lowered his tall frame onto a chair next to the bed.

"I heard her run to her room," Carrie said. "Carrying the envelopes, I presume."

"Yes." Grant took one of Carrie's frail hands in both of his. "She's going to tell us what Josh has to say after she reads the letter and the telegram." He paused. "I was just thinking that should Josh want to marry our girl, how far away she would be from us in Oregon."

"Funny, I was thinking the same thing."

"If it should happen, honey, I've already laid the groundwork for someone to live with us and take care of you and the household."

"Oh?"

"You remember Bessie Williams — the widow who does the janitorial work at the bank?"

"Does she want to leave the bank?"

"She mentioned one day that she'd like to be a live-in maid in someone's home, and I told her to hang on, we might have a job for her. I explained the situation with Jessica and Josh. Bessie's willing to wait, so the foundation has been laid. With my raise in salary, we can afford to pay Bessie fairly."

"Talk about mixed emotions," Carrie said, shaking her head slowly. "I want Jessica and Josh to marry, but if it happens, I'm going to miss her something awful."

"I know what you mean."

"I appreciate you telling me about Bessie, though. She's a dear. I'd love to have her with us if the Lord leads Jessica to Oregon."

For a few moments, there was not a sound in the room as they digested what they had just discussed and sent a prayer to the Lord for grace and guidance as they awaited their daughter's news.

Jessica closed the bedroom door behind her and tore open the envelope. She had only read a few lines when her eyes filled with tears. "Oh, thank You, Lord Jesus! Thank You, thank You, thank You!"

"Grant, maybe you'd better go check on

her. If this is bad news . . ."

Grant was just rising from the chair beside the bed when they both heard Jessica's door open, followed by rapid footsteps. She fairly hurled herself into the room, her face shiny with tears.

"Aw, baby," Grant said, "what's the matter?"

A smile spread over Jessica's face. "Nothing's the matter, Daddy. Josh says he's in love with me. He says the friendship love he had for me began to change when we saw each other in Fairfax, and he says there's never been anybody but me for him, and there never will be! He says — Well, let me read you the letter."

Carrie began weeping silently as she shared her daughter's joy.

"Before you read us the letter, what was the telegram about?" Grant asked.

"I'll tell you after I read you the letter. It'll make sense then."

Jessica choked up a few times while reading Josh's declaration of love and his marriage proposal. By the time she finished the letter, her mother's face was tear-streaked.

Grant chuckled. "So you'll be his mail order bride, huh? I thought you said you'd never be one!"

"I'll be *Josh's* mail order bride!"

Grant opened his arms, and Jessica rushed to him for a hug. Then she bent over to embrace her mother. "Oh, Mama, he's in love with me! Josh is in love with me! I'm going to be his wife! Praise the Lord!"

Carrie held her close, and as they mingled their tears, she said, "Daddy and I have prayed for this moment, honey. We're so happy for you!"

"All right, tell us about the telegram," Grant said.

"Well, you heard in the letter that Josh said if I will accept his proposal, he'll send the money for my travel expenses."

"Yes?"

"When I opened the telegram, it said at the very beginning that if I hadn't yet received the letter, I should wait till I did to read the telegram. Anyhow, he said that if I accept his proposal and come to Oregon City, he's made arrangements for me to stay in Pastor and Mrs. Farrington's home until the wedding. It's a long telegram. Josh said that Mrs. Farrington is looking forward to my coming . . . that she'll teach me some things about being a pastor's wife while I'm staying with them."

"That would be a great help to you," Carrie said.

"It's a bit frightening to think of being a pastor's wife, but with Mrs. Farrington's help and advice, I know it will be easier.

"Josh says we'll set the wedding date after I arrive. And he says that when he receives my reply — if it's a positive one — he'll buy a house just outside of town that's being vacated in about three weeks. Hoping and praying I will say yes, he's already put earnest money on it. So . . . I'm going to write to Josh and tell him that I will marry him, but that I can't come till Mama's back on her feet again."

"No, honey," Carrie said. "You can't put this off. The two of you deserve to be together. You must go to Josh right away."

"But Mama, I can't just up and leave you! Especially now that Dr. Stafford has said you can't cook anymore. You've still got Daniel and David to feed and clean up after. Who would do the housework? I —"

"Wait a minute, honey. Tell her, Daddy."

"Jessica, the Lord knew this was going to happen, and He has already provided someone — Bessie Williams — to move into the house and do the cooking and the housework. She'll also be right here to look after your mother."

Jessica's face pinched. "I . . . I'm a little scared all of a sudden."

"That's only natural," Carrie said. "When a young bird takes its flight out of the nest, it's bound to be a little frightened. You know Daddy and I will miss you terribly, but we have no doubt this is God's will, and we want you to be married to Josh. We'll be so proud, knowing you are in the Lord's service."

"The hardest part about all of this is that Mama and I won't be able to come to the wedding," Grant said as he wiped tears from his cheeks. "It would just be too much to attempt a trip like that."

"I know, Daddy. I wish you could both be there, but I know it's not possible."

"Ah, but when she gets better," Grant said, "we'll be out there to visit you."

"That will be wonderful!"

Grant looked into Jessica's eyes. "Honey, I'm not in a hurry to get rid of you, but Josh deserves a quick reply, don't you think?"

"I'll write a letter this afternoon."

"How about you dictate a quick reply and let me send him a telegram?"

"Oh, Daddy! Would you do that?"

Grant looked at Carrie. "What do you think, Mama?"

"I agree. That sweet boy deserves his answer as soon as possible. A telegram is the way to go."

It was Thursday, June 1, 1872. Josh Cornell and Casey Harmon were working together at the lumber mill, cutting bark from logs that had been brought down from the camp. While they planed the bark off, Josh talked to Casey about the spiritual growth he was seeing in Casey's life. The two men were becoming close friends.

"So you've been reading your Bible an hour every morning and every night, eh?"

Casey nodded. "Can't get enough of it."

"I can tell you're in the Book a lot, the way you answer questions when I fire them at you. You're getting doctrinally stable plenty fast for a new convert."

"I'm trying. Of course, Jed and I do a lot of studying together at night, too."

"There's another fella who's grown fast in his Christian life. I'm glad you two can room together."

Their attention was drawn to Mary Ann Cornell, who was walking toward them carrying a yellow envelope.

"Josh, that sister of yours is the prettiest girl in the whole world."

Josh's eyebrows arched. "Oh? And

you've seen all the girls in the world? Well, I can tell you about one in Colorado who's just as pretty."

"I know. You have. About sixty thousand times."

"Sixty thousand? Casey, haven't I told you a hundred billion times not to exaggerate?"

"What's so funny?" Mary Ann asked as she drew up.

"Just some of my strange humor, sis. What've you got there?"

"Telegram for a Mr. Joshua Cornell. Comes from Denver, Colorado."

"Really? Let me have it!"

Mary Ann swung the envelope behind her back and jutted her graceful jaw. "Only if you tell Casey and me what Jessica says."

"Oh, no you don't, girl! It's private business. Come on, hand it over!"

Mary Ann giggled and handed the envelope to her brother.

Josh ripped it open and unfolded the yellow sheet of paper. His eyes grew wide and then filled with tears. He waved the paper over his head, shouting, "Whoope-e-e! Praise God! Hallelujah! I'm going to be Jessica's husband! Casey, you'll have to work alone for a little while. I'm going into town and send Jessica a telegram. Mary

Ann, tell Dad I'll be back to work in an hour or so. And . . . and tell him why I'm going into town, will you?"

"Sure, big brother." She raised up on her tiptoes and kissed his cheek. "Congratulations." She turned and went back in the direction of the office.

"One thing before I go, Casey. Ah . . . make that two things. Number one. God used your testimony to bring Rick Kuchler and Mike Olmstead to Jesus last Sunday in the meeting at the camp. You really handled it well, and I liked the way you used Scripture in your testimony."

"Thank you. And this means . . . ?"

"This means I want you to get busy and prepare a sermon. I want you to preach it a week from next Sunday at the camp."

Casey's face lost color. "Me? Preach a sermon?"

"You came close to preaching when you gave your testimony. Will you do it?"

"Well . . . I reckon I could do that."

"Good! Now, number two. Mary Ann."

"What about her?"

"You've got a big ol' crush on her."

The young man ducked his head and blushed.

"Want to know a little secret? She's got a crush on you, too."

Casey's red face went pale. "You mean it?"

"I overheard her talking to one of her friends a couple of days ago. She really thinks you're handsome and very charming."

"Really?"

"Yep. Go slow, but get in motion, boy."

Casey took a deep breath. "I'll do it. Thanks for telling me."

"You're entirely welcome," said Josh, turning away.

Josh had taken only a few steps when Casey said, "Josh . . . thanks for number one, too. Thanks for having enough confidence in me to ask me to preach."

"You're welcome," Josh said with a wink.

20

On Saturday, June 3, Lydia Price couldn't help but notice the lilt in Josh Cornell's walk and the light in his eyes as he worked around her yard all morning.

It was almost noon when he tapped on her back door and called through the screen, "All done, Lydia. And the food smells as good as always!"

"Come on in, Josh," Lydia called from the kitchen.

Josh sniffed the air as he entered the kitchen and pronounced, "Potato soup!"

Lydia smiled at him over her shoulder. "You know where the water bucket is. Wash your hands. Soup's just about ready."

Lydia filled glasses with cool lemonade and ladled hot soup into the bowls. Josh led them in thanking the Lord for the food, and they began to eat.

"All right, Joshua . . . what's happened?"

He raised his eyebrows. "Pardon me?"

"I think I know you quite well, Josh. You're always happy in the Lord, and you're a cheerful person by nature, but today I see more happiness and cheer than usual. Want to share it?"

Josh gave her a wide smile. "I'm getting married!"

"Married! I didn't even know you were engaged."

"Well, it happened too fast for a formal engagement."

"I guess it did. I haven't seen you with any young lady at church, and you've never told me about being in love. Come on, now, who is she?"

"You haven't met her. Jessica lives in Colorado."

"Oh, I see. Long distance romance, eh?"

"I guess you could call it that."

"How long have you known her?"

"Since I was twelve and she was seven."

"Really? Talk about childhood sweethearts. Tell me about her."

While they ate, Josh told her about his relationship with Jessica from the days at Fort Union, New Mexico, up to the present. She would be arriving in Oregon City on June 22, on the Wells Fargo stage from Ogden, Utah, and would stay at the Farringtons' home until the wedding.

"Have you set a date?" Lydia asked.

"Not yet. We'll do that when Jessica gets here." His grin grew into a chuckle.

"What's so funny?"

"Jessica had a close friend who became one of those mail order brides."

"Oh?"

"And when this friend told Jessica she was considering becoming a mail order bride, Jessica said she would never do such a thing. But I told her that if she accepted my proposal and came to Oregon and married me, that would make her a mail order bride. And she'll soon be on her way!" He laughed again.

Lydia laughed with him. "She must be a wonderful girl."

"That she is, Lydia. Wonderful, beautiful inside and out, and everything I want in a wife."

"I'm happy for you. You haven't told me your Jessica's last name."

"A real common one. Smith. She's Jessica Smith."

A faraway look came into Lydia's eyes. "Oh, now isn't that something?"

"What?"

"I almost had Smith for my married name. I was engaged to an army officer named Smith. He was killed in the Mexican War."

Josh thought for a moment, then said, "But the Lord, who guides His children's lives, already had Dr. Price picked out for you."

"The Lord never makes mistakes, Josh. Even after bringing Clay and me together and giving us a precious marriage, He saw fit to take him from me and let me live the rest of my days as a widow. I must accept this as God's will for my life."

Josh reached across the table for her hand. "I wouldn't be too sure of that."

"Hmm?"

"Spending the rest of your life as a widow. I doubt you'll do that."

"What do you mean?"

"You're a very lovely lady, and you're only in your midforties. It would surprise me if the Lord didn't bring some real nice Christian man into your life. You deserve to be happy and have a full life yet."

Lydia warmed him with a smile. "You're a sweet boy, Josh. Thank you for trying to encourage me. I'll admit this widow's life is a lonely one, even though I have my church and so many friends."

"I'm sure it is. Of course, when that man comes into your life and you marry him, he'll take care of the place and look after you, and I'll be out of my Saturday morning job."

Lydia laughed.

"And more than the job, I'll miss these scrumptious lunches!"

The ten days prior to Jessica's departure were busy and emotionally full from daylight till she fell asleep at night. On the day her father bought her railroad and stagecoach tickets, she sent a letter to Brenda Simmons, telling her she was going to Oregon City to marry Josh Cornell.

In the following days, it became routine for Jessica to sit beside Carrie's bed and reminisce about the past — sometimes with tears — and talk of Jessica's future.

On her good days, Carrie did what she could to help Jessica sew and prepare her wedding dress. They also made tea towels and embroidered pillowcases, tablecloths, and napkins, which Jessica would take in the small trunk Grant had bought her.

"Honey, let me give you some advice on being a wife," Carrie said as they embroidered napkins one afternoon.

Jessica smiled. "Coming from the most wonderful wife and mother in the world, I will pay close attention."

"Jessica, always keep the Lord first in your heart, and everything else will fall into place. You and Josh are desperately in love, just like your daddy and I were, and still are. In one beautiful sense, you will be one flesh. But you are still two different individuals, and you will have differences of opinion at times. Because you're human, there will arise times when you'll even have arguments."

"You and Daddy never argue."

"Something else for me to admonish you about. When God gives you children, and you and Josh have your disagreements, never let your children see it."

"Oh, so that's it."

"Now, let me remind you of some Scriptures that will help keep things right in your marriage, even when serious disagreements arise and threaten to become arguments. Proverbs 15:1 says, 'A soft answer turneth away wrath: but grievous words stir up anger.' When husbands and wives snap at each other, it only makes things worse. God knows what He's talking about."

"Yes, Mama."

"And when you do get angry at Josh, remember Ephesians 4:26: 'Let not the sun go down upon your wrath.' Don't you and Josh ever go to sleep mad at each other. Talk it out until you can pray together and settle your differences before you go to sleep. Wrath has a way of growing if it's left to fester. I know that right now it seems impossible that you and Josh could have a disagreement and even become angry at each other. But it happens, even in Christian marriages. This is why God has given His children advice in His Word. Understand?"

Jessica nodded.

"Something else," Carrie said. "You've heard this many times from our pastors over the years, but I want to bring it up again. God has structured the home with the husband as its head. That doesn't mean He looks at women as inferior to men, but in His great wisdom, he knows that anything with two heads is a freak. Paul wrote in Ephesians that Christ is the head of the church. The church has one head — Jesus Christ. And Paul also said the husband is the head of the wife, and that she is to submit to him as to the Lord. There is one head in the home — the husband. Along with his God-given place as the head of the home, the husband also has God-given responsibilities. You understand that, don't you?"

"Yes, Mama."

"God has given you a wonderful, godly man to marry, honey. If you will always submit yourself to Josh, you will become in his eyes like the submissive wife in that marvelous thirty-first chapter of Proverbs: 'Her price is far above rubies. The heart of her husband doth safely trust in her.' "

Jessica's eyes misted. "Oh, Mama, I want to be the very best wife I can be to Josh. Thank you for telling me these things."

As the days drew nearer for Jessica's departure, Grant also gave his daughter sage advice on marriage. And Daniel and David spent extra time with their sister. The bond between Jessica and her family deepened in those few days, and as with all things done in God's will and God's time, He gave them immeasurable peace and grace.

On the morning of June 14, the boys loaded Jessica's trunk and luggage into the family buggy. Grant had arranged that after putting Jessica on the train, they would all go to the boardinghouse where Bessie Williams lived and bring her home with them to begin her duties.

Carrie was not feeling at all well, but she was determined to go to the depot with the rest of the family to see Jessica off. She wanted it to be as joyous an occasion for her daughter as possible. In the privacy of the master bedroom, she dressed herself carefully, fixed her hair in an upsweep before the mirror, and pinched color into her pale cheeks.

Soon the Smiths were on their way to town, with Daniel at the reins. It was a tight fit, sitting among Jessica's luggage and boxes.

They arrived at Denver's Union Station some forty minutes before departure time. Grant saw that Jessica's belongings were checked in the baggage coach, all except for her small overnight bag, then rejoined the family on the platform.

"Well, Jess, it looks like you're gonna do what you said you wouldn't," Daniel said.

"What's that?"

"Become one of those abominable mail order brides!"

"Well, at least I'm getting married. That's more than will probably happen to you!"

Daniel was about to come back with a wisecrack when the conductor shouted, "All aboard!"

Passengers began to move toward the line of coaches.

Suddenly the light mood the Smiths had prolonged was over. Jessica wept as she gave hugs and kisses to her teary-eyed brothers, telling them she loved them.

When she turned to her parents, she found them losing their own battle with tears.

Carrie embraced her daughter, holding her close, and said, "You be happy, honey. Please write often. And I promise, as soon as I'm well enough to travel and Daddy can get the time off, we'll be on our way to Oregon City to visit you."

Jessica's whole body shook. "I'll be looking forward to it, Mama. I love you."

"I love you, honey." Carrie smiled at Jessica with a God-given radiance and kissed her tenderly on each cheek. "Go with my blessing, and have as much happiness in your marriage as I have in mine."

Jessica turned to her father, and he held her close. "I'll miss you, sweetheart . . . more than you'll ever know." Grant took his daughter's tear-streaked face in both hands and gently wiped away the moisture. "I love you," he said, and kissed her cheek.

"I'll miss you too, Daddy. I love you."

"All aboar-r-rd!" came the conductor's call once more. The bell on the big engine was clanging.

Grant motioned for Carrie and the boys to come close. For a brief moment, the family was knit tightly around Jessica, arms locked together.

They heard the final boarding call.

Jessica's face was wet with tears as she picked up her overnight bag and headed toward the train. Inside the coach, she found a seat on the depot side. She placed her bag in the overhead rack then slid over to be next to the window.

Her family was huddled together, and she could see that the boys were supporting Carrie. Jessica stuck her hand out the open window and waved just as the engine whistle let out a blast. Steam hissed from the bowels of the boiler. The steel wheels began to move and the train lunged forward. As it chugged out of the station, Jessica leaned from the open window and waved until her loved ones were just a blur among all the other people on the platform.

Soon the train was in open country, traveling due north toward Cheyenne City, where she would transfer to another train for Ogden, Utah. Jessica eased back on the seat and let her mind settle on the man she loved and the happy life ahead of her as they served the Lord together as husband and wife.

It was almost two o'clock in the afternoon on June 22 when Josh Cornell drove the family buggy onto Cornell Lumber

Mill property and headed for the office building. He smiled to himself when he saw his sister standing on the porch, talking to Casey Harmon. Josh got their attention as he swung the buggy in front of the office and reined in smartly.

"I thought you were supposed to be working up at the camp," he said, grinning at Casey.

"I am," Casey said. "Luke needed a volunteer to come down here with a message for your dad. He's busy right now, so I gave the message to his beautiful secretary."

Josh stepped out of the buggy and moved toward them. "Sure was nice of you to volunteer, Casey."

Casey shrugged. "Somebody had to do it."

"Of course, the fact that you would get to see Dad's secretary had nothing to do with this sacrificial gesture."

Casey and Mary Ann grinned at each other, then Casey said, "Oh, maybe a little."

Josh shook his head. "What lengths some men will go to in order to spend time with a pretty girl."

"Tell me, Josh, can you blame me?"

"Casey, ol' pal, you're a mess, you know that?"

Brett Cornell and one of the mill workers came out the door. The worker greeted the young people and then headed for one of the outbuildings.

"You ready to go, Josh?" Brett said.

"Sure am. Casey's got a message for you from Luke. I'll help baby sister into the buggy while he delivers it."

When Mary Ann was settled on the front seat, she said, "My big brother looks awfully excited."

"That's putting it mildly. I'm about to explode."

"I can't wait to see her," Mary Ann said. "You suppose she'll know me?"

"I don't know. It's been a long time, and you've changed a lot . . . but so has Jessica. Both of you have gotten more beautiful."

"Bye, Mary Ann!" called Casey as he headed for his horse.

She waved. "Bye, Casey."

Brett climbed in the back of the buggy. "All right, kids, let's go pick up your mother and head for that stage station!"

Twenty minutes later, Josh pulled the buggy up near the Wells Fargo office. The whole family alighted and made their way to where the stage would stop.

Jessica was enthralled by the beauty of

the majestic Cascade Range. Like her, the other four passengers had never been to Oregon before, and they all marveled at the sight. As the stagecoach descended out of the mountains and followed the well-beaten trail through giant conifer trees, the driver called, "Oregon City . . . straight ahead!"

Five more minutes of driving brought them into town, and when the stage turned onto Main Street, which was lined with two-story, false-fronted buildings of clapboard, Jessica's mouth went dry and her heart banged her ribs.

The stage rolled up the broad street for two blocks, then slowed as it approached the Wells Fargo office. Suddenly, Jessica saw the man she loved waiting at the edge of the boardwalk, looking more handsome than ever. His parents stood behind him with a grown-up and lovely Mary Ann.

The stage came to a halt, and the Wells Fargo agent moved past the Cornell family to open the door. "Welcome to Oregon City, folks!"

Jessica was the closest to the door. As she started to rise from the seat, the agent offered his hand. "I'll help you out, ma'am."

"Pardon me, Ralph," said Josh, crowding

close, "but I'll help this young lady."

"Oh, sure, Josh. I forgot your fiancée was to be on this stage."

"It's all right. Thanks for being a gentleman." He leaned into the coach and said, "May I help you out, Miss Smith?"

Jessica took his hand and said, "Of course, Reverend Cornell."

When Jessica's feet touched ground, Josh took her in his arms. "At last. I can hardly believe you're really here, I've waited so long. Would you mind if the future groom kissed his future bride?"

"Of course not."

After the discreet kiss, Brett, Martha, and Mary Ann moved forward and gave Jessica a warm welcome. While Brett and Martha were embracing their future daughter-in-law, Pastor and Mrs. Farrington appeared, and Josh introduced them to Jessica.

"Josh," Farrington said, "we'll take your family and Jessica's luggage in the wagon so you can take Jessica to see her new home before bringing her to our place."

Jessica held on to Josh's arm as the happy couple drove through town. When they pulled up into the small driveway, Jessica gasped. "Oh, Josh, it's beautiful!"

It was a small, one-story frame house with a recent coat of creamy yellow paint, white trim, and a gray roof. As Josh helped her from the buggy, Jessica eyed the inviting wraparound porch on three sides, and was already planning the flowers that would adorn the porch and yard.

Josh led her through the door and into the parlor.

"This furniture looks brand-new," Jessica said. "You didn't buy it with the house?"

"No, ma'am. I bought it all new."

In addition to the parlor, there were two bedrooms, a kitchen with eating space, and a small study for Josh. As they went from room to room, Jessica commented that their tastes in furniture were very much alike.

"Oh, darling," Jessica said when they returned to the parlor, "it's just perfect for us!"

"You really like it?"

"It's a fairy palace! You've made me the happiest girl in the world!"

Their lips came together in a sweet, tender kiss that carried the promise of a world of love and joy beyond compare.

Josh took her by the hand. "Well, that's the tour, m'lady. I'm sure there are things you'll want to do to the house to give it your own flair."

"Well, I can see a few things I'd change, like maybe dress up the windows the way I want them, and a few other things here and there. Would that be all right?"

"Of course. That's what I want you to do. After all, it's your house. You fix it up just like you want it."

This time they kissed longer and with more feeling. When they pulled back, Josh continued to hold Jessica in his arms as she said, "It's a very pretty house, darling, but the sweet presence of the Lord and the love we have for each other will make it a home."

Josh agreed wholeheartedly and kissed her again.

21

The pleasing aroma of dinner wafted outside when Pastor Farrington opened the door and invited Josh and Jessica in. They could hear voices coming from the rear of the house.

"Maddie, Josh and Jessica are here!" Farrington called.

Brett got up from the couch in the parlor, and the three women appeared in the hallway outside the kitchen door. Madeline could see Jessica looking around timidly, apprehension in her eyes, and her heart went out to her. The poor dear. She rushed forward to greet her.

"Welcome, children! Josh, you can go sit with the men in the parlor. Dinner will be ready in about forty-five minutes." She looked over her shoulder at Martha and Mary Ann. "Ladies, if you will stay with the cooking, I'd like to take Jessica to see her room."

"We'll take care of it, Maddie," Martha said.

Jessica felt Madeline's arm slip around

her waist as the older woman said, "Come, dear, let me show you your room." Madeline guided Jessica down the hall to an open door just beyond her sewing room. "Here we are, Jessica."

"Oh, Mrs. Farrington, it's lovely!"

The deep feather bed looked so tempting to her tired body that she could scarcely take her eyes off it. With an inward sigh she pulled her gaze away and took in the rest of the room. She spied her trunk, overnight bag, and boxes in the corner by the window.

The coverlet, drapes, and overstuffed chair were of the same material — a blue-and-white background with a sprinkling of soft mauve and pink flowers twined together by vines and leaves. A white eyelet bedskirt peeked from underneath the spread, and the same white eyelet was at the windows.

There was a gleaming oak dresser with a large mirror on the wall above it, a nightstand next to the bed, and a large clothespress in a corner. Next to the clothespress stood a washstand with a basin and a pitcher of water. Colorful hand towels hung on a small rack behind it. Flowered rugs in muted colors covered part of the gleaming hardwood, and various delicate accessories adorned the room.

Jessica took hold of Madeline's hand. "This is all so beautiful. Thank you so much for taking me in."

"Honey, this is your very own room for as long as you need to stay."

"I think I'll tell Josh this room has to go to our house, or the wedding's off!"

Madeline laughed. "I'm glad you like it, dear." She noticed Jessica eyeing the wash basin and pitcher.

"Would you like to freshen up?"

"If you don't mind. It's been a long, dusty trip from Ogden."

"All right. I'll get on back to the kitchen. There's plenty of time before dinner for you to change and get your breath."

"I won't take the time to change clothes, but I would like to wash the dust off my face. I'll be out in a few minutes."

Jessica poured water into the bowl on the washstand. As she pressed a towel to her face, she stepped toward the dresser. She looked into the gold-framed mirror and saw a tired girl with happy eyes. She patted and tidied her hair with damp hands and then began brushing the dust and wrinkles from her dress as best she could. Her eyes trailed to the overstuffed chair. She walked over to it and slowly lowered herself into its cushiony depths.

Almost instantly her head drooped and her eyes closed. She jerked upright and reluctantly left the plush chair, promising herself to come back to it as soon as possible. Moving back to the mirror, she gave her cheeks a good pinch to bring some color into them, then left the room.

Madeline was placing a steaming bowl of gravy on the table when Jessica entered the dining room.

"You can go into the parlor, honey," Madeline said. "Mary Ann's in there. Martha and I have it just about ready."

"Is there anything I can do?"

"It's all right, dear, thank you. You go ahead and join the others."

When Jessica entered the parlor, Josh went to her. "Honey, are you all right? You look a little peaked."

"I'm just a bit tired. Other than that, I'm fine."

"Dinner is served, folks!" Madeline announced by the parlor door.

A bouquet of summer flowers and tall, flickering candles graced the center of the dining room table. Madeline loved to cook and had outdone herself for this occasion. While the meal progressed, the Cornells asked about Jessica's family.

"Daniel is planning on going to college to prepare for a business career. David has his heart set on a military career and, like my father did, he's making plans to go to West Point."

"Commendable for both of them," Brett said.

"They're fine boys, Mr. Cornell. I'm very proud of them."

Jessica explained to the Farringtons that her father had been a major when she and her family were at Fort Union, and that at the Battle of Glorieta Pass, he was hit with shrapnel in his left leg which forced him to retire from military service. He was now a banker.

Her lips began to tremble when she explained her mother's situation and what the doctor in Denver was doing to help her. "Dr. Stafford spoke optimistically when he examined Mama recently. I appreciate his attempt to keep her hopes up, as well as the rest of the family's, but I'm . . . I'm really afraid Mama is not going to live a lot longer."

Josh slipped an arm around her shoulders.

"Jessica," Pastor Farrington said, "I'll put your mother on the prayer list at church, and on Sunday, I'll tell our people about her. I'm sure you agree there are no limitations on the Lord. If He wants to heal your mother of this disease, He can do it."

"Thank you, Pastor. Yes, I believe He can, and I appreciate your concern very much."

Farrington then said, "Josh, you and Jessica need to set your wedding date sometime soon. It would be good if the two of you were married for at least several months before you become pastor. This sweet girl needs some time to adjust to married life before she makes the big adjustment to being a pastor's wife."

"I understand, Pastor," Josh said.

"What I am about to say has to remain between us at this point," Farrington said as he ran his gaze over the faces at the table, "but I feel you should know. As Maddie and I have prayed about when to step aside, we feel the Lord is telling us to do it early next spring. We've come up with an exact date — the first Sunday of April. Both of us have peace from God that my last Sunday as pastor will be April 7."

Josh looked at Jessica. "We'll discuss it right away, Pastor, and come up with the wedding date."

"I'm ready," Jessica said with a smile.

When the meal was over, the men retired to the parlor, and the women cleared the table and washed dishes in the kitchen. Later, in order to give Josh and Jessica a few minutes alone, everyone but the young couple returned to the dining room. Josh and Jessica held hands as they sat on a love seat in the parlor.

"How about I take you to one of our fine eating establishments tomorrow evening?" Josh said. "I'll bring a calendar, and we can talk about the wedding date then."

"Sounds good to me." Jessica's eyes began to droop.

Josh touched her cheek. "You need to get to bed, sweet lady. I don't want to leave you, but I can tell you're completely worn out."

When the door closed behind the Cornell family, Jessica thanked the Farringtons once again for letting her stay in their home, then went to her room. She leaned against her closed door for a moment and whispered, "Thank You, Lord! Thank You for all Your blessings!"

She moved from the door and looked askance at her luggage, knowing she should unpack. Her jaded body rebelled at the idea. She gave in to her fatigue, opened her overnight bag, took out a clean night-gown, and moments later was dressed for bed. She unpinned her hair, gave it a quick brushing, then picked up her Bible and climbed into bed, propping pillows behind her.

She turned to Proverbs 31, and after a few minutes she closed the Bible and laid it on the nightstand. "That's what I want Josh to feel about me, dear Lord. Far above rubies."

Jessica snuggled into the feather tick. She felt a momentary wave of loneliness wash over her at the thought of her family, then prayed for God's blessing on them and gave thanks for the Master's tender care. Soon she was sleeping soundly as silver moonlight bathed her in its soft glow.

When Jessica awakened, she could tell by the sun's position in the sky that she had slept quite late. Madeline was in the kitchen when Jessica appeared.

"Good morning, dear," Madeline said. "I was just having my second cup of coffee. Come, sit down. I've got your breakfast simmering here on the stove."

"It's almost 'good afternoon,' Mrs. Farrington. I'm sorry. I never oversleep. I don't know what —"

"Honey, you were a very tired young lady last night. I didn't waken you because I knew you needed some extra sleep."

Jessica ate breakfast then wrote to her parents, letting them know she had arrived safely in Oregon City and had been warmly received by everyone. Madeline walked to the post office with her, and on the way, told her they would start "Pastor's Wife's School" when they returned home. For the entire afternoon, the two women sat in the parlor as Madeline began preparing Jessica for the responsibilities and sacrifices that lay ahead in her role as a pastor's wife.

That evening, Josh took Jessica to the Meadowlark Café for dinner and to discuss wedding plans.

"Is there a particular day of the week you'd like to get married?" he asked.

"I like Sunday afternoon weddings."

"Well, guess what? So do I."

"Then let's make it on a Sunday afternoon."

"We want to be proper in the length of our courtship, of course. Seems most folks think an engagement should last about six months. But since we have known each other for twelve years, I figure we don't have to wait that long. What do you think?"

"I was thinking the same thing."

"And you heard Pastor Farrington say we should be married for several months before I become pastor of the church." Josh handed her a small calendar he had taken from his pocket. "I figure a two-month courtship would be sufficient. We could get married, say, Sunday, August 27. That would be a little over two months from now. From the first of September to the seventh of April comes out to a few days over seven months. In my estimation, anything less than seven months wouldn't be 'several.' What do you think?"

Jessica studied the calendar for a moment, turning it over to look at the year 1873. She smiled and said, "Oh, I agree a thousand percent. Anything less than seven months wouldn't be several months. You are so right, darling." Her eyes were sparkling.

Josh reached across the table and took her hand. "Then we'll tell Pastor that we want our wedding on Sunday, August 27."

They left the café and took a moonlight walk outside of town.

"Mrs. Farrington and I started what she

calls 'Pastor's Wife's School' today."

"So soon?"

"There's more to learn than I ever imagined. She's such a precious lady, Josh. I know what she teaches me will be invaluable."

"God bless her. I'm sure thankful for Pastor Farrington, too. They're both wonderful people. So when is your next session?"

"Tomorrow."

"Morning or afternoon?"

"Afternoon. Why?"

"Well, I haven't told you about my Saturday morning job."

"You mean on top of working three days for your father and three days for the church, plus Sundays at the camp, you have a job on Saturday mornings?"

Josh's eyes widened, and he snapped his fingers. "Oh, Jessica. There's something I meant to tell you in one of my letters, but I forgot. Remember I told you about Casey Harmon?"

"Mm-hmm. I've prayed for his salvation, as you asked."

"Well, he did get saved!"

"Praise the Lord!"

"You know how some people get saved, and some people really get saved? Casey really got saved. I've already had him preach at the camp. He's doing great. I can't wait for you to meet him."

"I'll look forward to it."

"And something else. Since Casey got saved, he and Mary Ann have struck up a romance. It wouldn't surprise me if things worked out between them and they end up married. I think the Lord may call Casey to preach."

"Wouldn't that be something! Josh, you were going to tell me about your Saturday morning job."

"Well, yes, but it's not exactly a job. I'm working off a debt I owe."

"What kind of debt, darling?"

"A debt to a man who's in heaven, and to his widow, who lives here in town. Her name is Lydia Price. Her husband was the town's physician until he died quite suddenly last August."

"Oh, that's too bad. And the debt?"

Josh explained how loving and generous the Prices had been to him, then said, "The debt is a debt of love. I work at paying this debt by doing yard work and odd jobs for Lydia on Saturday mornings."

"Josh, you're so wonderful," Jessica said, reaching up to caress his cheek. "The Bible speaks about caring for widows. I'm glad you're willing to take care of Mrs. Price."

"I'd like you to go with me in the morning to meet her."

"Oh, I'd love to."

It was just after eight o'clock Saturday morning when Josh and Jessica stood before Lydia Price's home. Jessica marveled at the beauty of the huge two-story house, with its corner turret, lace curtains in each window, the wide wraparound porch, and a yard full of trees, well-trimmed bushes, and flower gardens.

"What a massive house, Josh! Is Mrs. Price going to keep living in it? I'd think she'd want something smaller."

"I don't know if she's planning to sell it. She's never said anything about moving."

Jessica looked around the yard as they approached the front porch. "You've done a great job on the shrubbery. Did you plant the flowers?"

"Lydia helped me. She pretty well takes care of the flowers."

They moved onto the porch and found the door open. "Hello, Lydia!" Josh called through the screen door. "It's Josh! I've got her with me!"

Jessica looked at him. "She knows about us?"

"Mm-hmm."

They heard footsteps, and when Lydia opened the screen door, her smile was lustrous. "Oh, Josh! She's just as beautiful as you said she was. Hello, Jessica. Come in."

Jessica could hardly take her eyes off Lydia as she passed through the door. She was a beautiful woman. Her emerald green eyes were soft and warm, and she had styled her light brown hair in an upsweep that brought out her femininity. There was a slight hint of gray at her temples.

"Jessica . . . Lydia," Josh said, "you both know about each other; now meet each other."

Lydia embraced the younger woman, saying, "I'm so happy for you and Josh. He told me how you first met at Fort Union when you were children. I think it's wonderful how the Lord planned your lives and brought you together after all this time."

Josh excused himself, saying he would get to work on the yard. Lydia took Jessica into the kitchen and poured them both a cup of coffee. While they sat at the table, she asked about the Smith family.

Jessica told Lydia about Daniel and

David and their plans for the future. She explained that her father had been a major in the army until he was seriously wounded in the Civil War and had to retire from the military. He was now a loan officer in a Denver bank. And Jessica told Lydia about her mother's consumption, and of how she prayed for her healing several times a day.

"Oh, I'm so sorry to hear about your mother. I'll put her on my prayer list. What's her name?"

"Carrie. She's a wonderful lady, Mrs. Price. It means a lot to me that you will pray for her. I know the Lord can heal her."

"I'll join you in praying for her healing. Jesus is the Great Physician, and He can do it. Carrie Smith will be lifted to the throne of grace every day, I promise."

"Thank you so much. Mrs. Price, Josh told me about your husband being taken last August. I'm so sorry."

Lydia's eyes turned misty. "I miss him terribly. But the Lord never makes mistakes. He had His reasons for taking Clay to be with Him."

"Of course. But I'm sure you're lonely."

"At times. I stay as busy as I can so I don't have a lot of time to think about being alone. I teach a girls' Sunday school class, and I teach children's Bible clubs in various homes as a ministry of our church, year-round." Lydia saw Jessica's eyes light up, and she smiled. "You seem very interested in what I'm talking about."

"Oh, I am! I taught a Sunday school class at my church in Denver. I loved it."

"Oh, Jessica, I need an assistant to help me with my Sunday school class and with the Bible clubs. Would you consider being that person?"

"I sure will! Josh and I are going to meet with Pastor Farrington at the church this afternoon — to set our wedding date and talk about my joining the church tomorrow."

"Good! Then I'll talk to pastor after the service about you helping me. I know he'll be very happy about this."

"Me, too!" Jessica rubbed her palms together with excitement. "I'll still help you when I'm the pastor's wife, too."

"Oh, praise the Lord for answered prayer! So what date are you and Josh planning for the wedding?"

"The afternoon of Sunday, August 27."

"Marvelous! You two look so good together."

Jessica giggled. "That's because the Lord

made us for each other."

On Saturday afternoon, the happy couple met with Pastor Farrington, and they set the date for the wedding. They discussed Jessica's joining the church, and Farrington told her how glad he was to have her become a member.

The next day, the people of the church welcomed Jessica to the services, and when she joined the church, they welcomed her again. She was especially happy to meet Casey Harmon, who was now assisting a teacher in a boys' class . . . and had Mary Ann Cornell at his side.

In the afternoon, Jessica went to the lumber camp with Josh, Casey, and the musicians. The lumbermen and their wives, who had a great love for Josh, gave her a royal welcome.

As the weeks passed, Madeline Farrington continued to give Jessica all the help she could to prepare her for the role of pastor's wife. She warned Jessica that her youth would be a problem at times, but laughed as she said the only way to get over being young was to live to get older. Madeline had insisted that Jessica address her as Maddie. The two were becoming close friends.

Another relationship was growing strong — the relationship between Jessica and Lydia. Jessica dearly loved working with Lydia in both the Sunday school class and the Bible clubs. The more time they spent together, the more they loved each other and the stronger the bond became between them. Jessica was now addressing Lydia by her first name, as Lydia had requested.

They made Saturday mornings their lesson preparation time, and then both Josh and Jessica ate lunch with Lydia when the work was done.

One Saturday morning in late July, the two women were sitting at the kitchen table, Bibles open in front of them. They were teaching a series on the Ten Commandments to the girls' Sunday school class, and the coming Sunday would be on the Fifth Commandment.

Lydia read the verse aloud, and when she looked up, she saw tears in Jessica's eyes. "Honey, what's the matter?"

"I miss those two people I'm supposed to honor."

Lydia left her chair and hugged Jessica. "I know it's hard to be away from them, especially with your dear mother so ill."

"I know I'm supposed to be here. The Lord has His hand on Josh and me, but I sure do miss Mama and Daddy."

"Sure you do, honey." Lydia kissed her cheek. "Believe me, I'll do everything I can to make up for the mother side."

"Oh, Lydia, that means more than I can tell you." Jessica sniffed. "You are so much like a mother to me."

Lydia pulled back so she could look at Jessica through her own tear-filled eyes. "I learned early in my marriage that I would never be able to bear children. I've never had the joy of being a mother. Could . . . could I — Well, I would never presume to take your mother's place, but since she's in Colorado and I'm here, could I be your Oregon mother?"

Jessica hugged her. "Oh yes! I'd love that!" She eased back in the chair. "I call my mother Mama. Could I call you Mom?"

"You sure can, honey! You sure can!"

When the tears were dried and the two women were ready to continue working on the lesson, Jessica looked across the table at Lydia and said, "Mom?"

A wide smile graced Lydia's mouth. "Yes, dear?"

"My heart has been heavy for you. I know you handle it quite well, but at times you seem so lonely. With Dr. Price gone, there have to be times when this house seems empty. Have you ever considered marrying again?"

"Oh, I've thought about it. In fact, that man of yours has brought it up. He seems to think the Lord is going to send some knight in shining armor into my life who will sweep me off my feet and take away my loneliness."

Jessica smiled. They could both hear Josh outside in the yard, trimming bushes.

"If God has a plan like that," Lydia said, "He will bring it to pass at the right time, like He always does. I have to get over Clay first, and that's going to take a while. Jessica, he was a wonderful Christian man, and a good husband. I still miss him terribly."

"I know you do, Mom. I wish I could've known him."

Lydia thought about sharing with Jessica that she went through a crushing experience when another man she was engaged to was killed in the Mexican War. But after a moment, she decided it would sound as though she wanted sympathy, so she let it pass.

22

Grant Smith's sons stood beside him as he leaned over Carrie's hospital bed, holding her hand.

Carrie looked up at Grant with dull, dark-circled eyes. "Please don't write Jessica about this, darling. It's just a little setback. I'll get better. There's no reason to worry her."

"All right, honey. When I write her this week, I won't tell her you're in the hospital. But if you're still in next week —"

"I won't be. I'll be home in a few days. I know you believe Jessica has a right to know what's going on here, but there's no reason to upset her needlessly. You can tell her I was in the hospital after I'm home again."

Grant leaned over and kissed her cheek. "All right, we'll do it your way. The boys and I will be back this evening."

Both of Carrie's sons kissed her, then left her hospital room. When they were outside, Daniel said, "Dad, I'm trying to keep an optimistic attitude about Mama, but I've got this ball of ice in the middle of my chest."

"Me too," David said. "I don't think she's going to live much longer."

"We've kept your mother in prayer every day. We mustn't give up hope. We've got to keep on praying."

Josh and Jessica made plans for the wedding ceremony, using many of Madeline's wise suggestions. They could hardly contain their excitement as they talked of life after they were married.

Jessica had been working on their house during the daytime, putting up new drapes and curtains and adding little changes in each room. Josh loved what she was doing and was eager for the day they could make the house their home.

Late on a Thursday afternoon in early August, Jessica was working in the kitchen when she heard Josh call from the front door, "Hello-o-o! I was told that the most beautiful woman in the world is in this house. Where is she?"

Jessica appeared in the short hallway with a scrub cloth in her hand. "She left. Will I do?"

Josh laughed as he took her in his arms. "She did not leave; she's right here in my arms!" After he kissed her, Josh said, "Where have you been scrubbing this time?"

"Come into the kitchen. I'll show you."

After Josh bragged on how much cleaner the kitchen looked, he took an envelope out of his hip pocket and handed it to her. "I stopped by the post office for the mail. Here's a letter from your dad."

Josh watched Jessica closely as she unfolded the letter and read it silently. After reading a few lines, her expression changed.

"Something wrong?"

"Mama's been in the hospital. She's home now and is doing better. Daddy says that, at Mama's request, he didn't write to tell me she'd taken a turn for the worse."

"Well, praise the Lord she's better."

"Daddy says they'll all be with us in spirit on August 27. He thanks me for the letters and for those little notes you sometimes add at the bottom. He says they're very encouraging to Mama. He closes by saying they all send their love and that he loves and misses his 'sweet baby girl.' "

"You have a wonderful family, honey," Josh said. "I sure wish they could be here for the wedding." As he spoke, he pulled a second letter from his hip pocket. "Here's one from your best friend."

"Brenda? Oh, you didn't tell me you had a letter from Brenda!"

Josh shrugged. "Sure I did. Just now."

"Joshua Cornell, you are impossible!" She laughed as she took the envelope and tore it open.

The letter from Brenda Simmons was brief. When Jessica had finished reading it, she said, "Josh, she's such a sweetie. She and Gil were so glad to hear that we'd set the wedding date, and wish they could be here. And look at this."

She brought a slip of paper into Josh's view.

"A check?"

"Yes. A wedding gift. A hundred dollars, made out to Mr. or Mrs. Joshua Cornell. Since there is no Mrs. Joshua Cornell yet, you'll have to cash it."

"Oh, good! I need a new hat, and a new pair of boots, and a couple of new shirts, and —"

"We'll use it to buy some more things for the house that I talked to you about."

Josh threw up his hands. "My daddy told me it would be like this. Poor, helpless men henpecked before they even become husbands!"

Jessica put a mock scowl on her face.

"Poor, helpless men, eh? Well, let's see if you're helpless if I want to kiss you."

"Oh yes, I'm at your mercy."

Josh got his kiss.

The weeks passed quickly for the young couple. The Lord was blessing their church work and the services at the lumber camp. Casey Harmon did so well at preaching that Josh was now alternating with him regularly on Sunday afternoons. Mary Ann faithfully attended the camp services. It was evident that she and Casey had fallen in love.

On the night of August 26, Jessica slept fitfully. Toward morning she came groggily awake and turned over in the bed. She barely opened one eye and looked toward the window. It was still dark outside. She was about to drift off to sleep again when her eyes popped wide open. She sat straight up and gasped in a low whisper, "It's my wedding day!"

A smile lit her rosy face. She stretched her arms and legs, then slid out of bed and donned her robe. She padded carefully to the nightstand and found the small pile of matches next to the lantern. She fired the wick, and the room filled with a gentle yellow glow. The clock on the wall showed that it was only five minutes after three o'clock.

Jessica eased into the chair beside her bed, her thoughts filled with visions of the wedding and all the preparations that had been made. Suddenly a bittersweet melancholia stole through her as she thought of her family, and especially of her ailing mother. Memories of her growing-up years flooded her mind, and she cherished the closeness each member of her family had always enjoyed with one another. How she longed to have them with her on this most special day!

Tears hovered on her long lashes then slid down her cheeks, dropping onto her folded hands. She gave herself permission to mourn for a short time, then bowed her head and sought God's grace and comfort. When the "peace that passeth all understanding" flooded her heart and mind, she thanked her Lord for His tender comfort and told Him she loved Him from the depths of her soul. She took a handkerchief from the pocket of her robe and dried all traces of tears from her face.

She smiled as she recalled the wedding practice the previous night. Josh had chosen Casey Harmon to be his best man.

Three other young married men from the camp, who had been saved under Josh's preaching, were his groomsmen.

Lydia Price had joyfully consented to be Jessica's matron of honor. She looked dazzling, even at the practice. Mary Ann Cornell and two other young ladies in the church made up the bridesmaids. A seven-year-old boy and his six-year-old sister — children of one of the church families — were ring bearer and flower girl.

Jessica had chosen Dr. Emmett Fraser, one of the deacons in the church, to give her away.

Her smile widened. Everyone had done a beautiful job, and she had no doubt they would follow through in the same way at the ceremony.

The church was decorated with brilliant summer flowers. The soft flames of gleaming white candles sent out a muted glow over the faces of friends and family who gathered to witness the happy occasion. The pews filled rapidly while the organist softly played hymns. People from the lumber camp were there, as well as townspeople.

Madeline Farrington and Lydia Price attended Jessica in a small chamber off the vestibule. Jessica's hair, wedding dress, and veil looked exquisite. Madeline excused herself to make sure the rest of the wedding party was ready.

While the faint strains of organ music filtered into the room, Jessica took a final look at herself in the full-length mirror on the wall. Lydia, dressed in deep green silk, appeared in the mirror behind her.

"Mom, I'm sort of shaky inside," Jessica said, drawing in a deep breath.

"That goes with being a bride, honey. Enjoy it."

Jessica met Lydia's eyes in the mirror and grinned. Then looking at herself again, she said, "Guess I'm as ready as I can be."

There was a tap at the door, and Lydia moved quickly to open it a few inches. She could see people filing into the auditorium as Madeline said, "Lydia, there's someone out here who would like to have a few seconds with Jessica."

Lydia peered past Madeline and saw a young couple standing there. The young woman moved close and said, "Ma'am, I'm Jessica's best friend. I only need a half minute to let her know I'm here."

Jessica heard the familiar voice and darted to the door. "Brenda! I didn't know you were coming!"

"May I see you a moment?"

"Of course!"

Brenda motioned over her shoulder. "Jessica, that's Gil."

Gil smiled but made no move to come in. "Hi, Jessica! I'll see you later."

"Yes! Nice to meet you, Gil."

Brenda came inside the room, where the best friends embraced for a long moment; then Jessica introduced Brenda to "Mom" Price, saying that Lydia had been like a mother to her ever since she arrived in Oregon City.

"I'll go join the rest of the bridal party," Lydia said. "You know when to come out."

"Yes." Jessica hugged Lydia and thanked her for her help.

When the door closed again, Brenda said, "You look beautiful! I know you need a few minutes to settle yourself, so I'll slide on out of here too."

Jessica's eyes turned misty. "Oh, Brenda, thank you for coming. What a wonderful surprise!"

"I told Gil he had to bring me, or I wouldn't cook another meal for him! So . . . here I am!"

Jessica giggled, hugging her friend again.

"I'd better get out there," Brenda said, "or Gil and I won't be able to find a seat."

When the door closed behind Brenda, Jessica remained standing in the middle of the room, her hands clasped tight. She was a vision of loveliness in pale ivory satin trimmed in fine lace. Because her mother had helped her make the dress, she almost felt Carrie's presence.

Jessica's jet-black hair was gathered high on her head with ringlets cascading down the back. The simple gossamer veil fell gracefully over her hair and the shimmering satin of her gown.

She moved to the curtained window overlooking the side street and looked out through the filmy material into the brilliant sunshine.

"Mama . . . Daddy . . . I know you're thinking of me right now. And though you can't hear my voice, you can hear my heart. I love you both. Thank you for raising me in the nurture and admonition of the Lord. Thank you for teaching me, from as far back as I can remember, about Jesus and His love, and how He went to the cross to make a way of salvation for me. Thank you for loving each other, and for the love you always demonstrated to my brothers and me. You've always set a good example of what a marriage can and should be, and with God's grace and guidance, my marriage will be as sweet and fulfilling as yours. I love you both with all my heart."

After a moment of silence — except for the low strains of the organ coming from the auditorium — Jessica lifted a prayer toward heaven, then moved toward the door. As she picked up her small white Bible tied with ivory satin streamers and topped with a bouquet, her ears caught the change in tempo of the organ music, signaling the bridal party to get in place. Jessica opened the door to find everyone in their assigned positions, with Madeline looking on.

Dr. Emmett Fraser was there, wearing a wide smile. "My, don't you look lovely," he said.

Jessica thanked him, blushing, then turned her attention to her matron of honor. Lydia looked at her with a question in her kind eyes. Jessica nodded, and a gentle smile skimmed her face, lighting her dark brown eyes from within.

Jessica took hold of Dr. Fraser's arm and said, "Thank you for doing this."

"I am deeply honored to have the privilege."

The organ slid into the gentle strains of the wedding march, and Madeline told the ushers to open the doors. As the doors swung open, every wedding guest turned to look.

When Jessica and Dr. Fraser passed by Madeline, Jessica whispered, "Thank you, Maddie," then stopped at the threshold to wait for her cue.

As the procession made its way down the aisle, Jessica looked past them to Josh, who stood with his groomsmen. It was like a dream. How many times had a scene like this passed across the screen of her mind? But this was no dream. The God of heaven had made her dream a reality. *Thank You, Lord!* she said in her heart. *Thank You!*

The bridesmaids and the matron of honor moved up the steps onto the platform, where the silver-haired pastor stood, a beaming smile on his face. When the only man left on the floor at the altar was the groom, the organ swelled in volume, ringing out the familiar notes to "Here Comes the Bride."

Jessica began the long walk down the aisle, her hand resting in the crook of Dr. Fraser's arm. Flower girl and ring bearer preceded her and her escort.

The guests rose from their seats. Jessica slowly placed one satin-clad foot in front of the other. She blinked when her eyes met Brenda's through the veil. What a joy to have her best friend come to her wedding, all the way from Nevada!

Soon they were near the front, and the two children were climbing the steps together. Jessica's eyes met Josh's, and a radiant smile lit up her face, reflecting the joy shining on his. Jessica finished the walk without taking her gaze from Josh's face.

The bride was given to the groom by Dr. Fraser, and Jessica placed her hand in the crook of Josh's arm. Together they ascended the steps to the platform where the wedding party and the pastor stood.

The ceremony performed by Pastor Farrington was a touching one, in which the Lord Jesus Christ was exalted and the relationship between a husband and wife likened to the relationship between Christ and His church.

When the ceremony was over, the young unmarried women gathered for the toss of the bride's bouquet. Mary Ann Cornell caught it.

As the weeks passed, Pastor Farrington spent a great deal of time teaching Josh about being a pastor. He wanted the young man to be as prepared as possible for the load he would shoulder come April of next year.

Jessica and Lydia were growing closer as they taught their Bible clubs and the Sunday school class. Jessica also spent many hours each week with Madeline, making calls on the sick and learning from Madeline's example about being a pastor's wife.

More than anything, Jessica loved being Mrs. Joshua Cornell. Her longtime dream had become a reality, and she was an excellent wife and homemaker. Josh worked long and hard, and her deep desire was to give him a sanctuary when he entered their front door and closed out the world. There was such joy in her heart that she carried out her household chores singing or humming thanks to God for His goodness. Though often weary from her work, she felt a contentment in jobs well done.

She listened intently for Josh's step on the porch each evening as she prepared supper. Once he was home, all was right with her world. Jessica loved her life, though loneliness for her family often crept in. The newlyweds fell deeper in love each day and enjoyed married life to the fullest.

Jessica went regularly with Josh and the rest of the gospel team to the Sunday afternoon services at the lumber camp. Mary Ann also went, and she and Jessica often sang solos and duets before the sermon.

The only real cloud on Jessica's horizon was her mother's lingering illness. Letters continued to go back and forth between Jessica and her father. The Smiths were glad to know that she was superbly happy being married to Josh and serving the Lord in Oregon.

In mid-October a letter came from Daniel announcing that he was getting married in December to a girl in the church whose family had moved to Denver from Iowa. Grant had mentioned Susan Burke in a couple of his recent letters, so Jessica and Josh were not surprised to learn that wedding bells were in the offing. In the same envelope was a letter from David, telling them he would be graduating from high school a year early and would soon be writing to his congressman about an appointment to West Point. David closed his letter by saying they really needed to be praying for Mama. She was getting worse again.

A few days later, another letter came from Grant. The Cornells were at the supper table when Jessica read the letter to Josh. When the tears started down her cheeks, Josh left his chair and knelt beside her, saying, "Sweetheart, I'm sorry. I wish I could take the pain from your heart."

"Oh, Josh. I have so hoped that the Lord was going to make Mama better."

Josh held her for a long moment, then said, "I want to show you a verse of Scripture that has stood out in my mind for the past few days."

He hurried to the cupboard, where they kept a Bible for reading at the table. He knelt beside her again, flipped pages, and laid the Bible before her. "Psalm 18:30. Can you see to read it?"

Jessica wiped the tears from her eyes. "I can now."

"Read it to me."

" 'As for God, his way is perfect: the word of the Lord is tried: he is a buckler to all those that trust in him.' "

"We have to trust God to work His will in our lives and in the lives of our loved ones. Only His will is what's right for us. Isn't that right?"

Jessica met his loving gaze. "Yes."

"We have prayed continuously for your mother's healing, haven't we?"

"Yes," she said, sniffing.

"Well, honey, our precious God is now testing us to see if we will trust that His way is perfect, even if it doesn't look perfect to us. Does that make sense?"

It took her a moment to reply. "Yes, it makes sense. The Lord wants us to believe Him and His Word, in spite of circumstances and what we think is best."

"That's it. Without faith, it is impossible to please Him. He wants our faith in regard to your mother. We must trust that His way is perfect and believe that He will do what is best and right. Let's talk to Him right now about this."

When Josh had finished praying, Jessica wrapped her arms around him and said, "I love you, Josh. Thank you for showing me this verse. It has been a tremendous help."

Once again, Josh folded her into his strong arms. "Sweetheart, I love you more than you will ever know, and when you hurt, I hurt."

Jessica looked toward heaven and said, "Lord Jesus, thank You for giving me this wonderful man."

23

Autumn in Oregon took on a wintry look as November passed into December. Early in the third week of December, Josh and Jessica Cornell received a letter, written by both Daniel Smith and his new bride. He and Susan thanked them for the lovely wedding gift, and Susan told them how much she looked forward to the day she could meet Daniel's sister and brother-in-law.

Daniel informed them that Carrie had not been able to attend his wedding. She was simply too weak to leave her bed.

Christmas came and went, as did New Year's Day. A letter from Grant in early February held a note of encouragement. Carrie had actually been out of bed and on her feet some. Bessie Williams was taking good care of her, and Dr. Stafford seemed encouraged.

This news eased some of Jessica's concern for her mother, in the midst of preparations for Pastor Farrington's retirement and Josh's installation as pastor of the church.

On March 29, 1873, Jessica went to the

general store in Oregon City for a few groceries. On the way home, she stopped at the post office and was given a letter from her father.

When Josh came home at suppertime, he saw the glum look on his wife's face. "What's wrong, honey?" he said as he hugged her.

She leaned her head against his chest. "A letter came from Daddy today."

"Your mama?"

"She's back in the hospital. Daddy says we shouldn't be alarmed, but he felt we should know. The letter was written on the twenty-first. He said she was stable. But that was eight days ago."

Josh kissed the top of her head. "I think you should go to her, sweetheart."

Jessica pulled back to look in his eyes. "I can't, Josh. You're going to become pastor a week from Sunday. I must be here with you. If I only knew —"

"Knew what?"

"If Mama was still stable, or even still in the hospital."

"I'll send a wire in the morning and ask your father to give us a quick answer."

"Oh, thank you. It will help if I know she's not worse. But Josh, even if she is, I must be here when you become pastor."

"Let's see what we can find out tomorrow."

Grant's wire came back late in the afternoon the next day. Carrie was still in the hospital but was holding her own. Dr. Stafford was watching her closely. Grant would send a wire if there was any significant change. He also told Josh how proud he was that he was about to become pastor of the church.

Relieved that her mother was not worse, Jessica said, "April 7 is going to be such a wonderful day, Josh."

"Honey, I appreciate you so much. And I'm glad you want to be here for the big day. But if your mother gets worse, you're heading for Denver immediately after your husband becomes pastor."

April 7 came, and after the Sunday evening service, Lester Farrington officially resigned. It was only a formality, but in the business meeting the church voted 100 percent to call Joshua Cornell as their new pastor.

On the following Saturday, Josh and Jessica returned to their house after eating lunch with Lydia and found the Western Union messenger on their porch. Josh signed for the telegram, and the messenger went on his way.

When they were inside the house, Josh looked at his wife's pale face and said, "Do you want me to open it?"

Jessica closed her eyes and nodded.

Josh's shoulders slumped as he read the message.

"Your mama has taken a severe turn for the worse, honey. She's dying. The doctor says it's only a matter of days. Your daddy is asking if both of us, or at least you, can come. He says to hurry if you want to see your mother while she's still alive."

Josh grabbed Jessica as her knees gave way and hugged her to himself.

"Honey, we'll both go," Josh said. "I'll talk to Brother Farrington, explain the situation, and ask if he will look after the church while I'm gone."

"Oh, thank you, Josh. I can face this much easier if you're with me."

"I'll go see him right now. But before I do, I'll run and bring Lydia to be with you. Can you stay alone long enough for me to bring her?"

She nodded. "It will really help if I can talk to Mom right now."

The two women were seated on the couch when Josh returned home. Lydia had an arm around Jessica, whose eyes were swollen from weeping.

"Everything's set," he said quietly. "Brother Farrington will look after the church while we're gone. He asked if I minded if he switched off with Casey, since Casey's proving to be quite a preacher. I agreed to that, of course."

"God has His hand on that young man," Lydia said.

"No question about it."

"He's been a blessing to you, darling," Jessica said. "It's wonderful to see one of your own sons in the Lord develop like he has."

"For sure," said Josh, sitting on a chair, facing them. "Honey, I went over to the Wells Fargo office and set us up for the trip. The first stage to Ogden is Monday morning at eight o'clock. We'll be in Ogden on Wednesday in time to catch the late train to Cheyenne City. We'll take the morning train to Denver on Thursday and be there at 10:45."

"Thank you for going to all this trouble."

Josh dropped to one knee in front of Jessica and took her hand. "Sweetheart, it's no trouble. You're my wife, and that sweet lady in Denver is very special to me. We'll get to her just as soon as possible." Josh turned to Lydia. "And you are very special to me too. Thank you for being so good to Jessica."

"You're welcome, Josh. I love Jessica, and it's my privilege to be of whatever help I can."

That evening, Josh and Jessica went to his parents' home and told them the situation. While Brett led them in prayer, Mary Ann and Martha placed their arms around Jessica.

From the pulpit the next day, Josh explained the situation to the congregation. Everyone was sympathetic, and at the close of both the morning and evening services, the people passed by at the door and spoke words of love and comfort to their pastor's wife, and told both of them they would be holding them up in prayer.

Josh and Jessica arrived in Denver Thursday morning on schedule, rented a horse and buggy, and hurried to Mile High Hospital. Josh kept a solid hold on Jessica's hand as they approached the desk. He greeted the lady behind it and said cautiously, "Ma'am, we're here from Oregon to see a patient, Mrs. Carrie Smith. Is she . . . ?"

"Mrs. Smith is in room 112, sir," the receptionist said. "Her family is with her at the moment."

"Thank you," Josh said, and led a trembling Jessica past the desk into the hall.

They came to the room, and Josh paused before the door. "Are you all right, honey?"

Jessica took a deep breath, then nodded. "Yes. Jesus is very near."

Josh put an arm around her waist and pushed open the door.

Grant and David were on one side of the bed; Daniel and Susan on the other.

Tears filled Grant's eyes as he rushed to his daughter and put his arms around her. "Sweetheart, I'm so glad you're here!" he said, keeping his voice to a whisper. "I've been telling your mama you were coming. She's asleep right now, but we'll wake her shortly."

While Grant and Jessica were talking in low tones, David welcomed Josh and introduced him to his wife.

After Jessica had hugged her brothers, she turned to the sister-in-law she had never met and whispered, "Hello, Susan. It's so nice to finally meet you."

"Nice to meet you, too," said Susan, and they held on to each other for a long moment.

Jessica kept her arm around Susan as she looked at her father. "How's she doing, Daddy?"

"She's worse. We really didn't expect her to be here this long."

Jessica let go of Susan and moved to the bed. Josh drew up beside her. She bit down hard on her lower lip as she looked at her dying mother. Carrie was so tiny now, she hardly made a bump in the blanket covering her body. Her once round, rosy cheeks were sunken, and the skin covering them was waxy pale.

Carrie stirred, groaning as she opened her pain-filled eyes. Her lips had a faint blue cast, but when she focused on the face of her daughter, they widened in a smile. "Oh, my precious Jessica!" she said, raising a hand toward her daughter.

Jessica smiled directly into her mother's eyes as she clasped the shaky hand. "Hello, sweet Mama," she said softly. "I love you."

"Daddy said you were coming."

"Josh is here too, Mama."

Carrie's dull eyes found Josh's face as he bent low and said, "Hello, Mama."

Carrie swallowed with difficulty and pressed another smile on her lips. "Josh. I'm so glad . . . you're here."

Carrie looked into Jessica's eyes. "I . . . I had to wait till —" Her words were interrupted with a hacking cough. The others gathered close to the bed.

When Carrie stopped coughing, she went around the circle, telling each one in a voice barely above a whisper that she loved them. Each one spoke in turn, saying the same to her. As Josh took Jessica in his arms, he could tell the Lord was giving her inward peace and strength.

Carrie beckoned Grant to move closer. He bent over her, inches from her face. She lifted a thin, trembling hand and caressed his face. "I love you, darling."

Grant blinked at his tears and took the hand in his own. He raised it to his lips and placed a kiss in her palm. Never taking his eyes from hers, he whispered, "I love you, my precious."

With a wan smile on her face, Carrie peacefully closed her eyes and slipped from her husband's hands into the hands of hovering angels, who carried her into the glorious presence of her loving Father on high.

There was a long pause as the family stood beside the bed, weeping quietly. Then Grant tucked the frail, lifeless hand under the covers and said, "She's with Jesus now."

The family collected in a circle, arms around each other. Grant turned to Jessica. "I know what your mother meant to say when the cough interrupted. She had to wait till she saw you one more time before she could go to heaven."

Jessica hugged her father tight. "I'm so glad the Lord let Josh and me come. We have all eternity to be with her when we meet her in heaven, but these were precious moments. But I can't wish her back, Daddy. She's with Jesus, and she's out of this frail body."

Josh and Jessica took a liking to Daniel's wife, Susan, who fit into the family perfectly. They were all a great comfort to Grant when the funeral was held two days later. Josh had a part in the service, which was a special blessing to Jessica.

Daniel and Susan would be leaving for Ohio within a couple of weeks. Susan had an uncle who owned a large manufacturing company in Columbus and had offered Daniel a good job so he could go to school and get his business degree.

David had just received word of his appointment to the United States Military Academy at West Point and would be leaving for New York in August.

On the night before they would begin their journey home, Josh and Jessica sat in the Smith parlor with Grant. Colorado's nights were still quite cold in April, and a fire was crackling in the fireplace.

"Dad," said Josh, "Jessica and I have been discussing something, and we'd like to talk to you about it."

"Sure, son, what is it?"

"Well, since Daniel and Susan are going to Ohio, and David will be going to West Point . . . we'd like for you to come to Oregon City and live with us."

"You mean you'd want your father-in-law living under your roof?"

"Sure. We've got a spare bedroom."

"We'd love to have you, Daddy," Jessica said.

"Aw, kids, I'd just be underfoot. If I came, I'd buy my own place."

"Well, that would be all right too, Daddy."

"But I sure can't retire. I'm not even fifty, let alone retirement age."

"That wouldn't be a problem, Dad," Josh said. "I'm sure my father would give you a job in the office at the mill. Or if you wanted to stay in banking, I'm sure you'd have no problem getting a good job in one of Oregon City's banks. We'd sure love to have you close to us."

"We sure would," Jessica said. "What do you say?"

"I'd love that. Of course, I'll have to settle my affairs in Denver first, including the sale of this house. It might take several months."

"But you'll pray about it and consider it?" Jessica said.

"I will. I actually like the idea. I don't think it will take a whole lot of prayer or very much considering. I'll keep in touch with you about it."

Josh and Jessica arrived in Oregon City on a Saturday afternoon. On Sunday, the people of the church welcomed their pastor and his wife home, and spoke their condolences when they learned that Jessica's mother had died.

On Monday evening, Martha Cornell cooked a nice meal and invited the younger Cornells, as well as the Farringtons, Lydia Price, and Casey Harmon for dinner.

While they were eating, Jessica said, "Josh and I have been so busy since we got back that we haven't had a chance to tell you the news about Daddy."

"What news is that?" Brett asked.

There was a trill in Jessica's voice as she said, "He's coming here to live!"

"Really?" Martha said.

"He sure is," Josh said. "Jessica and I talked to him about coming here, and I don't think there's any question he'll do it. He'll need a job, Dad. I told him you'd make a place for him in the office at the mill, or that he could get a job at one of the banks."

Brett chuckled. "With his banking experience, it won't be hard, the way the banks are growing. Or if he'd like to work for me, I most certainly can use him."

"This is wonderful," Lydia said. "Jessica, I'll look forward to meeting your father."

"Oh, you'll love him, Mom. Daddy's a real prince, even if I do say so myself."

"The rest of us can attest to that, honey," Martha said.

"So, any idea when he'll be here?" Brett asked.

"He definitely won't come till after David leaves for West Point. And then, of course, he'll have to sell his house. Anyway, it sure will be great when he gets here."

Josh and Jessica had brought Lydia in their buggy to the Cornells' house for supper. As they drove across town afterward to take Lydia home, Jessica spoke of how happy she would be to have her father living in Oregon City. Josh also said how much he loved Dad Smith and what a blessing it would be to have him near.

As they turned the corner of the block where Lydia's house was, Jessica spoke of how much she would miss her mother, and she began to cry. Josh pulled the buggy to a halt in front of the big white house, and Lydia said, "Before I go in, Jessica, I want to say something to you."

"Certainly, Mom," Jessica said, using a handkerchief to dab at her eyes.

Lydia cupped Jessica's face in her hands and looked at her by the light of the porch lamp. "You've honored me by allowing me to be your Oregon mom . . . and I have loved it. Now that —" She cleared her throat. "Now that the Lord has taken your precious mother to be with Him . . . could I be a little *more* mom to you?"

Jessica put her arms around her, kissed her cheek, and said, "Oh, yes! A little more mom . . . I like the sound of that."

Both women were shedding tears as Lydia waved from the front door and the buggy drove away.

Life went back to normal in Oregon City. Josh and Jessica were happy in their ministry, in spite of its trials and pressures. Souls were coming to the Lord, both at the church and the lumber camp. Christians were maturing, and the church was growing.

In mid-May, the Farringtons bid their friends in Oregon City good-bye and moved to Wisconsin, where their oldest son and his family lived.

On the last Sunday night in May, Casey walked the aisle after Pastor Josh Cornell's sermon. He told Josh that God had called him to preach and wanted him in the ministry full time. He knew the Lord wanted him to go to the same seminary where his pastor had received his education. The congregation expressed great joy when Josh had Casey repeat this to them.

Casey then asked if he could say something else to the church, and Josh gave him the floor. With light glistening in his eyes, Casey announced that he and Mary Ann had just become officially engaged. Before proposing to Mary Ann, Casey had privately received permission from her parents. They wanted to have their wedding in early August and would leave for the seminary in Virginia later that month.

Josh was thrilled at the news, and told the people that although the engagement period would not be as long as was usually considered proper, his sister and Casey were strong, mature Christians and deserved to be married before they went off to seminary. There was applause from the people, showing their agreement.

The next day, Lydia and Jessica were walking back to Lydia's house after finishing a Bible club session. When they came in sight of the house, Lydia said, "Jessica, I've been thinking and praying about something. The savings account that Clay and I had is still quite substantial, but I need to generate some income so it doesn't run out in a few years."

"Mm-hmm?"

"Imagine a sign on the front porch, honey. It says, 'Boardinghouse.' "

"Boardinghouse! You're going to turn your home into a boardinghouse?"

"I'll live on the bottom floor. That will leave six rooms to rent out upstairs. That will certainly help my finances."

"That's a great idea, Mom, considering all the people moving into Oregon City. But won't it take a lot of work?"

"Yes, and I've already talked to Jake Blane and Harvey Roberts at church about it, just to see what they think and how much it would cost for the alterations. They agreed that it's a great idea, and they'll do it for me at their cost."

"Wonderful! You'll make a great boardinghouse cook and hostess."

Josh and Jessica heard from Grant from time to time. He assured them he was coming to Oregon City once David was gone and the house was sold.

The Casey Harmon-Mary Ann Cornell wedding took place in early August, and they left for Virginia two weeks later. It was an emotional time for the Cornell family, and especially for Josh and Casey, whose hearts were entwined in the bonds of Calvary.

In early February of 1874, Josh and Jessica received a letter from her father that the house had sold and he was on his way west. He had sold all the furniture with the house and would stay in their home only as long as it took to buy a new house and furnish it.

Josh and Jessica were at the Wells Fargo office when the stage from Ogden pulled in several days later. After greetings and hugs, Josh placed Grant Smith's luggage in the back of the buggy, and they headed off through Oregon City as the sun went down over the hills. Jessica was sitting between the two men on the front seat.

"Now, kids," Grant said, "I want you to know that I deeply appreciate the offer to live under your roof, if I so desire, but like I've been saying in my letters, I really need to get my own house. So just as soon as I can buy one, or have one built, I'll be out of your way."

"Dad," Josh said, "you could never be in our way."

"I appreciate that, son, but —"

They happened to be on the street where Lydia lived. Grant's attention was drawn to the big white house and the sign hanging from the porch.

"Well, lookee there," he said, pointing with his chin.

"What, Daddy?"

"Right there. The sign at the bottom says Vacancy. That's what I'll do, kids. I'll take a room in that boardinghouse till I can get my own place."

"Well, it would give you more privacy than we can offer at our house," Jessica said. "It just so happens that we know the lady who owns that boardinghouse. She's a widow and a fine Christian. She belongs to our church. In fact, do you remember that

I mentioned in some of my letters that I'm teaching Bible clubs with a lady, and that I also help her teach a girls' Sunday school class?"

"Sure."

"Well, that's where the lady lives. She and I have become so close, I've been calling her my Oregon mom. She's been such a help to me with Mama's sickness and death."

"God bless her," Grant said. "I'll look forward to meeting Mrs. —"

"Price."

"I'll look forward to meeting Mrs. Price."

"Tell you what, Daddy," Jessica said. "You stay with us tonight. I'll go talk to her tomorrow and get you the best room she has available."

"Thanks, honey. I really appreciate that."

"Nothing's too good for my daddy," she said, leaning toward him and kissing his cheek.

Josh turned the corner and headed down another street. "Well, honey," he said, "I guess since your daddy is going to take a room at the boardinghouse, we can tell him."

"Tell me what?"

Jessica giggled. "We . . . ah . . . we would

413

have had to move you elsewhere in a few months if you had moved in with us, Daddy."

Grant's eyebrows arched. "Oh? And why is that?"

"Because that room we were going to put you in will have to become a nursery."

"A nursery? You mean — ?"

"You're going to be a grandfather in early September!"

Grant lifted his hat, swung it around in the air, and shouted, "Whoopee! Hallelujah! I'm gonna be a grandpa!"

Josh and Jessica didn't tell Grant that Martha had prepared a delicious meal to welcome him to Oregon City until they pulled up in front of the Brett Cornell house.

The reunion was a sweet one. After tender words were spoken about Carrie, the conversation went to the old days at Fort Union.

Brett told Grant that once he was settled, he would show him what he had in the way of a job in the mill office, and if that wasn't what Grant wanted, he would introduce him to both bank presidents. One way or another, Grant Smith had a job.

The next morning, Jessica cooked a hearty breakfast for her two men, then Josh took his father-in-law to the church for a tour. Jessica went to secure her father's room at the boardinghouse. When Josh and Grant returned, they would all take Grant and his luggage to his new abode.

A smiling Jessica was waiting for them when they entered the house. She hugged them both and said, "It's all set, Daddy. My Oregon mom has all but two rooms rented and will give you whichever one you want — on the east so the sunrise comes through your window, or on the west so you can get a good look at the sunsets. Other than that, they are exactly alike."

"Well, I guess I'll take the sunrise room. Did you already give her my name and sign me up?"

"No. I figured I'd let you take care of that."

"Well, let's go! I'm anxious to meet this Mrs. Price who has been so good to my daughter."

Jessica laughed. "I guarantee you, Daddy, you'll love her!"

24

Josh guided the buggy into Lydia's driveway. "Might as well go to the back. She'll no doubt be in the kitchen."

"No doubt," agreed Jessica, hanging onto her father's arm.

While Grant worked his way out of the buggy, cumbered by his cane, Josh helped Jessica out on his side. As they moved up the steps of the back porch, Josh called, "Hello-o-o! It's your favorite pastor and his wife. We've got your new boarder."

"Come on in. I'm in the kitchen."

Josh grinned as he opened the screen door. "Didn't I tell you she'd be in the kitchen?"

Father and daughter chuckled. Josh let both of them precede him, then closed the screen door and followed on Grant's heels as he limped along on his cane. When they stepped into the large kitchen, Lydia was on her tiptoes with her back toward them, taking a glass bowl down from the cupboard.

"Mom, I want you to meet Daddy," Jessica said.

When Lydia turned around, she froze. The bowl slipped from her fingers and crashed to the floor, sending broken pieces in every direction. She didn't seem to be aware of it as she gripped the cupboard for support.

Grant, too, was frozen in his tracks.

Josh and Jessica looked on, exchanging bewildered glances.

Grant still seemed the same handsome young man in Lydia's haunted, staring eyes as he had been the last time she saw him. Her voice cracked and a sort of broken sob escaped from somewhere deep inside her.

"Grant! Is it . . . is it really you? I thought you were dead! They — the army told me you were killed in Mexico!"

"Lydia . . . I . . . I —"

Jessica looked on with wide eyes. "Daddy . . . Mom . . . you two know each other?"

"Jessica," Grant said, "Lydia and I were engaged to be married before the Mexican-American War."

Tears welled up in Lydia's eyes and began to spill down her cheeks.

Grant let his cane fall to the floor as he limped to her amid the broken pieces of glass. Suddenly they were in each other's arms, weeping.

While they held each other, their words tumbled out in a rush. Grant explained about being wounded and the imprisonment that lasted for over three years. He told her of the day he came home and that her shocked parents informed him that she had married and gone out West.

"Oh, Grant!" Lydia sobbed. "It's like I'm dreaming! This can't be real! It just can't be real."

He held her close, while tears streamed down his cheeks. "It's real, Lydia, it's real! I . . . I never thought I'd see you again this side of heaven."

Josh and Jessica held each other and let their own tears flow.

"Josh, I can't believe this," Jessica said. "I remember Daddy talking to Grandma and Grandpa Smith one time years ago about the girl he almost married. But never in my wildest dreams would I have guessed it was Lydia!"

The emotion and astonishment went on for better than an hour as Grant and Lydia sat at the kitchen table and talked. Josh and Jessica sat with them, listening.

Finally, Lydia told them she would have to prepare lunch for her boardinghouse guests. She would prepare enough food for them, too, and they would eat after the guests were finished. Grant said they would take his things up to the sunrise room, if it was all right, and they would come back after Lydia had served her boarders.

When Lydia and her special guests sat down to eat lunch at one o'clock, she and Grant told Jessica and Josh the story of their young love for each other — all the way up to the day they parted when he went off to fight in the Mexican War.

In the months that followed, Jessica's heart glowed when she saw her father and her adopted mom together. Grant had been in Oregon City barely a week when he accepted the job as office manager of the Cornell Lumber Company.

One Sunday night in June, after church, Grant and Lydia walked home together. When they reached the house, she said, "Would you like some coffee before you go up to your room?"

"I won't pass up an invitation like that."

As they sat at the kitchen table, Grant said, "Tell me about Clay."

"Really?"

"Yes. I'd like to hear all about him. Josh

has told me he was a wonderful man."

Lydia went back to how and when she had met Clay Price and told him of their life together until the day Clay died suddenly of heart failure. She then said, "I already know a great deal about Carrie from Jessica, and I know she was a wonderful woman. Tell me how you met her and how it all came together for you."

When Grant had finished his story, bringing it up to the day Carrie died, Lydia said, "I wish I could have known her. Is Jessica like her mother?"

"Very much so. Same sweet personality. Same unselfish person, always ready to do for others." He smiled. "Just like you."

Lydia blushed.

Grant sipped coffee, then said, "Lydia, I was just thinking . . ."

"About what?"

"Your mother's choice words about us that night our family had supper at your house. Remember?"

"Yes." She nodded, a faraway look capturing her eyes. "Mother said, 'Your love is a tender flame. Time will prove if it is the genuine, lasting kind upon which to build a marriage.'" Lydia wiped the tears that had gathered in her eyes. "And I remember what you said, Grant. 'I know the tender flame between Lydia and me is genuine. It will grow stronger as time passes.' "

Grant ran splayed fingers through his thick silver hair, blinking against the excess moisture in his own eyes. "And I remember what you said, Lydia. 'Life can bring along things we never planned on, but when it comes to my love for Grant, I know it is the genuine thing. I have no doubt at all that the Lord has chosen us for each other, and that He has given us the true, lasting kind of love.' Remember that?"

"Yes. Yes, I do."

Grant took her hand in his. "Lydia, the Lord knows the end from the beginning. We both knew on that night the kind of love He had given us. He also knew — and planned — my imprisonment. He gave you a good husband, and you had many years of happiness together. He also brought Carrie into my life. She was a wonderful wife and gave me three precious children. You know about Daniel and David."

"Yes. And Daniel's Susan."

Grant nodded. "Marvelous girl. Lydia . . ."

"Yes?"

"I've heard nothing about children of yours. Are there any?"

Lydia shook her head. "Shortly after

marrying Clay, I found out that I would never be able to give him any children."

"Oh. I'm sorry."

"No need to be. 'As for God, his way is perfect.' "

Grant's shimmering eyes lit up. "Psalm 18:30!"

"Pastor John Britton used that verse to comfort me when word came from the army that you had been killed. I've clung to it many a time since."

Grant smiled shakily. "He used the same verse for me when I came home and learned that you had married the young doctor and moved to the West. And I, too, have clung to it over the years." He thought on it a moment, then said, "Lydia, the Lord put the tender flame in our hearts for each other. Then in His wisdom, He let the Mexicans put me in prison for all that time, then made a way so my fellow prisoners and I could escape. He gave us precious and wonderful mates, then, in His wisdom, took them to heaven."

"Yes, Grant, and His way is perfect. In His wisdom, our wonderful Lord has done what you might call a miracle. It's a big country, you know. Only His hand could have brought us together here in Oregon City."

"That's right."

"And something else to think about . . ."

"Hmm?"

"Jessica. And your sons, too. If you had come home from the war and we had married, I wouldn't have been able to give you children. There would be no Daniel and David, whom I know are wonderful boys."

Grant's eyes widened. "You're right, Lydia! I wouldn't have my sons. They indeed are wonderful boys. And . . . and I wouldn't have that precious Jessica. Oh, God is so good! His way is perfect!"

"And I wouldn't have that sweet Jessica, either! She's such a bright spot in my life. Because of her, I almost have a daughter. Carrie was her mother . . . her mama, Grant, and I would never try to take her place in Jessica's heart, or yours, for that matter. But because God's way is perfect, I have a precious girl who calls me her mom!"

"Lydia, my sweet," Grant said, looking her straight in the eye, "we both had good marriages, and we dearly loved our mates. We still have love for them, though they've gone to heaven."

"Oh yes."

"But we are still here on earth because of God's perfect way. And deep inside this man's heart, because God has willed it so, the tender flame still burns."

Lydia squeezed his hand. "And deep inside this woman's heart, because God has willed it so, the tender flame still burns."

Grant left his chair and knelt before her. "Lydia, will you marry me?"

Love light shimmered in Lydia's tear-filled eyes. "Yes, I will marry you!"

Instantly they were on their feet and in each other's arms. After a sweet kiss, Grant said, "This is great! I can't keep it in! Let's go announce our engagement to Jessica and Josh."

Lydia glanced at the clock. "But, darling, they're in bed asleep. It's almost midnight."

"So? We'll wake 'em up!"

Lydia laughed. "All right! Let's wake them up!"